ENSHALLAH

M.M. Terrence

ISBN 978–0–6152–2428–2
Published by Stand Up America, USA
Bigfork, Montana
Printed in the United States of America

ACKNOWLEDGEMENTS:

Stand Up America:
Major General Paul Vallely, US Army (ret)
Chairman/CEO, Stand Up America USA
and his team who made this project possible.

*****

Erika Cooper for her editing expertise and friendship.

*****

To family and friends who have patiently waited.

*****

Last, but not least,
For WJM always

PROLOGUE

The young woman bent low against her husband, carefully protecting the blanket wrapped newborn baby with her body.

The Navy Sea Stallion was closer now, slowly dropping down from the black night sky, guided by the pulsing light held in the man's hand. Crouching down, the two figures turned away as the helicopter's backlash whipped debris at their backs.

A figure jumped down from above.

"Peace be with you brother. Let's go!" Strong arms lifted them into the helicopter, its rotor never losing r.p.m.s. They were up and flying instantly.

The Yemeni's wife wept silently, knowing that she was leaving her homeland forever. She would not see it again. As the helicopter gained altitude her husband looked down at the rugged mountains of his country and then at his newborn son cradled in his wife's arms. He was sure. Whatever they had to face in their new country, life would not only be better for them, but for their child. Enshallah.

M A P

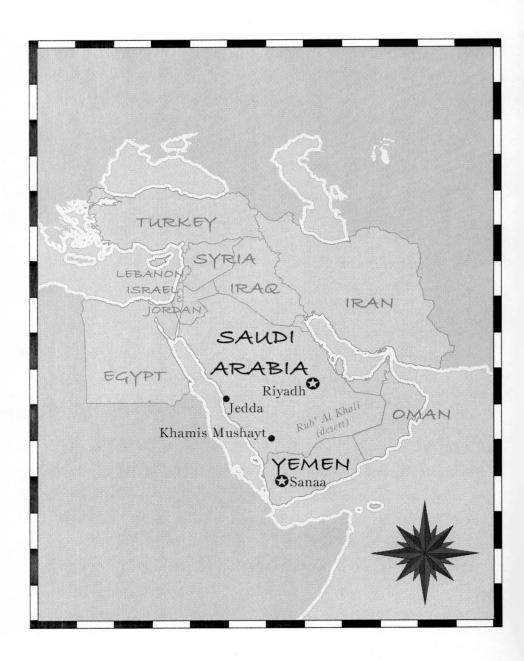

FOREWORD

T he old bastard sent word for her to come at once.

Yasi strode quickly out of the dusty wadi where the goat herd was grazing, climbed hand over hand up the rocky cliff side and trotted to the front of the old man's tent. The young woman kneeled down in the sand with her head lowered and waited, panting slightly. The sun baked her body, the black wool abaya she wore covered her from head to foot and intensified the sweltering desert heat. She closed her eyes and fought off a feeling of queasiness.

The sound of footsteps caused her to look up. A young boy jumped into a nearby pickup truck and drove away. She noted the tribe's water tanker truck was still parked where it had been the day she'd arrived, almost three weeks earlier. It was probably close to empty now, and would soon be replaced with a full one.

The old Bedouin stepped out of his tent and slashed at Yasi's head with a horsewhip, addressing her coarsely.

"Daughter of whores, you are to read this paper I will give to you. You will read it now, in front of me and then I will burn it. I cannot read, but I have been told it is terrible and justified news for you. I hope it tears your heart from your body."

He threw a folded newspaper at her head, hitting her hard in the face. She picked it up from the gravel packed ground and squinted painfully at the front page, her eyes tearing from the sun's glare. A photo of a well dressed, smiling middle-aged couple came into focus. The man was proudly holding a plaque while a beautiful woman looked lovingly at him.

Her heart skipped as she inhaled. It was a photo of her mother and father. She blinked, trying to focus her eyes. What were they doing? Scanning the large print at the top of the paper, the Arabic headline seared its message into her brain:

'PUBLISHER AND WIFE FOUND DEAD IN DOWNTOWN DETROIT. RANDOM MURDERS NOW TOTAL 12!'

Air rushed from her body. She felt herself sinking into the ground. The paper she had read was her father's newspaper, "Sadeek". It had been published in Dearborn, Michigan only five days earlier, but the story accompanying the headline didn't make sense. Her eyes had devoured the article faster than her brain could interpret the words. She read the article again, this time more slowly, making a supreme effort to comprehend what at first, seemed to be nonsense. The newspaper stated her parents were dead. It said they had been murdered. How? Why? She forced herself to mentally check each word, hoping she had made an error in translation. The hair on the back of her neck prickled as a dot of white hot fear grew in her gut.

"The bodies of two wealthy Dearborn citizens were found in their late model Cadillac in a drug infested neighborhood close to the Rouge Steel Plant. Adel al Amar and his wife, Suhair were discovered during a routine traffic patrol. They appeared to have been severely beaten and shot to death by an unknown assailant or assailants sometime late on Saturday night. Their car had been set on fire, their bodies badly burned. Police said robbery was probably the motive. No suspects have been identified at this time. Police are canvassing the neighborhood for possible witnesses. Mr. Amar was the publisher of the Arab/English newspaper, 'Sadeek'."

My God! Her mother and father were dead. They had been murdered last week while she was captive in this godforsaken desert. She had not been there to help them and now, she would never see them again. She blinked while she gripped the newspaper tightly. Controlling her breathing, she tried to make sense of what she just read. Her eyes drifted down to a handwritten note taped to the bottom of the paper's front page. Written in perfect English cursive was a message addressed to her:

"Yasmina, my pet. It was not a random murder. It was me.
They suffered before they died, as will you. This is only my first installment
of pain to you."

It was signed with the letter "M" done in calligraphy.

She understood. She now knew who it was. She forced herself to remain motionless on her knees, fighting the urge to get up and run. Her training materialized, its rhetoric reciting in her head.

"Control. Show no emotion. Give the enemy nothing. Stay calm. Center within."

As her emotions began to war with her reasoning she fought off the urge to scream and howl at the sky. She wanted to claw the old man's face until only blood and bone were left. The rote exercises repeated in her head.

"You are the control. Show the enemy nothing."

The old Bedouin peered at her with heightened expectation, his toothless mouth parted in smiling anticipation. She finished reading and purposely looked up at him with flat, emotionless eyes. Disappointed with her reaction, he snatched the newspaper out of her hands and stomped angrily back toward his tent, lifting the entrance flap so that she could see him drop it into the fire. She remained motionless, staring straight ahead. He came back out of the tent and cuffed her. "Get back to the goats immediately. Get back to work, you filthy bitch!"

She got to her feet and walked away briskly, heading toward the edge of the mesa, a half mile away. So, this was the surprise Mohammed told her he would deliver to her. The last night in Riyadh, when he discovered she was an agent, he brutalized her and then ordered the murder of her parents. The bastard killed her mother and father and now he planned to murder her.

It was a display of omnipotence. He was proving he could kill anyone close to her. This was an example of the ancient tribal custom of killing all blood relatives of an enemy's family, so no one could exact retribution in the future. She remembered his smug smile as a jolt of rage exploded unexpectedly inside of her, causing her to hyperventilate. She tried to manage her breathing by cupping her hands over her mouth, but instead, she started to hiccup. She gagged as bile retched up into her throat, her stomach emptying out onto the sand. Her body shook, her functions out of control. She felt like an exploding nova, pieces of her being spun off in all directions. She was in danger of losing control.

"Goddamn him to everlasting Hell!" She bellowed the curse.

The rage grew and roiled throughout her body and mind, causing her to lose track of her surroundings. She entered the recesses of her being, oblivious to the day's heat as well as her need for water. She focused her mind on her enemy's face and voice. The agony within her howled with injustice that Mohammed was still breathing after the torture and killing of her innocent parents. He was an abomination to her and to all living things.

Hate wasn't a complex enough word for the emotion she felt. She would escape from here and hunt him down. When she took him prisoner, she would make sure all useful information about al Qaeda was sucked from his brain. The drugs used could damage a detainee's memory, rendering a prisoner mentally incompetent, but she wouldn't allow that to happen. Yasi would make sure the technicians kept Mohammed mentally aware as they ripped apart his brain.

She made herself a promise. She would not only be the main architect of his death, but also the instrument of his extermination. Before his execution, the payback would be far worse than anything he could imagine. As a bonus, she promised herself he would suffer. He would be conscious of every second of his impending doom, feel each tremor of fear, and scream her name as he took his last breath. There would be no opportunity for him to escape final retribution.

Her mind shifted. She realized that in order to escape and pay the bastard back, she had to take control. She took her rage and began to turn it. As her resolution hardened her mind cleared. Adrenalin poured into her body and she stopped shaking. In a few seconds she knew what she had to do.

Reaching the edge of the mesa, Yasi pushed a large boulder off a ledge and watched it crash onto the ground twenty feet below, shattering a rock formation of black mica, just like a window pane. It would do. A jagged piece of mica is more lethal than a box cutter. Desert rock shards constantly shred the rugged truck tires of even the most experienced long distance desert drivers. Razor sharp, they are prevalent throughout the region. Truckers who supply Bedouin camps complain that their trips are often filled with delays once they drive off-road. The water tankers repeatedly arrive with slashed tires, and new tires must be put on before they can begin their return trip. Drivers always carry two, and sometimes three, additional tires on top of their trucks to insure their ability to drive home.

During the past weeks, Yasi had picked up small pieces of mica and felt their razor sharp edges. She mentally catalogued it for future use. Today, when she crashed the granite boulder down onto the desert floor, dozens of shards had broken loose.

The tribe's goat herd had wandered into an adjacent series of sand gullies, and paid no attention to the crash. The goats were busy chewing on the tough salt bushes that lined the wadi, scavenging for blades of grass. Armallah, the Bedouin woman who was her appointed jailer did hear the noise, looked up and saw Yasi standing on the top of the cliff.

Yasi raced down the cliff face toward the pile of newly created mica shards and saw the large abaya clad woman marching quickly toward her. The old man had ordered her to return to the goats immediately, and she had disobeyed. She knew the fat woman would now try to punish her.

Reaching the bottom of the cliff, Yasi stooped down quickly and appeared to tug at her long robe. Pretending to adjust her abaya, she cut the foot long end of her rawhide wrist thong off with a piece of mica. She then wound the strip quickly around the blunt end of a twelve inch long razor-edged shard, creating a lethal dagger.

"Where have you been, you stinking slut?" Armallah screamed as she approached. Yasi knew as soon as they were closer, the woman would reach out and yank at the leather thong that had been, up until a moment ago, tightly tied around Yasi's right wrist. Armallah would use it to pull her captive down to the ground. Once Yasi was forced onto her knees, the Arab woman would beat her until she grew tired of inflicting blows with her whip. Yasi watched the distance between them lessen. A huge, ugly woman with broken teeth and mottled skin, Armallah had made it her duty to be the young American's torturer. She was the only unmarried sister of the old Bedouin, and tradition dictated that without a husband to provide for her she must remain with her brother's family. His wives treated her as a destitute outcast. Berated for her laziness, she was the most despised female in a family run by women who had no status themselves. Illiterate and frightened of anything Western, the Bedouin's two old wives had been disgusted by the sight of their female American captive and gladly gave the responsibility of being her jailer to Armallah. They wanted nothing to do with the girl, except to collect the bounty on her life when she was killed.

At first, Armallah's brutal beatings had nearly broken the young American, but Yasi learned to curl her body into a tight ball so that most of the force of the camel whip landed on her back, instead of her face and head. Over the weeks the welts bled and swelled, abating into hard, wide ridges of scar tissue.

The place where the two women met was below the level of the mesa where the Bedouin camp was set up, well out of sight of the tents. Armallah reached Yasi, and without a word, grabbed her wrist thong, preparing to pull down on it. Abruptly, she stopped moving. Her head snapped up as she cried, "Eowww!" Her mouth opened and closed. She yelled again, "What has stung me?" Armallah stared down at her bloody right palm with a puzzled expression, trying to understand what had just happened to her. Yasi quickly sidestepped behind her and yanked the woman's head viciously to one side while she expertly slit her throat. At the exact moment Armallah realized her right palm had been sliced in two, she was gargling in her own blood.

Yasmina felt no emotion as she looked down at her dying torturer struggling to breathe. Armallah kicked her legs out one at a time, rolling her huge body back and forth, a seeming mountain of black wool. Flecks of blood frothed from her nose and mouth, her hands and arms flailing uselessly at her sides, grunting sounds emanating from her now gaping throat. She stared sightlessly into the blazing sun.

Shifting attention from her victim, Yasi took the stone dagger into her left hand and quickly began to dig out the rest of the rawhide piece that had been knotted tightly around her right wrist since the first day she arrived as a captive at the camp. After three weeks, it had embedded itself almost a half inch into her flesh. She saw the wound would take time to heal, but that it wasn't dangerous. Armallah died as Yasi stood over her rewinding and knotting the remains of her rawhide wrist strap carefully around the hilt of the bloody dagger while knotting it tightly into place. Glancing up at the sun she judged it to be a half hour before the noon prayer. There was still enough time. She took off at a slow trot and headed up the cliff to the old man's tent.

She knew the old Bedouin would pray alone at noon. Muslim women are forbidden to pray in the same place as men. His two wives would either pray by themselves, or just ignore prayer time and continue their chores. If he was devout, he would prostrate himself facing toward Mecca and recite his prayers. If he wasn't, he would be asleep. Either way, his wives would not come to his tent to serve the noon meal until he summoned them. She made her way to the back side of the men's tent and easily cut through the woven goat hair wall. She peered into the dimness of the interior, giving her eyes time to adjust to the darkness.

The old man was asleep on the carpet strewn floor, lying on his back and snoring loudly. She carefully widened the cloth slit and slid through silently.

The viselike grip crushing down on his mouth and nose caused the Bedu to jump awake with pain and try to call out. He struggled to sit up, but his body was pinned to the floor. The head and face of the person straddling him was swathed in black wool and only the eyes of the attacker could be seen. They were as black as night and glinted with what looked like amusement. He heard a whispering voice, clear and unmistakably female, breathe into his face. The voice spoke to him in his own dialect of the Sharourah, spewing out an age old curse of the Bedouin.

"Son of a dog whose whore of a bitch mother gave him birth. What you have wanted to do to me and to my kind I will now do to you. You are a dead man. You and your seed will be scoured from this earth. Your livestock will die, and the earth will be salted so that no part of you or the swine that are a part of you can survive."

His eyes widened with recognition as he made one last superhuman effort to throw off the body on top of him. The dagger in Yasi's right hand flashed below his chin and left a crimson smile oozing on his throat. As he began to drown in his own blood, he frantically tried to stop the bleeding by clutching his neck tightly with both hands, his eyes wide with terror, his mouth a wide gaping maw of blood. He stared at her with surprise and hatred, his need to kill her as primal as his need to live.

She stood up and watched dispassionately as he rolled from side to side thrashing out the last moments of his life. His intended cries for help emerged only as strangled sounds, while his blood quickly ran in thick fingers onto the carpets, spilling the last of his life into the soft desert sand. "Shut up dog!" She spat down on him.

She looked at his feet and wondered if his boots might fit her. While he died she pulled off his boots and socks. Sitting on the rug she tried them on. They fit well enough. She took a loaded revolver from his belt, and then noticed a storage chest in the corner of the tent. She searched it for ammunition. It was there. She took two boxes of twenty rounds each. The sheik's chest also held old trousers, shirts and a belt. She stripped off her blood soaked abaya and ragged shift and stuffed them under a carpet. Putting on the dead man's clothes she placed a gutra, or Bedouin style headdress, on her head and wound it around the lower front of her face. Only her eyes showed. She stuck the revolver in her belt alongside a dagger that she found stored in the chest. When she finished dressing she looked the epitome of a Bedouin fighter.

As Yasi was closing the lid of the box her eye caught a glimmer of something shiny, tucked back into one of the corners. Lifting a shirt she found a stack of gold coins piled neatly at the bottom of the box. It was the gold the old man had been given the day she was delivered to him as his prisoner. The coins were the initial payment for her mutilation and murder. They were a down payment for the systematic amputation of her fingers and, afterward, her death by beheading. She took one of the coins and put it into her pocket silently vowing to return the gold to Mohammed personally. Another quick look around the tent netted her a goatskin water carrier and a cell phone. The phone had been left with the old man so Mohammed could stay in contact with him. There was only a weak signal available at the present encampment, but the battery light indicated full power. She slipped the cell into her trouser pocket and exited the tent.

Speed was going to be an important factor in her escape and she hoped that the stationary water tanker parked in front of the tents would start. She had to get away as quickly as she could. She didn't know when a replacement water tanker was due to arrive, or when Mohammed would dispatch men to witness her first scheduled amputation.

The Bedouin's two old wives trembled and shook at the entrance of the women's tent. They quickly covered their faces as Yasi walked out and pointed a revolver at them.

"On your knees mothers of dogs." She snarled as she walked a few paces past them to the tanker, the pistol cocked and pointed in their direction.

"Don't move, or I swear to God that I will kill you."

She opened the driver's door, saw the keys hanging in the ignition and climbed in, starting the truck. The gas gauge was on the half full mark. "Good," she mumbled. While the engine idled, she jumped down from the driver's seat and walked back toward the old women, her gun now aimed at their bellies. She motioned for them to get down. They knelt in the sand wavering back and forth and wailing loudly.

"Please be to God, son of the desert. Do not hurt us. We are old women who wish you no harm."

Yasi could smell their fear. One of them soiled herself. Both of them begged loudly, groveling at her feet.

"Mercy, oh warrior of the jihad. We are but mere women who beg for your mercy. Take any of our water that you need to sustain you and any of our animals that you see fit, but spare us our lives and sacred honor."

It took a minute for Yasi to sort it out. The women had not seen her since the morning Mohammed had dumped her at the old Bedouin's feet, three weeks earlier. They had hidden themselves and watched, intrigued by the badly beaten and bloody young Western woman, puzzled at first as to why she was put under their husband's control. During the past weeks, Yasi tended the flocks as Armallah's prisoner, more than a mile away from the camp. At night, on the old man's orders, she was tied to a stake and kept out of sight of the womens' tent. They had not seen her again. It was logical that they had no idea what she looked like.

Yasi's voice was pitched low, her throat hoarse from lack of water. With her head and most of her face covered by a gutra, the women could not tell she was female. The old man's clothes hung loosely on Yasi's thin frame, giving her a shapeless form. The women recognized their husband's clothes were being worn by a stranger, and his pistol was aimed at them. Bedouins did not surrender their weapons, and no man would let a stranger approach his wives. This meant their husband had been killed. In their narrow concept of the world, no woman would be capable of killing a man and taking control. They thought Yasi was a brigand, and they were terrified of being raped. She shook her head in disgust as she ordered the old women into their tent. Following them inside, she told them to lie face down in the corner and not to move. They wept and shook uncontrollably, but did as they were told. She knew there was nothing to fear from them.

Yasi walked over to the cold fire pit. There was a slab of dried goat meat hanging on a chain above the pit and she sliced off a hunk. She took some goat butter from one of the containers stacked on the floor and slathered it on the dried meat, sticking the pieces into her pocket. Yasi kicked at the rest of the containers until she noticed salt topple out of one of them. She picked up the salt canister and walked back outside where she carefully emptied the salt in a circle at the front of the tent, grinding the white crystals into the dirt with her boot.

Striding back toward the tanker truck, she stopped and filled the goatskin from the communal water trough and then tipped the large container over. Precious gallons of water spilled over the hard packed earth and began to disappear. A few moments in the afternoon sun would obliterate any trace of moisture.

The survival of modern Bedouin flocks and herds was predicated on having water tankers follow them from place to place. In earlier times the only way to graze animals was to go where natural wells were located. Traditionally, nomadic tribes used the same grazing routes, following the sparse desert grasses even when water was hard to find. In the past it had been a precarious existence, at best.

The Saudis were one of the first to build an extensive number of cell phone towers throughout their desert country, marketing cheap phones to their people. Because of a hefty government subsidy even the poor could afford a phone, and the huge number of towers allowed for cell phone service throughout a large portion of the country. Now, a Bedouin had only to call on his cell phone for water to be delivered to his encampment in a tanker truck. For some tribes, it was contracted for and delivered based upon the month to month location of the herds. Without water few things could survive. The desert offered both life and death, but water was life.

Yasi knew eventually, the two old women would be found, either dead or alive. It didn't matter. At their age there wasn't a seed of life left in either of them. During her nighttime captivity, Yasi overheard the women talking in their tent, their voices drifting over the quiet desert sand. They lamented the deaths of their children and wailed in misery. They had lost all them of them over the years from either disease or tribal warfare. There was no future for their bloodline.

Yasi knew in a few days not only was a water tanker due to arrive, but men would be dispatched to witness her initial torture. Until then, both humans and animals left in the camp would suffer. Tonight the livestock would be thirsty. Tomorrow, desperate for water, they would wander into the desert. Within three days, they would be dead. By symbolically salting the earth, she had fulfilled her curse to her dead jailer. It was too bad she couldn't track down the bastards who attacked on 9/11 and retaliate using tribal vengeance. She hoped the old Bedouin she just killed rotted in some eclectic Hell alongside his ugly sister. She hurried to the truck and got in.

The highway was a shimmering ribbon of black tarmac, stretching northeast toward the capital city of Riyadh, but, as she put the truck in gear, she turned south. She didn't know how long the southern road would last, but she knew that the country of Yemen lay southwest of where she was, and Yemen was where she was going. Enshallah.

CHAPTER I

Dearborn, Michigan sits thousands of miles from the Middle East, snug on the outskirts of the Midwestern industrial city of Detroit. A whirlpool of ethnicity, it is a haven for the diverse cultures flourishing within its neighborhoods.

To a world traveler, Dearborn might resemble the suburbs of any prosperous, modern Middle Eastern city. Of the over two hundred thousand people of Middle Eastern descent living in Michigan, thirty thousand choose to live in the Detroit suburb of Dearborn. With Iraqi, Lebanese, Palestinian and Yemeni nationalities among others, the suburb acts as a mixing bowl, reflecting each nation's cultural traditions and preferences. Residents wear both Western and traditional Middle Eastern dress, and while Iraqi girls modestly cover their hair, Lebanese women don't. Although the predominant religion represented is Islam, there are thousands of Chaldeans, Coptic, and Lebanese Christians among the immigrant population. Operating as a microcosm of internationalism, Dearborn's streets are filled with small stores stocked with commodities from America, as well as delicacies imported from their native lands. It is a kaleidoscope of smells, sights and sounds.

Adel al Amar was a tall man with an aristocratic bearing. Soft spoken with a purposeful demeanor, he maintained a gentle aloofness about him, placing him slightly apart from others. Fifty years old and lean bodied, he gave the appearance of a man who still possessed youthful strength and agility. His gray hair curled tightly around his forehead, and a well tended goatee added solemnity to the fine lines on his face. He saw the world through a large pair of soft brown eyes that suggested an ingrained intelligence and curiosity about all things. Normally, he emanated a quiet confidence and it was only after a person closely studied his face that the deeply etched lines around his eyes offered some hint of past struggles.

He had immigrated to America twenty-five years earlier, and was a naturalized U.S. citizen. Adel started his newspaper, "Sadeek"(Friend), shortly after arriving in Michigan and realized he was the only adult in his neighborhood who could read both English and Arabic. At that time, Dearborn's population desperately needed an Arabic/English newspaper and his initial effort quickly grew from a thin, two page newsletter type bulletin to a full fledged newspaper with three sections. In a short time it became the main source of both local and international news for new Arab immigrants, as well as first generation Americans. Adel's "Sadeek" insured that Arabic speaking Dearborn residents had the opportunity to read national and world news in their native tongue while they were struggling to learn the difficult new language of English.

A rarity in his chosen profession as a journalist, he was the most truthful man most people knew. Intellectually inquisitive about everything, he never let his newspaper staff complete their writing of a story without answering every question a reader might have. He was adamant that all news be verified by unimpeachable sources and double checked by editors for accuracy. His employees revered him for his professionalism, and marveled at his high standard of ethics.

He was an egalitarian and treated "Sadeek's" most menial employee with the same courtesy as he treated his senior editors. Although modest in dress and manners, he was not descended from the working classes, but was rather one of the most wealthy and well educated men in Michigan, having attended universities both in the Middle East and the United States. An example of the New World's immigrant noblesse oblige class, he believed that he not only had a duty to be principled in business, but charitable to those less fortunate. He contributed generously to the good of the community and encouraged others to follow his example.

Honored and admired among his peers, he was known as a thoughtful conservative leader who advocated positive change while adhering to traditional Middle Eastern mores. His intellect and sense of innate fairness put him in demand as an advisor to many politicians and business leaders. Locally, he was the voice of moderation in all things relating to Dearborn's diverse Middle Eastern community while nationally he was revered as a rising political star who would represent a centrist position on Middle Eastern issues.

On the surface he seemed a man given over to Western ideas and beliefs, but those closest to him knew that an integral part of him would always belong to his tribe and his birth country. Although a genuine American patriot, a piece of him would always be a part of the country of Yemen and the ancient Arab world of his birth. Adel and his wife were ardent supporters of their adopted country and felt their immigration to America had been one of the greatest blessings of their lives. They loved the United States for many reasons, mostly for the opportunities their American children would have; opportunities only dreamed about in the world they'd left years before.

Born the third male heir in a large and prosperous family of traders in Yemen, Adel was tutored at home and educated in mathematics, science and languages. His instructor thought him a bright and willing student, but intellectually lazy. When of age, he was encouraged by his father to attend university in Egypt and to study Sharia or religious law. In a culture where tradition required the family leadership pass to the oldest male heir, Adel's father hoped he would find a place for his third son teaching. Adel displayed the proper academic prowess and graduated with the school's highest honors but stunned his family when he chose not to continue the career path of a teacher. While still a student he had accidentally found out his chosen future lay in a completely opposite direction.

Egypt in the 1970's was a country locked in the throes of developing its own unique style of nationalism. Deeply interested in international affairs, Adel volunteered to do research to assist one of the university's prominent professors for a campus wide discussion highlighting the decadence and depravation of Western culture and America, in particular. In preparation for the debate, one of the books he had chosen to read contained copies of the American Declaration of Independence and the Constitution of The United States of America. When Adel read the Arabic translations of the documents he was sure they had not been translated correctly and paid a local English scholar to translate them again. The man confirmed the first translations were accurate, and Adel condescendingly dismissed the philosophy they highlighted as naïve and foolish. The principal political tenet he could not fathom was a statement written into the American Declaration of Independence. When he read the phrase, "All men are created equal," he thought it bizarre and untruthful. There was a hierarchy to the world, and he had been taught all men knew their place. The powerful ruled and the poor remained poor.

Using the resources of the university library he began to research eighteenth century English law. He was interested to learn how England's political government and monarchy had erred contributing to the gross mismanagement of their American colonies, losing them in the progression of growth and evolution. He discovered a book on American heroes and his curiosity was piqued when he read how the Revolutionary War hero George Washington rejected being made a king at the end of the American War of Independence. Adel wondered why a man would refuse to become a king. The altruistic George Washington was an intriguing figure.

After reading his fifth book on the early history of the American Colonies and their political development, he was disappointed to find out there were no more reference books available to him within the university. The librarians told him there were none in their inventory. Scouring the city's used bookstores he found a few more and eagerly devoured information in them. The more he read, the more he became fascinated by the unique political treatises of the founding fathers of colonial America.

He learned the thirteen colonies of the then infant United States had never turned away from their initial revolutionary ideas of freedom and equality, but had progressively evolved over the years into a modern democratic republic that offered even broader individual rights to its citizenry. How was it possible that America, a country barely two hundred years old, could guarantee incredible personal freedom and suffrage for its entire people? If the freedom of an American citizen was as it seemed, was that the reason the United States had become so powerful? What he read created a stirring within him unlike anything he had ever felt. He was compelled to learn more.

As a university student in Egypt in 1978 Adel's view of the world was in direct opposition to an American college student's view. American students were free to read everything and anything they wished. Adel was limited to what books the government permitted the university to procure. In America, students occasionally rioted, disrupting universities when they politically disagreed with them. Their professors expressed opposition views at will, dissenting as a matter of common practice. In Egypt, professors who taught at the university were on the government dole. If they chose to disagree with their government's politics they could not only lose their jobs, but be put in prison.

Adel read about the huge demonstrations against the Viet Nam War during the 1960's and how the actions of ordinary American citizens and a free press had influenced their government's political actions. He could not quite grasp how it had worked, but he knew it had been the freedom of the American people that brought it about.

In Egypt people whispered about political corruption within the safety of their homes or offices, but did not dare mention it openly. Fear of reprisal was universal. Religious clerics received stipends from the government and reinforced rote instruction in the mosques. Students were encouraged to repeat only what was taught to them and individual thinking was discouraged. The Koran was literally treated as the only truth in the world, and many Western books were banned. In 1978, there were no maps in any university library that showed the existence of the country of Israel.

During this time, the city of Cairo was bursting at its seams. Overcome with a population explosion and not enough housing, many homeless people were forced to live on the streets. With no jobs available, hundreds begged for alms. Raised with the values of his class,

Adel was not particularly concerned with the sufferings of the poor and lived in a well furnished garden apartment close to the university. He and his friends led self-satisfying lives of study, conversation and dining. As part of the moneyed class, they felt living well was their inherited right. Adel was descended from one of the most powerful families in Yemen, and the mundane problems of daily existence were not his concern. Everything he needed had been provided to him by his family or their retainers. It was the way of his world. In the future, he would hold a position of power and influence within his country, and in turn, take care of the men who loyally served his family. His tribe traced their roots back to the biblical city of Eden and to the ancient kings and queens of Yemen. They were Muslim, but were derived from a moderate sect who had intermarried with ancient settlers from India.

Returning home after graduation Adel greatly displeased his father when he expressed his wish not to continue his education in Egypt. He desperately wanted to study in America. When he attempted to address this issue with his father, the old man angrily waved him away.

"You are a young fool, ungrateful for all that I have given you. Get out of my sight!"

As Adel left the room, Jamal al Amar wondered what it was that he had seen glowing in his son's eyes. Was it the glint of a new zealot, or a young man yearning to embrace the decadence and evil of the West? He didn't like the enthusiasm his son exhibited when he talked about the Great Satan of America and decided Adel would begin to work at home, immediately. There would be no more discussion of an overseas trip.

As the days passed, Adel dutifully began monotonous tasks associated with expanding his family's extensive trading business. He and his older brothers traveled throughout the region, visiting new villages. They sat and drank coffee with the village elders, presented their portfolios, and then politely listened to the chieftain's demand for "baksheesh" or a bribe. They also bestowed baksheesh on the municipal bureaucrats and gave alms to the village poor.

"You don't seem very enthusiastic about our work Adel." His older brother Razul snorted as they were leaving the last village to be visited before returning home.

Adel shook his head. "I don't know how you and Bezar do this, day after day. It's just so....."

"Boring?" chimed in Bezar, a big smile on his face, patting Adel on the back. But Razul's tone stayed serious. "Yes, I see that what we do seems too ordinary for a university educated boy. You've had the opportunity to study in Egypt, and read all the books. You even studied about the great Satan all while we worked like mice at home, currying favor with potential trade partners. Well, let me tell you little brother, the al Amars were once a great warrior tribe and now we are even greater businessmen. Good solid commerce is what makes us strong, and we will make a master trader out of you, yet." He threw his arm around Adel's shoulders and hugged him closely, grinning from ear to ear.

After their return, Jamal's sons dutifully reported to their father on the business trades they tried to develop and awaited his judgment. Afterward, his brothers went to their respective homes and Adel returned to his room to study his books on the West, dreaming of one day being able to see the place that had captured his imagination.

The only newspaper published in North Yemen was run by the national government. It reported what the government dictated, nothing more. The newspaper's editor was amused to see that a son of one of the wealthiest tribal families had written to the paper complaining about living conditions of his fellow countrymen. Adel had written to the paper many times, criticizing the existence of a Marxist state on Yemen's southern tier, demanding an end to the slave trade that was permitted to exist, and exhorting the country's leadership to provide better education and health care for its people. Yemen was not a wealthy country. Most of its population existed at the subsistence level. Although each tribe and sheik was responsible for the welfare of their own people, resources were scarce and allocated in a haphazard way. Many people died of disease and hunger everyday.

Adel listened carefully to what the clerics were preaching in the mosques. It wasn't what they said. It was what they did not say that disturbed him. He'd heard the local Imams extol the greatness of the Yemeni government, and the evil of the West, but nothing was mentioned about improving the plight of the desolate poor. When Adel questioned the clerics they answered him curtly, barely tolerating his interference. His incessant questioning infuriated them and they complained bitterly to his family.

Jamal summoned his son to his study. He was reading when Adel walked in, and never looked up from his letter.

"Adel you have given me much displeasure. It is a sorry thing to be a man of my age and to have a son who disobeys."

"Father? I do not understand."

"I am reading a letter from the chief Imam of our province. He has written that you have challenged clerics in the mosques and you have taken it upon yourself to instruct them as to what they should be teaching in the mosque." The old man raised his head and looked straight into Adel's eyes. "Are you so brilliant that you dare to instruct men who have taught religious law for all their lives?"

Adel solemnly replied. "The things I said only concerned our country's people who are sick and starving. Our country is in disarray.

Father I wanted to…"

"Enough!" Jamal spat the word. "You are to occupy yourself with the business of our family. Period. End of argument. That is my wish. Nothing else should be of interest you. I am weary of you not being enthusiastic about your responsibilities. You will stop going to the mosques, and you will concentrate only on your duties as a son and brother. Now leave me." His father looked back down at the letter on his desk and began to write.

Adel had wilted under the old man's outburst. He felt the same frustration and anger rise in the back of his throat that he had at their last meeting. He turned briskly and left his father's house.

Hoping to stabilize the political front, the American Consul in Yemen sent a hand picked emissary into the villages to speak to various powerful tribal families. The representative was tasked with asking them for their assistance in organizing a plan to disarm the Marxist South, and help design a unification treaty that would be acceptable to both sides. The United States was looking for tribal leaders who could offer advice on how to negotiate with the tribes in the south in order to begin the process of reunification. America did not want Yemen to be united by war, but rather to have North Yemen economically absorb and pacify South Yemen. The tribes therefore had to first heal their own rifts, with America financing the effort. When compared to the north, South Yemen was being left far behind in economic development. Marxist doctrine had proven anathema to its people. Poverty and starvation were at peak levels in South Yemen at the same time North Yemen was economically expanding. It was simple fact that daily life was better for the people of North Yemen.

At first, Adel's father had refused to see the Yemeni who was the American's paid messenger. Although the man's tribe was known to him,

Jamal harbored distrust for anyone who would let Infidels direct his actions. Once he learned, however, that he would be paid handsomely for receiving the envoy, he graciously granted an audience.

As was the custom, Adel was seated on the floor of the audience chamber next to his father's chair. He listened intently as the emissary eloquently put forth the American point of view and was surprised to hear him state the United States wanted nothing from Yemen other than friendship. His father, however, showed no interest, rudely looking away and yawning during the short dissertation. The man finished his briefing, turned to one of the sheik's retainers and handed him a bag of coins. Jamal got up and left the room. Adel had been enthralled by what the man said and wanted to know more. He caught up to the speaker in the palace courtyard.

"Peace be upon you. I am Adel, the son of Jamal Al Amar of the Maerb." He held the man haughtily with his eyes.

"And peace be upon you," the man bowed differentially. "I am Achmed al Badr of the al-Jouf. What can I do for you young master?"

"Some of what you said inside interests me, but I want to know more about America's true motives. What does it want of us as a people? Can the United States think us to be so stupid as to believe it cares what happens to our country without some kind of payment in return? Is it arrogance that surpasses their greed? What are their honest plans, and how dare this foreign power try to interfere in our country?"

Achmed smiled tolerantly at the young man's fervor. "I think you have asked more questions of me than I can deliver answers to. Besides, Americans are best judged when they speak for themselves. However, I do know someone who can answer all of your questions. He is the chief of all the Americans in Yemen, and my friend besides. Will you meet me on Tuesday, next week?"

"Tell me where," Adel answered.

"The American Consulate in Sanaa. After evening prayer."

"I will be there."

On Tuesday afternoon Adel left his village and drove one of his family's trucks to his country's capital city of Sanaa.

The American Consulate occupied an older office building in the city. It was located in the same square that housed the city's main mosque. As Adel arrived, the mosque was emptying after evening prayer. Groups of men were hurrying home, or back to work to reopen their shops for the evening. All of the buildings surrounding the square had been built in an older time, and were showing their age after decades of hard use. As Adel approached his destination he was surprised at how ordinary looking the American building was in comparison to the others.

Ingeniously, the building's simple weathered facade hid advanced electronic surveillance gear and state of the art unseen protective measures. A modern concrete and glass addition at the front of the building's entrance now blocked direct access to what had been the original front door. As he got closer he saw two uniformed men standing in what looked to be a glass booth and was surprised he recognized who they were. They were American Marines. He had read about them in one of his books. He remembered the book said they were the bravest and most ferocious of all American fighting men. His eyes widened when he saw them glance up at his approach. He wondered if they would speak Arabic to him or expect him to speak English. When he saw they were armed, his throat went dry.

As a matter of routine, pressure sensors buried in the sidewalks and the adjacent buildings to the consulate had picked up Adel as a potential target as soon as he had left the center of the main square and headed toward the consulate. His photograph was taken with hidden cameras and within hours his image would be faxed worldwide to all agencies that had data on terrorists. In a short time any terrorist image that matched his would be returned. He was photographed again from all sides as he approached the glass booth. Based upon the photographic details of his face and body an electronic file was started, estimating his age, weight and nationality. During the same time, an x-ray machine scanned his body for weapons.

The darker skinned Marine looked at him and spoke to him in perfect Arabic.

"Marharba. May we help you?"

"I am Adel al Amar of the Maerb. I have come to see Achmed al Badr of the al Jouf."

"One moment, please." The guard spoke into a telephone and pushed a button.

A few minutes passed. He heard a sharp metallic sound as the steel door of the consulate slowly opened, revealing a smiling Achmed who embraced him as a long lost brother.

Achmed led Adel into an elevator and then out onto the top floor of the building and down a wide hallway. He chatted happily, thanking Adel for keeping his appointment, and asked politely about his father's health and his travel to Sanaa. Adel barely acknowledged the questions as he tried to absorb what he was seeing. There were large notices printed in English and Arabic neatly displayed on the walls, pictures of American soldiers in uniforms posted throughout the corridor. After a few paces, they stopped at a wooden door. Achmed tapped lightly, opened it and preceded Adel through the doorway.

"Mr. Hunter Farrington, American Counsel General, may I present Adel al Amar, son of Sheik Jamal Al Amar of the Maerb?"

Achmed bowed to the American and smiled at Adel. "I will await you outside, young friend." He exited the room, closing the door behind him.

Adel watched a small man walk out from behind a large desk. With a friendly smile the older man held out his right hand and said in non-accented Arabic, "I welcome you to the American Consulate. I understand you wish to have some questions answered about America, and I hope to be of service to you. Thank you for your interest in my country." Adel tentatively took the American's hand and, when motioned to a chair, sat down. Hunter sat down across from him.

The office was large and well furnished with two overstuffed chairs and assorted tables. The room's table lamps gave it a shadowy but comfortable feel in the evening's darkness. Adel looked at the walls and noted they were covered with photographs, awards and plaques. Most of them were in English, and he could not read them, but his eyes finally rested upon a framed Arabic proverb done in exquisite calligraphy.

"Arrogance diminishes wisdom"

Hunter noticed the direction of his gaze. "Ah, yes, I try to remember that, and many other truths the proverbs tell us. It's a struggle not to be a fool. But, please tell me, how did you develop an interest in my country? You are of the generation that doesn't usually have a liking for the Western world." Hunter smiled, shook a cigarette out from a pack, offered Adel one, and then lit both.

Adel leaned forward, his elbows on his knees and exhaled. His voice was strident.

"Why are you interested in helping Yemen to unite? Why would our unification benefit the United States? What is your real purpose? Do you think us fools, or worse?"

Hunter sat comfortably, smoking his cigarette. He could feel the tension in the young man release with each word he spoke and waited for him to finish. Adel continued. "I studied Political Law at the University of Cairo under a man who was the head of the Department of Islamic Studies, and a dedicated extremist. He hates everything about the West and America in particular for being secular. It was his theory that God would reach out and destroy all Infidels and non-believers. While I was doing research for him in preparation to lead an anti-American rally I read the American Declaration of Independence and Constitution. At first, I didn't believe the documents were valid. I know now that they are, but I wonder if what is written in them is honestly put into practice by Americans or is only an international perception of your politics. I am also honestly intrigued with the political evolution of your country from a British colony to a world power."

Hunter smiled and began to talk slowly.

As the evening waned, an honest give and take of ideas transpired between the older Stanford University educated American Consul, who had entered the Foreign Service when he was Adel's age, and the skittish young Yemeni who wanted to learn more about America. They met often after that, and it benefited them both. Each week Adel telephoned his new friend and made an appointment to meet with him. He would drive from his village into the city of Sanaa late in the afternoon, conduct his business errands and arrive at the American Consulate after evening prayer. The two men would talk long into the night, each one's questions complementing the other's answers. Adel was eager to discuss and debate world politics with his American friend and quickly learned about new and innovative geopolitical ideas that spun his head with their complexity.

Hunter's range of interests fascinated the young Yemeni. The older man was not only extraordinarily well educated, but a voracious reader to boot. He had an intense curiosity about everything and a desire to learn. Adel warmed to Hunter's honest inquisitiveness about Yemen and began to share his knowledge on the political thinking of the tribal sheiks. He taught the American the history of his own tribe as well as the cultural mores of the region around his home village and Sanaa.

Hunter's State Department colleagues didn't know he was descended from an American aristocracy of sorts. During his years as a career diplomat he never divulged his family's status or his wealth. As a young man he had applied to study at Stanford University rather than attend his family's traditional choice of Harvard. In a further insult to his Wall Street banker father, he chose to major in Political Science instead of Business.

Intrigued by international politics and the art of diplomacy, he won a post-graduate grant to study for a Masters Degree in International Relations at American University. He wrote his thesis on "Middle Eastern and Arabic Historical Precedents Encouraging the Future Spread of Islamic Fundamentalism." At the same time as he completed his post graduate work, he applied to the Foreign Service. His acceptance into the State Department program filled him with wild enthusiasm, but his excitement was soon diminished by his father's reaction.

As the founder and senior partner in Farrington Investments, Sinclair Farrington was an impatient man given to short sentences and a shorter temper. He was a small, sparse man whose life's interest was making money and placing it in large piles inside a bank vault. Although a millionaire many times over, he lived to make more money. A totally cheerless man he had a long suffering wife whom he dismissed as too soft hearted and frivolous, and a son whom he considered a failure.

Ethel Farrington was a soft spoken gentle woman who busied herself with charitable good works and church duties while remaining vague and aloof from her husband and son. Normally, Ethel would not have argued with her husband, but it was her tenacity that succeeded in preventing Sinclair from cutting Hunter off financially while he was still a college student at Stanford. She convinced Sinclair Hunter's college choices were only a juvenile aberration and he would be a future asset to the family's business once he settled down and matured. All he needed was time.

The Farrington's had already moved to their lake home for the hot summer months when Hunter received his letter of acceptance to the Foreign Service. Hurrying out onto the country house's large porch area, he found his parents quietly reading.

"Father, mother. I've been accepted into the Foreign Service. My first assignment will be Paris!" His face was glowing with enthusiasm as he looked at each of them, waiting for their reaction. Sinclair puffed slowly on a cigar as he gazed out over the lush waterfront, saying nothing. Ethel fidgeted with her bible and murmured, "Oh my goodness. Paris. Is that Paris, France?" She asked timidly, her eyes darting from her son to her husband.

Hunter got down on his knees in front of her, and held her hands in his. "Yes, mother." He laughed quietly. "You will come and visit me and we will see all the wonderful things of that magnificent city. Together we'll learn all there is to know about the City of Light." His mother stared down at her feet, not answering.

Getting up off his knees he approached Sinclair. "Father, what do you think?" He asked. His eyes locked onto his father's face, his body stiff with suspense.

The old man puffed on his cigar slowly, taking a long time to answer. When he finally looked up he glared at his son. "What do I think? I think you have forgotten your promise to join our family's firm when you were finished with all of your nonsensical education. I think you've forgotten what, and more importantly who, has supported you in style, while you've wasted your time at school. Most of all, I think you have forgotten who you are. I think you never asked my permission to apply to the Foreign Service. You are not a fifty dollar a month government clerk. You are the heir to the Farrington fortune and have an obligation to help manage your family's business affairs. Now is the time for you to take your rightful post as a manager and a partner. If you do not, you will be the biggest disappointment of my life. That's what I think." Sinclair got up from his chair and stalked back into the house. Ethel wept quietly, dabbing her eyes with her handkerchief.

The family's final days together dragged by as the two men barely spoke, exchanging words only when it was unavoidable. Sinclair worked long hours at the office while Hunter methodically packed his belongings. Ethel stayed in her rooms, ill with the vapors. The day he departed for Europe Hunter kissed his mother goodbye, but never said goodbye to his father. He left him a short letter of farewell instead.

Hunter arrived in Paris as a junior attaché assigned to the American Embassy to assist the French with their Algerian problems. As the newest member of the American Embassy staff, he was formally presented to his colleagues at a weekly cocktail social hosted by the ambassador. There were dozens of people gathered in the large formal reception hall, but Hunter noticed only one. She was the embassy's French born Deputy Communications Director, Michelle Dubois. Petite and red-haired, she was known not only for her beauty, but her cleverness and razor sharp sense of humor. Hunter approached her at the first opportunity, mesmerized by her beauty.

"Mademoiselle Dubois, I don't think I've had the honor to make your acquaintance. I am Hunter Farrington." He reached out for her right hand and brushed his lips gently over the back of it.

"But of course we have been introduced." She laughed. "The Ambassador has just introduced you to the entire room. We are now old friends. Please call me Michelle." Her smile seemed to penetrate his soul and he fell in love. It took Michelle the rest of the week before she felt the same way.

They were married a few months later in a tiny country church on a rainy, warm Saturday afternoon in April, and set up housekeeping in a Left Bank apartment. Hunter had never been as happy. They both loved their work and on the few evenings they were at home, they either listened to classical music or entertained friends. Sometimes, Hunter would read Agatha Christie to Michelle, in French. Michelle laughed at his non-Parisian accent and teased that she could tell he was an American, but inwardly she was impressed with his grasp of her language and culture. Hunter already spoke four languages, two of them with no discernable accent. One of those was French, and the other was Arabic. He had begun studying Arabic while still an undergraduate in college, believing the newborn Middle Eastern petroleum industry had great business potential. As he became more intrigued by the history of the region and its diverse people, he continued his study of Arabic in graduate school. His new position in Paris now required he use the language daily with his Algerian counterparts.

By their first anniversary Michelle was pregnant. In their happiness, they excitedly planned for the birth of their child. The baby was to be born early in the coming New Year, but during a cold and rainy December Michelle became seriously ill. Hunter stayed by her side day and night in the hospital. Diagnosed with a deadly form of Influenza, both she and their unborn son perished. At twenty-five years old Hunter was a widower.

In desolation he traveled aimlessly around Europe and then, exhausted, headed to America. His mother had died from a massive stroke during the time Michelle had been ill. Upon his arrival home, he found his father stumbling in Dementia, the elder man barely able to recognize him. Sinclair was now fully retired and attended by a retinue of daily caregivers. The family business was successfully roaring along, earning more money than ever, due to competent executives.

The Farrington family attorney, Harold Tarrey requested to meet with Hunter at his first availability. Hunter met him the next day, in his parent's house.

"Hunter, I have been instructed by your father to give you information as to the dispensation of his estate."

"His estate? What are you talking about? He's still alive," Hunter responded, puzzled.

Tarrey patiently continued. "Some time ago, after your mother died, your father was still fully cognizant. Although he was able to conduct day to day business, he knew things were getting out of focus. He was aware he wasn't as quick witted and that something was wrong, but he hadn't been diagnosed yet. Somehow, he realized his condition would only worsen, and that he wanted to protect you as his heir. He arranged for me to design a trust for your family's assets. I accomplished what he ordered me to do and drew up the appropriate papers. He signed them three months ago. His physicians have now diagnosed him with Perpetual Dementia, therefore initiating the first phase of the trust. Because Sinclair is not capable of discussing this with you, it has therefore been left up to me to explain the details." The lawyer took a deep breath.

"While you are in the Foreign Service all assets of the Farrington firm will be administered by a dual trusteeship comprised of your family bank and your father's accountant. Both trustees will be supervised by me. Any expenses incurred by Sinclair and/or you will be paid by invoice to the accountant, and paid with the bank's approval. All profits created by the Farrington firm or any other profits created by the trust will be reinvested for future growth. I will conduct quarterly audits. When you are forty years old all assets will be turned over to you and you will be the sole trustee. Do you have any questions?" The lawyer waited.

"No." Hunter didn't care. He had no interest in any of it. After conferring with Harold about compensation for the caregivers to insure continued personal attention for his father, he bid his father and his country goodbye. He requested immediate assignment to the Middle East and was posted to Saudi Arabia as Junior Consular Officer in Riyadh. His father died the next year.

Time passed quickly as his assignments in the Middle East became more significant. Fifteen years from the day he left the United States for his first appointment he was named the American Consular General in Yemen. When he finally looked up from his State Department duties to reflect upon his promotion, he was also one of the richest men in the United States.

Hunter was intrigued by young Adel al Amar. The young man was bright, eager to learn, and an interested student of the world. He grasped political theorems easily while showing a real talent for learning English. His personality was as pleasing as it was dynamic, and Hunter found himself liking the boy. Sometimes he wondered if Adel conjured up poignant memories with his youthful enthusiasm, like a ghost from the past. Had he lived, Hunter's own son would have been only a handful of years younger than Adel. In truth, it was more than that. Hunter sensed something extraordinary in the youth. He had thoughtfully evaluated him, and knew that as a son of one of the most powerful tribal chiefs in Yemen, Adel might someday be an influential friend to the United States. With politics being as explosive as it was in the Middle East, you could never tell where people were going to wind up in the final tally. Adel might be a leader to reckon with in the future. Hunter decided to mentor the youngster.

The two men had been meeting with each other for about six months when both of them recognized the positive effects of their relationship. Hunter felt more energetic and interested in life than he had in years, and Adel had accrued more confidence in his own intellect, especially in his understanding of politics.

"Hunter what do you honestly think the future holds for my country?" Adel was leafing through a new book on the history of the Arab peoples and looked up to see Hunter writing notes in his journal.

"Hmm. That's a difficult question. I think that you're at a crossroads as a nation. First of all, you know that it is crucial that both partitioned pieces of your country unite forming one true nationality. It is not possible for Yemen to evolve as a nation in the modern world with a Communist government on its southern flank."

Adel smiled. "You Americans are so afraid of the Communists. Thousands of my countrymen migrated to the north because they knew they didn't want to stay within a Marxist government. I think because the fundamentals of Communist dogma are false, they will ultimately fail as an influence in the world. But, I don't want to have to wait and see the people of our south suffer until then. You politicians of the world move too slowly for my taste. This is why I am working for unification now."

Hunter replied slowly, carefully thinking through his words while looking at Adel.

"You're right. It is up to you and other patriots of Yemen to insure not only reunification, but the future direction of your country. You were once part of the Ottoman Empire and because of British national interests, later divided into two countries. Ancient history has shown you as an important people of the world, from before the Himyar Dynasty to the conversion of the Persians to Islam. You can be that again. Yemen can make a real contribution to the modern Middle East and you can play an important part in making that happen." Adel nodded his assent.

Later that month, Adel was driving home after an especially long evening get together with Hunter, when a group of mounted, armed tribesmen intercepted him. After being recognized, he was brusquely escorted to his home village. Upon his arrival in the town square his oldest brother Razul stepped forward from the crowd and reprimanded Adel.

"Adel al Amar, third son of Sheik Jamal of the Maerb, I admonish you for being absent from your tribe and your family this night. It is your responsibility as a member of our great family to remain by the side of your people during their time of need. Do you understand?" The men who escorted him home listened closely and nodded their approval. Adel stared questioningly at his brother trying to comprehend the real message he was sending. Finally, he was told.

"Our father, peace be upon him, has been taken to God this night and is already being mourned by the women. We do not know what caused his death, but he was praying when the great God summoned him. We will miss his leadership and his strength. God is great."

Razul leaned close to Adel's ear and hissed into it. "I looked for you everywhere. No one knew where you had gone. You are the last of our tribe to arrive. Where the hell have you been? Our people are terrified and need leadership. You will follow my orders from now on." Razul stomped out of the square.

To the villagers not only was the sheik of their tribe dead, but the head of their most powerful family was gone. The man who had led them for thirty years in peace and prosperity was no longer with them, and they desperately needed reassurance that their lives would remain stabilized, the tribe's status unchanged. Adel's oldest brother Razul had rightfully stepped in to fill the void of leadership as the oldest son of the dead sheik. It was his obligation to do so, but it was a frightening time for the tribesmen. Tribal continuity was vital. As the third son of Sheik Jamal, Adel should have been with his fellow tribesmen joining in the mourning for his father and displaying fealty to his brother.

He hurried into his father's house and entered a private study. He found Jamal's body laid out upon his day bed, freshly bathed and dressed in the finery of a Maerb sheik. The keening wail of the women reverberated off of the walls of the house. He knelt beside the body and said a prayer for the dead. As he lifted his head he looked up into his mother's eyes.

Fatima was tall and graceful, and, as her husband's first wife, the most powerful woman in the family. Adel was her third son and, despite that he was not of any great consequence in the family's order of things, she was very fond of him. She gently touched his shoulder as he stood up.

"Listen to me, my son. Remember and revere your father. Always keep in mind the great man that he was, and follow your brother Razul's lead in all things." He nodded and bowed to her.

"Come and see me after the mourning period. I have something of great importance to discuss with you."

As dictated by tradition, Razul had become tribal sheik upon his father's death. As the new leader, he ordered Adel to travel to the tribes of Communist South Yemen and bargain with them for new trade agreements. Adel was successful in procuring additional trade for his family. Using his business trips as an excuse, he lobbied on the side with local sheiks in South Yemen to accept the Americans' idea of unification. Before each trip he coordinated closely with Hunter and the consulate staff to prepare for his discussions. In response to his successes, the Communist government of South Yemen posted a death bounty on him and his family.

When her husband died, Fatima decided Adel would benefit by having a strong ally standing beside him. In order to succeed in life, he needed someone who would add to his stature in being a man and support him in all his endeavors. She sent word to her family to choose a bright and clever wife for her son, as soon as possible. As a sheik's daughter of the al Jouf tribe she could trace her bloodline back to the Queen of Sheba and made it clear to her relatives that only young women of exceptional quality would be acceptable to her as a daughter-in-law. Her family had wisely chosen Yasmina's mother, Suhair.

Suhair was the oldest daughter of a minor sheik of the al Jouf. Young and beautiful, she was her father's favorite, loved by her people for her kindness to the sick and the poor and her gentle personality. She was exceptionally bright and traditionally educated, possessing an inquiring mind as well as solid common sense; a seemingly perfect match for the daydreaming Adel.

His wedding had been arranged by his mother as soon as was permitted after the tribe's mourning period. Arrangements were quickly negotiated and agreed to by both families. Adel and Suhair met each other only once before their wedding day and fell in love at first sight.

Marriage was a revelation for restless Adel. For the first time in his life, he was happy. He adored his beautiful Suhair. He found himself sharing everything with her, especially the political ideas his American friend Hunter Farrington discussed with him. Suhair was eager to learn and began to study English and Arabic so that she could read Adel's books. As the months passed the young couple often discussed what they learned about America and wondered if they would ever be able to visit the fascinating country of freedom.

Adel began to bring Suhair with him to Hunter's evening sessions and watched in approval as she seemed to hang on every word the men debated in both Arabic and English. One night as they were debating the human rights outlined in the American Bill of Rights, Suhair timidly interrupted them. Her English was unsure so she addressed them in her home region's A'izzi-Adeni dialect.

"I think I hear you arguing about what men can and cannot do in America. I think that you are saying they have many guaranteed rights written in this document. Is that not so?" When they concurred, she continued. "Where are the rights for women written? I have heard nothing that gives women the right to do anything. Why is that?"

Hunter brightened and quipped approvingly. "Ah Suhair, how you would have loved meeting Abigail Adams. She was the wife of John Adams, one of the founding fathers of our country. As an outspoken advocate for women's rights she wanted women to be included in the constitution and have the right to vote in their new nation. Mrs. Adams was terribly disappointed when her husband and his colleagues failed to accomplish that."

"When did American women get the right to vote?" asked Suhair.

"The nineteenth amendment to the Constitution was passed in 1920," Hunter answered.

Suhair turned her head quizzically. "Why did it take so many generations?

"I don't know," he answered honestly.

Afterward, Hunter gave Suhair books to read on European and Middle Eastern Medieval law and history. The next time they met, he congratulated her on her grasp of historical principle as she proudly informed him that the books he had given her taught her that Muslim women's rights during the Middle Ages surpassed anything the Europeans allowed their women.

Adel and Suhair's world was idyllic, and when Suhair announced to Adel that she was pregnant, it was as if they were truly blessed. She gave birth to their son Fahd, a year from the date of their marriage. The baby was only a few weeks old when Hunter sent Adel an urgent summons to come to the consulate as soon as he could. Once they were alone, Hunter told him that the negotiations detailing the reunification of Yemen were almost completed and the outcome would be politically positive.

"But, this is all good news you have for me old friend," smiled Adel. "Why such an urgent summons?"

Hunter motioned for Adel to sit down. "You know the Southern Communists will relinquish control of the south for a price. They want millions of American dollars deposited in Swiss bank accounts for their personal use. That was never a problem. They have also demanded seats of power in the new unified government. That was a thorny issue to resolve, but again, not an insurmountable problem. We will work with both sides to see that is accomplished."

"What is it then?" Adel leaned forward, his interest piqued.

Hunter's voice was purposeful. "We found out that the Communists have put a bounty on your and your family. The Communist Imams have issued a fatwa targeting the destruction of your village. They did this to save face. They think these assassinations will show that they could not have been coerced into coming to the treaty table, but instead came in under their own accord."

Adel got to his feet and grabbed Hunter's arm. "Is there nothing you can do? I'm frightened for my people. You know my family is innocent of any involvement. I alone did the missions for you and your countrymen. You must help me to protect my people."

Hunter put his hand on Adel's arm. "I have given the order for our representatives to offer whatever it takes to rescind this fatwa and to pay a ransom for your family's safety. They will negotiate diligently with the Communists and eventually they will be successful, but we are afraid that some assassins may have already been dispatched. We just don't know. As your friend, I had to make you aware of what was happening."

Hunter looked at Adel solemnly. "I have assets available to me to protect you and your family. Should the occasion arise I will send an armed squad to supplement your village guards, and my people will watch all known border crossings closely watching for any unusual activity. Adel, listen to me closely. This is very important. I want you to know that the American government is offering political asylum to you and any members of your family who wish to immigrate to the United States. I'm asking you to seriously consider this offer. If not for your sake, for the sake of Suhair and little Fahd."

Adel was halfway out the door as Hunter finished speaking. He drove to his village and related to Razul and the elders of the tribe the news of the impending danger they faced. Precautions were initiated within the tribal guard and security was tightened on all approaching roads.

Three weeks later, Adel and Suhair and baby Fahd were at Hunter's consular office discussing details of their family's possible immigration to the United States when word of an attack on their village reached them. Hunter barked an order into the embassy phone. The two men raced down the stairs and out to the courtyard.

"Keep Suhair and Fahd with you," Adel yelled over his shoulder. "I will return for them later." Hunter strained to keep up with the twenty-five year old Adel and yelled back.

"I will. There's an armed escort waiting to accompany you at the gate. They are men who are loyal and will take orders." He stopped running, breathing heavily. Adel nodded that he understood as he sped through the gate with a truck full of armed men following him.

Arriving at his village two hours after the assault he found almost total devastation, many of the buildings still smoldering from where mortar shells had hit them. Men, women and children's bodies lay scattered throughout the streets, alongside their butchered livestock.

Adel found his mother and brothers' bodies. Each had been slaughtered in their own house, their throats slit from ear to ear. The village's crops had been cut down and burned. Salt was strewn heavily on the soil to prevent anything from growing in the future. Total war had enveloped the village of the al Amars and destruction was complete.

No one knew how many villagers managed to successfully escape into the mountains and survive the massacre. It would be years before verification of their individual existence reached Dearborn, Michigan but Adel al Amar never forgot about them or forgave himself for leaving them behind.

He and Suhair escaped to United States with their son. Hunter Farrington secretly watched over them as they traveled into the foothills behind the capital city of Sanaa and were airlifted out in the middle of the night to an American aircraft carrier. With Hunter's help they arrived safely in the United States and began to make a new life for themselves and their child. Over the years their impressive successes included more children, the accumulation of wealth and the respect of their adopted countrymen. They never returned to Yemen and never lived anywhere else except Dearborn, Michigan until the day they were murdered.

CHAPTER 2

Adel al Amar's office wall was covered with the affirmation of over twenty years of notable accomplishments. Framed awards hung in long rows, alongside numerous honorary degrees intermingled with signed photographs of politicians and statesmen.

As a publisher Adel presided over his weekly newspaper editorial meetings with principal staff members listening attentively as he enumerated the latest topics he wished them to write about. As editors, they had the tentative right to disagree and debate with him, but more times than not he won them over to his point of view with seemingly crystal clear logic. It was a foregone conclusion that he would always present both sides of an argument equally and without bias. Although perceived as a middle aged progressive by outsiders, he personally held to the traditional Middle Eastern views of duty to family and country to be fundamental in all things. Although not a devout man, he obeyed and respected the tenants of his religion. Preferring to be a catalyst for free thinking, he did not impose his personal ideology on anyone else.

Next to his beloved wife, his children were his life's passion and he adored them beyond words. As a father, he was a model of directed parentage. He never disciplined his three sons and daughter, but rather worked with each of them to create and develop individual goals. As a child achieved one set of goals, new ones were put in their place. His children thrived on the leap frog competition, growing solidly with quiet intellectual confidence. Adel was aware of the challenges they would face as adults and knew that, in order to survive, they would have to be contributing citizens of not only America, but the world. One of his primary objectives was to have them think for themselves, and take nothing for granted. His most revolutionary and utterly American belief was that his daughter Yasmina was equal in every way to his three sons. He expected the same excellence from her that he did from her brothers.

All of his children were leaders within their peer groups and schools. His oldest son Fahd attended the University of Michigan, graduated with honors and now taught mathematics at one of the best middle schools in the state. His younger twin sons were honor students in high school and already perceived the world as a positive place where they would make future contributions. His daughter Yasmina, was the second oldest and possibly his brightest child. She thrived and blossomed within the competitive world of her three brothers. Adel noted that when faced with a challenge she excelled beyond even his expectations. He remembered when she was fifteen years old she had fallen, breaking her arm. She did not complain about the initial pain of the fall or the discomfort of the bulky cast, but as soon as the cast was removed she exercised her muscles to the maximum so that she would not miss any athletic events. Her personal discipline was rigorous, and she allowed herself no excuses for failure.

His daughter would attend college in the east in September. To her parent's consternation, she had chosen a Catholic school, Georgetown

University. Although her father was aware that she was possessed of a strong personal character, he had some misgivings about his overly secular daughter being exposed to a powerful religion known for its ability to attract converts. He expressed his concerns to her one day while they were working together at the newspaper. Yasmina volunteered after school when she could, enjoying the private time with her father.

"Yasmina, do you really want to attend the very Catholic Georgetown University in Washington, D.C. for its curriculum or are you just testing your mother and me?" Adel addressed her from across the conference table, his eyes filled with warm amusement.

Yasmina stopped what she was doing and looked at him with a quizzical smile.

"Why'd you say that father? What's up?"

He smiled at her. "I think the religious dogma that created Georgetown University is a most powerful force. You are still very young and impressionable and might be unduly influenced by the Catholic religion. You know, it is not unheard of for people to change their beliefs after experiencing intellectual pressures, and you are not what I would term a religious Muslim. We will worry about you," he lifted his eyebrow.

"Oh father, you're too much!" Yasi responded back dismissively. She continued in a lecturing tone. "If you think that being exposed to, and learning intellectual arguments about a new religion will convert me to becoming a Catholic, you are selling me short. I should be insulted. Yes, I am a Muslim, and I'm not devout. That's a part of who I am. But, I am also a woman, an American and an al Amar. These are all powerful descriptions, but each one only defines a part of me. I am a conglomeration of more things than I can list and each of them is important. You've always told me that new ideas are to be searched out, investigated and examined. Why would that tenet change now?"

She continued.

"Listen father, although Georgetown University is a Catholic Church affiliated university, it is first and foremost a premier seat of learning. Religious leanings aside, it's one of the most prestigious colleges in the world in the field of International Relations. Good God in Heaven. Why would I settle for a lesser school to educate me because of what religion founded it over a hundred years ago? Georgetown didn't care that I wasn't a Catholic. They looked at my grades and my leadership abilities and evaluated me as a student who would succeed. I'm proud they placed me on their early admittance list. Your concerns are totally unfounded." She flipped her long hair impatiently as she ruffled the papers she was sorting.

"Yasmina," Adel admonished, hiding a smile. "Do not refer to God in such an off hand way. I see your point and I defer to it." The conversation ended and they both returned to their editing. Adel knew if he continued to argue about Georgetown, Yasmina's rebuttals would be logical and to the point. She had made up her mind. She was going to study International Relations at one of the foremost universities in the world, and had been pre-selected from thousands of qualified applicants. Why should she attend a different school because of his religious reservations? It fact, she was a Muslim, but his family was sophisticated in their devotion. He knew Yasmina was respectful of her religion and tolerant of others. If Georgetown University did not care what religion she practiced, why should she care what religion founded it? She was right. Adel let his concerns fade into the background.

Yasi, as she was called by her friends, was aware that had she lived in parts of the conservative Middle East, being born a woman was something she would have to overcome. Within her parent's ancient culture, being female would have marked her for a rigidly defined role. Even in present day Yemen, educated women did not compete against men, but chose traditional professions. Yemeni society preferred that women remain at home. Because she was raised by progressive parents in America during the early nineteen eighties, Yasi felt it was her birthright to have the opportunity to excel at anything she chose. When Adel and Suhair lectured their children on how proud they should be of their ancient tribal culture as well as modern American values, Yasi listened out of respect, but remained emotionally detached. Her mother and father hoped she would be proud to be an Arab-American, but the young woman considered herself an American. She had no interest in hearing about the outdated tribal traditionalism and mores that had been her parent's heritage. She felt her greatest strength came from being born in a free nation where she could accomplish any goal with hard work and talent.

Just eighteen years old, Yasmina al Amar stood five-foot-six inches tall with wavy shoulder length hair. Slim hipped and long legged, she was perfect physical mix of her parents. She had the lean body of her father, but the bone structure and large eyes of her mother. Her long legs were well muscled, the result of athletic competition in cross country, varsity soccer and local marathon races. Her forehead was broad and smooth with wide-set deep brown eyes that sparkled when she smiled. Her soft, angular face hinted at her Arabic tribal roots. A natural beauty, she could put on an oversized T-shirt and jeans, tuck her hair up into a cap, and pass for a teenaged boy.

A favorite family story tells of a time when she was fifteen years old. Dressed in boy's jeans and wearing a ball cap, she was walking home from the library when she stopped to watch a fast moving soccer game.

"Hey, brother! Do you play soccer? Do you wanna play?" A boy's voice carried over the fence to her. "We need a wing." Yasi saw the sideline coach nod okay. She ran onto the field. After scoring three goals and winning the game for her team, she took off her hat and let her long hair fall.

"Ow! You're a girl. The goals don't count. No fair!" The opposing team howled in self righteousness. "You're not a guy. No fair!" The referee waved the boys away, came up to her and shook her hand. "What's your name young lady?"

"Yasi al Amar." She answered straightforwardly.

"Well done, Yasi al Amar. We have an opening on this team, and I know any team would love to have you join them. You have a great left foot." The boys she had played with stood around him, nodding enthusiastically, cajoling her to sign up.

"I can't. Sorry. I live over by the country club and already play in a league, but thank you so much for asking. I've got to go now." She turned and jogged off.

Her favorite hobby was astronomy, an interest she shared with her oldest brother. She and Fahd spent many nights on the roof of their house peering through a used telescope they had bought in a resale store. They mapped the constellations that hovered above their Michigan street and watched the stars in the skies change positions from season to season. Her most cherished high school graduation present was an antique sextant her father gave her so that she could learn how to navigate from the sun, just like sailors had done for hundreds of years.

Her oldest brother always acted as her protector, and helped instill a feeling of invincibility within her. At age five, while on a picnic she snuck away from her mother and followed Fahd and his friends down a pathway to a local lake. The boys dove off an old dock into deep water, and did not notice tiny Yasmina running to join them. As they plunged into the icy depths, the cold water took their breath away and they surfaced laughing, swimming away from the shore.

In her effort to catch up, Yasi was running as she jumped into the water at the end of the dock. As she landed in a belly flop on top of the lake's surface, the air in her lungs was instantly expelled. The little girl sank down into the lake's murkiness, but instinctively flailed her arms and legs in a facsimile of how she had seen the boys swim. Hearing his mother's scream, Fahd looked back. He saw Yasi's head break the lake's surface yards away, and then disappear.

Swimming furiously, he reached the spot where she had gone under and dove down, finding her on his second try. She was under the surface, but still swimming strongly. Yasi had intuitively swum up toward the light, creating her one chance of being saved. As Fahd towed her to the bank of the lake, she continued to try to swim, moving her arms and legs in dog paddle fashion. Once safely on the lake shore, she did not cry but jumped into Suhair's lap wide eyed and shivering, her little arms tightly wrapping around her mother. After a few minutes of being coddled she walked up to Fahd and punched him hard on the leg.

"You didn't wait up," she pouted.

Yasi's oldest brother had been born in the country of Yemen, and became a naturalized American at the same time her parents did. As she grew up Fahd helped to convince her she was the best runner, the brightest student, and the prettiest girl in school. He was her most ardent cheerleader and best friend. When he married, she felt his happiness within her own heart. Now he was the father of a young daughter and lived within five miles of their parent's home in Dearborn. Her younger, twin brothers were in high school, and her mother's stated pride and joy.

Suhair called them the most handsome of her children and the children of her heart.

She and her twin brothers were born in Dearborn, Michigan. Having three brothers to grow up with gave Yasi a unique understanding of boys and their egos, and she more than held her own when it came to their bullying and teasing. Although it was the three of them against one of her, Yasi considered it an even match. Yasi's school grades were better than theirs and she constantly challenged their superior attitude with a strong brand of her own. Not only an honor student and Merit Scholarship finalist, she was president of her class and a member of student government. She lettered in track and field and soccer. Her love of running induced her to try out for both sports. She was captain of the woman's soccer team, assistant captain of the cross country team, and a junior champion in state marathon competition. Her leadership style was tempered with humor, laced with a large dose of self deprecation. It was a combination that made her popular with both students and teachers. She appeared to be a solid young woman who had set lofty goals for herself and would travel successfully on the road of life to achieve them.

Before high school, she began to participate in junior marathons and quickly advanced. Adel watched in awe as his daughter entered the competitions with a ferocity that brought back feelings of the warrior race that was locked deeply within him. When Yasmina ran, an untapped wildness was released. He could see a feeling of joy begin in her face and spread throughout her body as she was released from earth's normal restraints. Her physical power reminded him of the ferocity of old Yemeni tribesmen of his youth. Yasi possessed a steel-edged will to win, regardless of the price to get there. She seemed happiest when she was challenged to the maximum.

On days she did not have athletic practice or school activities she would hurry over to her father's office and work at whatever task was necessary to get the paper to press. She had helped out at the newspaper since she was a small girl, and learned to read and write Arabic by blocking the newspaper's columns. Eventually, she demonstrated a patient talent for attention to detail that was required to be a good proofreader. Her father always made time for her and was gratified when she asked him to be allowed to help. As she matured, she impressed Adel by asking intelligent and well thought out questions about the complex political situations printed in the paper.

They read the news together, discussed local and international politics and wondered about America's future interests. Just as Suhair had been his muse as a young man, Yasmina was now the catalyst that once again made Adel feel intellectually alive. He found himself looking forward to his daughter's office visits and often proudly discussed her precociousness with Suhair. Adel loved his daughter's mind, her insistence on finding out why something was the way it was, and encouraged her to find truth on all levels. Her questions would initiate intense give- and- take sessions between father and daughter, with Adel eagerly becoming both teacher and mentor. He would fill Yasmina with information and then challenge her to find her own answers to the questions she asked him. He wanted her to formulate her own opinions and learn to use him as only one of her sources.

One afternoon as Adel was proofreading the newspaper's editorial page Yasi asked him if he thought the Palestinians and the Israelis would ever make peace. "Yasmina, you might as well ask me if I know where King's Solomon's mine is. I have absolutely no idea……"

"But, you are in contact with both sides on a daily basis. They confer with you," she interrupted.

Adel continued. "What I do know however, is that leadership is the most important factor in any progress toward peace. In that, I mean the men who are the leaders of their countries are a crucial determiner of what their country can do. But there's a heavy price Middle Eastern leaders pay for political moderation. Remember Anwar Sadat of Egypt? In 1977 he was the first Arab leader to visit Israel and with Menachem Begin, signed the Camp David Peace Agreement. He won the Nobel Peace Prize for his efforts, but his negotiations with Israel were extremely unpopular at home. In 1981, when he tried to crack down on dissidents within Egypt, a Fundamentalist cleric by the name of Omar Abdel-Rahman issued a fatwa approving his assassination. He was gunned down at a military parade by army soldiers who were part of the Egyptian Islamic jihad. It was an unfortunate event. He was a good man. They should not have killed him. He understood that peace was more important than national pride. That doesn't happen very often." He spoke the last words quietly.

Yasmina responded, "So, I hear in your voice that you are not optimistic. But can't today's leaders be made to see reason? Men like you know peace is the only way to secure the future of the region."

"Men like me will try, but your generation must succeed if we leave off."

She nodded enthusiastically. "You're right. If you fail, we will succeed."

Because of her interest in his world of publishing, she filled his heart with hope for the future. His sons had not shown any interest in the paper, or in studying Middle Eastern politics. Yasmina, however, not only had the interest, but the talent. She was a perfect choice to continue in his footsteps. It would be a difficult road for her to travel, but if she chose to go down it, he would make sure that she had the training and the tools to accomplish her goal. Until then, she must continue her studies. Yasmina was scheduled to leave for college where her major in International Policies would be completed in a three year accelerated program, and she would segue immediately into the International Relations Master's Program. When she was finished her goal was to either enroll in the Foreign Service or to work for an international conglomerate. Adel hoped she would change her mind and work with him.

Yasmina's family history was unique. Surviving members of her father's family had emigrated from Yemen and followed him to America, but her mother Suhair had never seen any of her family or tribe again. It was not spoken of openly, but Adel confided to Yasmina his village in Yemen was destroyed because of his pro-Western political actions as a young man. He told her he had acted as an agent on behalf of the American government helping to unify Yemen. Because of that, the Communist government of South Yemen ordered the annihilation of his entire village. The ghosts of his people lived within him and he never forgot how fortunate he had been to escape to America.

Although Suhair al Amar was a traditionalist at heart, and considered her primary roll in life to be a wife and mother, she eagerly took advantage of the opportunity to earn a college degree in the United States. The years her children were in school she taught English as a second language to new immigrants, volunteering three times a week. She could have tried to raise her children more traditionally, as an adjunct to their American way of life, but insight told her that would be a mistake. She knew she had made the right decision to raise her offspring as modern Americans, but as she watched her young daughter develop, she became concerned that Yasmina regarded her Yemeni heritage as unimportant. Unlike her brothers, Yasmina thought the role of Arab women as inconsequential in the modern world and showed minimal interest in the genetic gifts she might have inherited from her ancestors. She was solely Western in her ideology. The youngster imagined herself an American woman born to parents who were immigrants from Yemen, as if her heritage was something she must rise above. Although Yasi adored her mother, and tried to emulate her great hearted dedication to family, she personally thought Suhair had never reached her true potential.

Suhair was aware of her daughter's intellectual precociousness. Knowing her children were safe and sound as Americans pleased her. They would be able to live in a place where personal initiative and hard work dictated success. In America men succeeded with their women standing beside them, not behind them. With all this, Suhair hoped as Yasmina matured she would develop a broader understanding of her inherited genetic gifts. She knew she couldn't dictate to her daughter, but would instead act as a reminder that she was more than just a child of immigrants. She needed to explore her undiscovered strengths and realize she was descended from a powerful line of warrior tribesmen.

As a young girl growing up in Yemen, Suhair had been protected by her parents from becoming individually and intellectually active. Instead, she was groomed to be become a wife and mother. As Suhair watched her children grow, she knew she had to encourage them to experience and explore the world.

Yasmina loved her mother's gentleness and responded to Suhair's sweet nature but, on a day to day basis she preferred the company of men. When she was not with her father, quizzing him about why things in the world were the way they were, she was with her older brother and his friends, demanding to be allowed to join in daredevil stunts. She had many friends in high school, but, most were boys. Her girl friends were either athletic team mates or school leaders. During her junior year in high school, her closest girl friend, Cheryl Huggand suggested they ask their parents to send them to an Outward Bound style boot camp during the school's month long summer vacation. Cheryl reasoned it would not only help them lose weight, but put them in shape for the upcoming athletic season.

Twenty-four hours after their arrival at the camp Yasi realized the summer course was going to be one of the most inspiring things she ever attempted. She responded with unbounded enthusiasm to the cadre's difficult list of month-long challenges. Each training day began at dawn and ended at sunset. Yasi's success in conquering the camp's targets was the the opposite of Cheryl's. Her friend was a reluctant recruit and failed to achieve daily goals that stressed both the attendees bodies and minds.

Each day early morning conditioning exercises alternated with hard physical training. White water rafting, tree and rock climbing, and courage slides made things exciting for Yasi, but miserable for Cheryl. Her friend left for home after the first week, using stomach flu as an excuse.

The day Yasi successfully climbed up to the top of a hundred-foot rock cliff and repelled back down, she felt a blast of adrenalin that was indescribable. She repeated the repel three times, only stopping because instructors would not allow her to continue. Confident she could complete whatever task the camp cadre asked her to do, she was now aware of personal accomplishment as an adjunct to physical hardship. Given correct instruction and proper physical conditioning, she could do anything. The course ended too soon for her liking.

Back at home, she and Cheryl were flipping through college brochures when Cheryl admitted she had been bored with the camp's physical conditioning and horrified by the difficult personal goals they were expected to accomplish.

"How did you ever last in that dump?" asked Cheryl shaking her head. "What a concentration camp. God! I mean, like, you know, every camp counselor thought he was like the crocodile guy. And the camp food was indescribable. I've never eaten so many different forms of grains and raisins. Yuk!" She grimaced in disgust.

Yasi's face was glowing. "Cher, I'll tell you. I had a blast. The day you left, we trekked ten miles cross country, climbed a huge Redwood and ate fresh trout we caught ourselves. I don't think I've ever had more fun. I agree that the morning PT sessions were sucky, but look at me; I'm slimmer than I've ever been. I feel great!" Yasi smiled and twirled around, showing off her figure.

"Well, you look like a boy," pouted Cheryl. "I mean, you lost weight I guess, but I think you lost it in your boobs. I can't see your boobs anymore. You didn't have a lot to start with, but ….."

Yasi peeked down her shirt front. "Yeah, well, I did lose it partly up there, I guess, but I can stuff something inside my bras to make up the difference. Look at this though; it's hard as a rock," she patted her butt proudly.

"I finally have a buff butt!" She turned sideways to Cheryl who smiled and nodded in agreement.

Suhair had noticed a change in her daughter immediately after her return from summer camp. She was more angular, especially in the face. Her arms had definition and she somehow seemed taller. Even her legs seemed longer. She moved with physical confidence and glowed with good health. Some of it was probably due to weight loss but more likely it was the result of her body reacting to weeks of hard physical training.

Yasmina had always been athletic and Suhair knew the reason why. It was genetic. Physical challenge played an important part of who she was and would become. Her body needed to be challenged, just as her mind did. Suhair smiled with pride. Yasmina was, after all, the granddaughter of a Yemeni princess who could trace her bloodline directly back to the Queen of Sheba. Her grandfather had been a powerful tribal chieftain and her ancestors were the fierce warrior tribesmen of Yemen. Her daughter was the fortunate recipient of a centuries old gene pool of survivors and winners, a treasure trove of natural selection. Suhair knew Yasmina would be a blazing success at whatever she chose to do, and a formidable adversary against anyone who chose to try and stop her, or be her enemy.

CHAPTER 3

Mohammed bin Fasheed stood a little over six feet tall with a body that was well proportioned and generously muscled. His curly black hair, dark skin and chiseled facial features reflected his Bedouin bloodlines. His lips were set in what seemed like a perpetual smirk and framed a mouth filled with perfectly enameled white teeth. On the surface, he appeared a genial and good natured man, but he was not. His coal black eyes were almost mesmerizing. They keenly observed the people and events happening around him. They were the eyes of a hunter.

Startlingly handsome, he moved with a masculine grace that suggested years of athletic and martial arts training. His English was American accented, and, depending upon his mood, his attire was either casual American or European. He appeared to regard women with exaggerated respect and treated them with almost archaic chivalry. His college friends knew him as the supreme ladies' man, renowned for hosting the best college parties in the state of California. At twenty-three years old, he seemed to always have a beautiful girl on his arm and an expensive sports car to drive. Typically, he was either on his way to a party or returning from one.

He had just finished his fifth year of lackluster undergraduate study at UCLA, completing the minimum requirements for a Bachelors degree. He would not attend his graduation, but would, instead, receive his diploma in absentia while back in Saudi Arabia. Mohammed had been recalled to Riyadh by his father to help with a family business crisis. As soon as the problem was resolved, he would return to the United States to begin his studies for an MBA at Georgetown University.

His father, Akbar bin Fasheed, was wealthy, even by oil rich Middle East standards. He owned a half dozen palaces in Saudi Arabia, estates in Europe and homes in America. A descendent of one of his country's most prominent families, his forebears had loyally served the royal family ever since their great grandfather had taken control of the country.

Over the years, the Fasheeds had been granted special privileges and opportunities, growing increasingly wealthy and powerful alongside their royal overseers. At first, the majority of their income was earned by managing and overseeing the investments of the royal family and collecting a percentage of the profits. Now, they owned conglomerates around the world in their own right while still serving their royal benefactors.

At nineteen years old, Mohammed's father, Akbar, had been the first young man of his tribe selected by the family's elders to be sent to college in the United States. This was with the concurrence of the royal family. Both families wanted to cement the profitable business relationship between them. When he completed his MBA, Akbar would become the youngest business advisor to the royal family, with the potential of becoming the most influential businessman on the Arabian Peninsula. By supervising a large portion of his country's financial portfolio, he would earn millions for his family and assure that they would also continue to prosper.

For six years, Akbar lived and studied in the United States, excelling academically and dutifully learning to manage his future responsibilities. His completed his undergraduate work at UCLA and earned his MBA from Wharton at the University of Pennsylvania in an accelerated program. During school breaks, he dutifully commuted back to his homeland, visited family and advised the elders as to how he planned to expand the businesses of his royal clients. Obedient to his family's wishes, he never stopped focusing on the goals of growth and the accumulation of wealth.

Akbar kept mistresses in New York and Paris, and although he had romantic liaisons while living in the United States, he never considered marrying an American woman. He thought Western women too flighty and hard to control, with preposterous ideas of equality. He did not want to dilute his pure Bedouin bloodline with the blood of an Infidel. Women were for breeding sons and Akbar was determined to have a large family of male heirs to help administer his future empire. Saudi tradition directed that he would wait and marry whomever his mother chose as a bride for him. Of her eight surviving sons, he was his mother's favorite, and he knew she would choose a woman from a powerful family for him to wed. With a rich and powerful bride, he would gain status and increase his wealth and, when his father died, as the eldest son, he would be named sheik.

The years passed as Akbar worked meticulously for success. He never forgot the lessons he learned as a student in America, especially the tenant, "No one watches your money better than you do." To that end, even though he employed gifted corporate managers, he traveled from one country to another, overseeing his far flung conglomerate, micromanaging his investments. His hard work and business acumen earned him the respect of the King and the senior princes of the royal family. They trusted him as they would a brother. Year after year, he generated sizeable profits for his family and his countrymen until he became the royal family's principal investment banker.

In recognition of the bond between them, the princes invited Akbar and his family to accompany them to their palaces within the Kingdom. In the summer, they traveled to Jedda on the Red Sea and to the cool mountain palaces of the Asir region. While they vacationed, he and the senior princes discussed future business plans. His children played with theirs, his wives were included in the royal princesses' shopping trips to London and Paris. He felt content.

Each of his four wives lived in their own mansion-sized house within the one mile square family compound in Riyadh. Akbar's personal palace was purposely built in the middle. As was customary, he lived alone. When he wanted to have sex with one of his wives, he summoned one to his bed. This system had blessed him with eighteen children, seven of them male.

Fawzi, his firstborn son, had been born a disappointment. He was the only child of Akbar and his first wife, Lala. She was his uncle's daughter, the child of his father's brother. She was his first cousin, but she was also the offspring of a marriage of first cousins. Often ill and under the constant care of doctors, she suffered through four miscarriages before their son had been born. The birth had been difficult and she had almost died during delivery. Doctors told Akbar that she would never survive another pregnancy.

From the moment of Fawzi's birth it was obvious the boy was mentally and physically handicapped. Jaundiced and physically underdeveloped, he needed intensive care during the first months of his life. After struggling through numerous childhood colds and pneumonia, his health remained frail. At six years old, he was only partially toilet trained and spoke in simple phrases. His physical and mental development had never caught up with the norms for his age.

Fawzi could be entertained by toddler's games and cartoon videos, but did not interact or respond well to people. He was difficult to teach. He spent the majority of each day being pampered and entertained by his mother's servants, sleeping in his bed with favorite toys. Pediatric specialists eventually confirmed what Akbar had concluded for himself. His oldest son would never be normal or be able to care for himself. He would have to be watched over for the rest of his life. The doctors diagnosed him as having an Autism Spectrum Disorder, to include physical handicaps.

Akbar had seen this condition in the children of other wealthy families. In past generations, purity of bloodlines was sometimes maintained by brothers marrying their sisters, and first cousins still married as a matter of course. The thought that incestuous marriage could be the cause of children being born mentally and physically impaired was never considered. Saudi men universally believed that it was a flaw in the mother's genes that caused the problem. In order to save face, some prominent families institutionalized their special needs children immediately after birth, never seeing them or acknowledging their existence.

In Fawzi's case, things would be handled with diplomacy and tact. Lala's father was not only a powerful sheik within the tribe, but Akbar's father's favorite brother. Although Akbar no longer had any interest in whether his small son lived or died, he chose not to send the boy away. Instead, he told Lala that she could do what she wanted with the child as long as he didn't have to see him.

Lala raised the boy quietly by herself and, for his own safety, purposely kept him far away from his father. She knew her husband had told her the truth. He would never want to see Fawzi again, or be reminded of his existence. She also knew that since she could no longer bear any more children, her husband would have no interest in bedding her. He would have divorced her if he could, but her family was too powerful. She contented herself with a future of supervising her son's welfare, shopping and gossiping with the women.

As Akbar looked to his other sons for an heir, he knew what traits he wanted his successor to have. His second born, Mohammed, caught his interest from the day he was born and seemed a likely choice. Mohammed was his son by his second wife, Basha'ir. A year after Fawzi's birth, a second marriage had been arranged for Akbar. Elder sheiks had decided that, for the tribe's security, adjacent lands of a neighboring tribe should be brought under their control. His uncles had chosen a thirteen-year-old girl from a large and devout Bedouin family. Her tribe's ancestral lands bordered the western region and would secure their holdings for generations. The tribal elders of both families signed an agreement and plans for the marriage began.

A shy, sensitive girl, Basha'ir had been hurriedly dispatched from her parent's home to her wedding in Riyadh. She traveled with her male relatives in a retinue appropriate to her father's status as a minor Bedouin sheik. Upon her arrival at Akbar's majestic compound, she was startled to see the opulence that awaited her and shyly stayed within the women's quarters. Her father was greatly pleased with the obvious wealth of the Fasheeds and the generous bride price offered for his daughter, and agreed to marry her immediately to Akbar. The wedding ceremony was brief. After they admonished Basha'ir to uphold her family's honor by being a good wife and mother, her father and uncles hurriedly left for home. Frightened and lonely, she clung to the one person she knew in the palace, her personal maid. The girl was two years older than she was.

As dictated by tradition, she had not met her husband privately until the night of the official marriage ceremony. Basha'ir had only the most basic knowledge of adult male anatomy, and had not been told of the practices that might occur during sexual intercourse. Her mother had instructed her to readily submit to her husband's will and to please him in all things, but she did not know what the consummation of her marriage would mean.

Akbar had been sexually active since he was ten years old. He had traveled a great deal and was now a sexually experienced man with deviant tastes. Although he gave an outwardly conservative appearance, over the years he made many trips to Beirut and was well known within the brothels of that city. At twenty-seven years old, he was at the height of his sexual powers. He knew his new wife would be a virgin, but he had already bedded many of those in the Lebanese brothels, and was not enticed by her innocence. He wanted Basha'ir to perform in bed exactly as he instructed her. Her first duty was to make the act of sexual intercourse pleasurable for him. From his perspective, the only other responsibility she had was to produce sons. He would sexually use her as he saw fit, and as often as he wished.

Basha'ir's first night as a wife was horrific. She had politely refused her servant's offering of a glass of juice laced with a narcotic before going to her bridal bed, and had been badly frightened and bruised as Akbar mounted her repeatedly throughout the night and the following days. When she awoke each morning, she became physically ill, filled with dread of the oncoming night's sexual attack. A month passed and she began to try and fend off his aggressiveness. She refused his demands and wept pitifully, begging him to leave her alone. The more withdrawn Basha'ir became, the more aggressive Akbar acted. He believed her sexual reluctance was conscious disobedience to his will and was a behavior that he would not tolerate from a woman. He repeatedly raped her, forcing her to submit to both vaginal and anal sex. In the mornings, her maid would administer to her wounds and give her a narcotic so that she could sleep. Two months after her wedding night, Basha'ir slashed her wrists but failed to die. On her husband's orders, she was put on a twenty-four hour suicide watch and kept in total isolation, away from everyone except her personal servant.

Family physicians conducted examinations of her physical wounds and counseled Akbar to have patience. She was very young and obviously frightened. They prescribed mood elevating drugs, along with exercise and hearty food. Over the next months, Basha'ir seemed to improve little, barely tolerating Akbar's sexual advances and weeping persistently upon sight of him. She begged him to return her to her family. Determined to crush her to his will, he flew her with him to his villa in Spain. Once there, his personal physician administered a daily dose of a powerful hallucinogenic to her. Basha'ir was so overpowered by the drug that she vacillated between moods of manic excitement and stupefying depression. She no longer knew what day it was, or cared what happened to her.

Akbar took the change in her behavior to be more accommodating and took her submission as an opportunity to introduce her to his world of sado-masochistic sex. She soon became addicted to the daily narcotic, and, when she discovered she was pregnant, tried once again to commit suicide. At the news of her pregnancy, Akbar ordered her to be sent back to Riyadh and placed back in her solitary room. She was guarded twenty-four hours a day until Mohammed was born.

During the birth of her son, Basha'ir hemorrhaged, the physicians barely able to stop the bleeding. She lay unconscious as her son was taken from her and given to a wet nurse.

The physicians pronounced the baby perfect in every way, even though he showed signs of addiction to the drugs that had been forced upon his mother. The doctors told Akbar that Basha'ir's womb had been perforated by the birth of the child and she would never be able to have another. On Akbar's orders, the doctors insured doses of prescription drugs continued to flow unabated into his wife so she could not attempt to take her life again. Basha'ir lingered in a drug induced haze, unable to comprehend that she had given birth and never asked to see her newborn son.

After he was assured his son would survive, Akbar decided he would divorce his rebellious wife. Infuriated that he already had one wife who could no longer breed, he did not want to pay to keep another. The law required he was obliged to support Basha'ir as long as they were married and maintain her lifestyle equal to his first wife's. He could divorce her by verbally stating three times that he wished to do so, but, under those circumstances, he would have to return her dowry to her father. Her dowry was worth far more than the bride price Akbar had paid. It included livestock, gold bullion, and the precious property the tribal elders had wanted. He would not forfeit such riches and could not allow her to kill herself, as his family's honor would be challenged.

Devising a plan, he summoned his counselors. Acting the part of an ill-treated husband, he charged Basha'ir with not properly executing her duties as a wife, as well as exhibiting salacious and immoral behavior. He accused her of being a drug addict, and an unfaithful wife. Therefore, he declared she was unfit as a mother. His retainers would testify to the truth of these charges, and Akbar had already ordered an itinerant goat herder to be murdered for his fictional part in Basha'ir's infidelity.

Declaring their newborn son as his true offspring and property, he would retain Mohammed as he made arrangements to have Basha'ir returned to her family in disgrace.

The consequence of the charges against her would cause her family to lose face and grievously dishonor them. Tribal custom dictated that, under those circumstances, her father could not ask for her dowry back. In order to save her family's honor, she would probably be killed or put in solitary confinement for the rest of her life. Akbar would retain her property.

Pitying her young mistress and distraught over what she had heard from Akbar's servants, her maid told Basha'ir about the charges against her. With the servant woman's help, Basha'ir hoarded enough of her medication to overdose and finally kill herself. In accordance with custom, she was buried in the desert in an unmarked grave. Mohammed never saw his birth mother. Akbar married again within a month of his fourteen-year-old wife's death.

Mohammed was initially raised by his wet nurse and her husband, but was taken away from them when he was three. Given to his father's brother, he was ignored within his uncle's family of ten sons and five daughters until Akbar summoned him to live at the palace when he was seven years old. He met the rest of his half brothers and sisters and Akbar's other wives for the first time, but did not see his father.

As he watched his son grow up, Akbar thought Mohammed to be the cleverest of all his sons, but far from perfect. He was bright and could be disarmingly charming but unfortunately exhibited unmanageable fits of rage. As a small boy, he would fly into a tantrum whenever he saw any of his half brothers and sisters being embraced by their mothers. He would throw rocks, attack them with his fists and spit in their faces. His half siblings were terrified of him and kept their distance. As he matured, his violent outbursts increased in their intensity and perversity. When he was not immediately obeyed or was denied what he wanted, he would strike out and inflict physical pain. A lonely, angry child, he was often foul mouthed and cruel. Almost daily, retainers of the Fasheed household were forced to protect themselves from the stinging blows of Mohammed's whip.

He ridiculed the servants' children and often forced them to perform dangerous acts for his own amusement. At times he ordered them to climb to the roof of the palace and jump off. At other times, he forced them to hold scorpions in their hands until they were stung. As the oldest of his father's sons, except for the dimwitted Fawzi, his word was always obeyed. He would bully and boss any child, regardless of their status within the family. His half sisters thought him fearsome and dangerous, and his half brothers hated him.

Whenever he and his younger brothers would pretend to be Bedouin bandits, they would charge each other on horseback, brandishing dulled scimitars. Mohammed would play the role of a lone desert marauder, and was always first to attack the others. He would beat his brothers on their heads and backs with his scimitar until they screamed in pain and surrendered. He never lost a mock battle against the six of them and would angrily strike back at his father's retainers when they dared to interfere and rescue the crying boys.

Tutors and servants would relay Mohammed's academic and behavioral progress to Akbar on a regular basis. Academically, he seemed to progress ahead of expectations, but emotionally he exhibited severe problems. Akbar was pleased with his academic prowess but wondered if the boy's errant behavior was caused by his mother having taken mind altering drugs during her pregnancy. In any case, he did not think that cruelty and zealotry were necessarily bad traits in a leader, and anger could be channeled with the right guidance.

Mohammed grew quickly and developed a well muscled body at a young age. He had a natural affinity for athletics and enjoyed pushing himself physically. He seemed impervious to pain and trained hard in self defense classes with his father's security guards, enjoying the rough behavior and coarse language of the men. The guards were impressed with his force of will and his high energy level and considered him an excellent student. His martial arts education included instruction in the use of weapons. He was trained to use everything from the ancient scimitar to the newest assault rifles and became an expert shot with a rifle while riding at a full gallop. He could bring down an Oryx antelope at 250 yards, or shoot a desert hare squatting in a wadi a quarter mile away.

Riding was one of his favorite pastimes, and he was fearless at it. He would race his purebred Arabians into the desert, recklessly galloping over areas that had slate and mica formations, in seemingly total disregard for his own safety. Often, his horses became injured and he would order them to be taken away, and a new one put in their place. Bedouins adored their Arabians above all else, but Mohammed never formed an attachment to any living thing, and remained detached from the stunning breed.

He enjoyed playing soccer and excelled at the sport, becoming one of the best players in the region. A ferocious competitor who often committed personal fouls, sometimes injuring opposing players, he was often thrown out of games for unsportsmanlike conduct on the field. As a consistently high scorer for his team, however, his ferocious play was taken to be unbridled enthusiasm by partisan fans. He had his first taste of celebrity as a soccer player and reveled in being admired by the stadium crowds. Off the field, he kept himself surrounded by a group of wealthy young men who wanted nothing more than to be amused by life.

During his childhood years, Akbar paid little attention to his son, his only interest the boy's monthly progress reports. As Mohammed matured, his father began to look more closely at him and he was given the best private tutors money could buy. Their initial reports showed that he had a natural talent for academics. Quick witted with good reasoning ability, he was lazy in his intellectual curiosity. He was gifted with a rare combination of a photographic memory, both in image and language, and he retained knowledge easily. At sixteen, he was conversant in three languages, had a basic knowledge of world history and was well schooled in classic Arabic poetry and religious law. He found the tenets of Islam confining, but the historical perspectives and the powerful message it projected to the masses fascinated him. He was not religious but professed piety when it was opportune. He was not particularly interested in politics but had grasped basic theories of economics and found them fascinating. His true interest was in the physical here and now and the wielding of power. He thoroughly enjoyed manipulating information and people.

Sexually active since he was a small boy, he would often have sex with the housemaids in the palace, or pay young boys in the village for their bodies. Once he tried to seduce one of his half sisters, but she became frightened and ran away, telling her mother. Her mother demanded that he be severely beaten, but Akbar dismissed his third wife's tirade as hysteria and ordered her to be silent.

On Mohammed's seventeenth birthday, Akbar summoned his son to his presence. The boy stood rigidly before him and looked evenly into his father's eyes. Neither of them showed any emotion. His father spoke:

"You were born my second son but I have decided to choose you as my heir. I have no doubt of your ability to follow me and become the head of our family. I have promised the King that you will be educated in the discipline of business and will continue our family's successful management of the royal family's investments. I am giving you the opportunity to devote your life to our family and our country, as I have devoted mine. If you accept this opportunity, you will become one of the most important men in the world, and one of the wealthiest. The responsibilities are immense, but so are the rewards. If you have any doubts that this is possible for you to accomplish, tell me now as I will expect no failure on your part in the future." His father waited.

"I accept. I will do what you ask." Mohammed bowed to the older man.

He left Saudi Arabia the same week and took up residence in the United States, making his home at his family's compound in southern California. His first year in America was dedicated to being tutored in college preparatory courses and learning about American mores and customs. He traveled like a rock star with his family's retainers carefully coddling him as they crisscrossed the vast American countryside, paying courtesy calls on his father's American business partners.

Mohammed thought Americans both amusing and generous. One on one, he liked them, but, as a people, he considered them naïve. They were childlike in their political and religious philosophies. He thought Americans too trusting in their democratic process, and lazy in their religious faith. He felt the word "lazy" seemed to fit them best. They were spoiled and overconfident. While they took on easy tasks, they deferred more difficult jobs to others. Mohammed thought it a dangerous flaw in their national character. He knew the United States did not graduate enough engineers, computer science majors, or scientists for their own needs. Instead, they had begun to import foreign nationals to fill hard science positions or worse, they outsourced their work to foreign countries. Americans were mortgaging their future because they were too lazy to buckle down and take the hard road with their children's education.

He thought of his own seared, harsh land of Arabia. Life was anything but easy there. His people survived in spite of intense heat, lack of water or fertile land. Food was wrested from the earth only after carefully engineered farms had watered and fertilized the parched desert. Billions of gallons of crude oil bubbling beneath the desert floor was Saudi Arabia's great leveler. If most things were available to the average American, all things were available to a wealthy Saudi. Money poured into the country's coffers as it filled the pockets of the upper class businessmen faster than they could spend it.

At eighteen, Mohammed began his undergraduate work as a student at UCLA. During school vacations, he commuted between family homes around the world, watching his father deal with the royal family as well as oversee the thriving businesses locked within their conglomerate. Mohammed thought the opportunities he had in studying his father's techniques were more valuable than studying in the American college he was attending. By his junior year, he found the university's curriculum unworthy of his time, and chose not to attend classes. He hired another student to sit in his classes and to take his exams. His generous personal allowance permitted him to not only pay his campus clone, but also bribe his father's retainers to keep their mouths shut.

During the day, he either slept or spent time at the beach. At night, he prowled the innumerable nightclubs of Hollywood. He bedded every male and female starlet who interested him. Hollywood had a surfeit of shallow, beautiful people whose only interest was in being entertained with new physical sensations and bad gossip. Drugs, sex, and personal agendas drew locals together to congratulate each other on their own brilliant choices and opinions. By hosting lavish parties, he financed their fantasies and reaped the rewards of easy sex and inner sanctum access.

While attending a fundraiser for Middle Eastern orphans, Mohammed met Farouk al Nasser, an Egyptian importer/exporter. Hollywood was the world's epicenter for hypocritical people who donated money to any cause that was politically in vogue at the moment. In return, they wanted their picture featured in the trade papers, accompanied by articles recounting the details of their generosity. During the party, Farouk impressed Mohammed with his verbal attacks on Americans and their international politics. Farouk almost shouted in the Californians' faces that they were the main reason there were so many Palestinian orphans in the world. His attacks on Israel and the United States were vitriolic, but the Americans made no effort to defend their government's policies or to take offense at his treatment of them. Mohammed was astounded to discover Farouk not only made the Americans feel guilty, but increased their donation levels. Over the next weeks, he watched and listened as Farouk preached the evils of the Western world at every charitable event they attended. The Egyptian would rant endlessly, beginning with America's moral degradation to damning the United States for choosing Israel as their ally, and turning their back on the Muslim world. Americans nodded their heads in agreement and regret while they pulled out their checkbooks.

Farouk and Mohammed were alone one night, chatting with each other, having just ordered a nightcap, when the Egyptian began an emotional outburst. He invoked God's name and sputtered that his vengeance would be wrought upon the United States in the near future. Mohammed laughed out loud. Zealots bored him. He had seen too many of them in his time, and all of them were ineffectual. He waved his hand in dismissal at the agitated man.

"But it is true my brother," Farouk protested. "There has never been such a wonderful and holy force. The warriors of the jihad will wrest power from the Americans and punish the Infidels for their evilness and their disbelief of the one true religion."

Farouk was sweating profusely. Unable to find a handkerchief, he wiped his forehead with the sleeve of his two thousand dollar suit. Looking around the room, he leaned toward Mohammed and spoke quietly.

"Our group believes that our order will bring retribution to the West and the Zionist dogs. We are part of an amazing movement. Loosely translated, it is called the base of jihad, or 'al Qaeda.'" Farouk detailed the movement's dogma that would bring destruction upon the Infidels of the Western world.

"I have only just begun to work with them to help finance our plans and have collected millions of dollars. There are tens of millions more to be had for the asking."

Mohammed leaned in closer to Farouk, instantly paying close attention. His interest increased when he saw his friend's eyes grow wide with excitement and enthusiasm while he detailed the millions he had already collected for his cause. The rhetoric had ceased being boring to Mohammed as soon as Farouk let it slip that millions of dollars were pouring in to the terrorist group's coffers in the Middle East and Asia. He told Mohammed he had run out of banks to put it in, and confided the Americans would never suspect or attempt to track the money as it would appear to be legal donations to charity. In actuality, millions were to be deducted from the charitable donations and set aside for the holy war. He also shared the information that not all the monies he collected were deposited for either charitable use or the terrorist's cause. As was customary with the traditional position of a go-between in the Middle East, he kept a fifteen percent finder's fee for all donations collected by him.

Mohammed chuckled inwardly. The scheme was brilliant. You took money from wealthy people. Some Muslims and Christians thought they were donating to a charity. Others were interested in furthering terror groups. You took their millions and kept fifteen percent for yourself. Never forgetting his wish to be one of the wealthiest and most powerful men in the world, he reveled in this newfound information and began to scheme how he could cut himself in on the financial action. He decided that Farouk's energy would be useful to him in the future and immediately feigned a devout interest in the new cause.

Looking earnestly concerned, he spoke to Farouk, "What you've told me is fascinating and obviously you're doing great work. May I offer my help to you and your organization? I would like to meet your warriors and, of course, be at your disposal for any future fundraising events. As you know, my family is well known and it would be a help to you to use their name in your fundraising."

Farouk was ecstatic to have Mohammed join him on the charity circuit and made the contacts immediately. For Mohammed, it all went exceedingly well. He shared finder's fees with his new friend and, within months, had collected millions of dollars for orphan and displaced person charities as well as Farouk's terrorists while adding almost a million dollars to his own account. It was the easiest money he had ever made.

Initially, al Qaeda only requested information about Mohammed's father's business partners in the United States and the government of Saudi Arabia. Mohammed willingly complied and was rewarded with a large cash deposit to a private bank account in Singapore. After their initial request, he fed them a continuing stream of information about Saudi Arabia as well as America, and more money flowed into his accounts. Farouk was as good as his word. After a few weeks, Mohammed was offered an important position within the terrorist hierarchy. Al Qaeda proposed he help funnel American donations as well as operational information to designated accounts and operatives around the world. Tasked to coordinate with Farouk, he would design and set up a covert network within the United States. In return, not only would he continue to be handsomely paid, but he would act as one of their covert handlers. He would be permitted to assist them in the selection of future American targets, and be privy to the initial planning of those attacks. All expenses would be readily paid by al Qaeda. Mohammed pretended to be honored by their offer and heartily accepted. His honest thoughts, however, were how much of his personal commissions would be added to bills he submitted to al Qaeda for payment. At this rate, it wouldn't take long for him to become richer. He returned to California in high spirits, but during his absence his father had sent an urgent message ordering him to return to Saudi Arabia immediately.

Akbar bin Fasheed looked worn and tired. His eyes were sunken with large black circles etched in the flesh below them. His speech was slightly slurred as he attempted to relate the disastrous events of the previous weeks to his son. Mohammed could see his father was very ill. Akbar had obviously ordered his son home because he didn't have the physical strength to deal with what was happening.

After taking a deep breath, his father spoke, "The Crown Prince has taken control of our entire operation in Damman." The old man conjured up an inner strength and continued. "Our people have been locked out of the natural gas fields as well as the oil refinery. Special security guards from the royal family have taken physical control of our property. I've ordered the site managers to remain close to the properties involved, but not to physically come in contact with the royal guards. My entreaties to the Crown Prince have not been responded to and the King is too ill to intervene."

The Crown Prince had taken control of the Fasheed family's largest and most lucrative conglomerate. Wholly owned by the Fasheeds with no part of the investment owned by the royal family, the prince had accomplished the takeover in one day by physically seizing the property with his personal armed guards. Word had reached Akbar after the fact.

There was no explanation for the prince's action. For some unknown reason, Akbar's influence with the royal family had been erased. His good friend the old king lay dying after having suffered a stroke. He had played no part in what had transpired. Mohammed knew the loss of their property was potentially devastating, not only to their personal business holdings, but also to their net worth. After their father's petition to the prince had been denied, Mohammed's half brothers had wrung their hands in desperation and petitioned the government, begging forgiveness for any offense their family may have committed. Staggered by the ineptitude of his younger sons, Akbar had summoned Mohammed home.

"You will go to the monthly majlis and demand an audience with the prince. He cannot dare to refuse you in front of the other sheiks."

Mohammed knew his father would never have permitted the surprise takeover if he had been well. He would have sensed a nuance of change in his treatment by the royals and would have bribed their retainers to get more information. Once he realized what was being planned, he would have sent word to other tribal leaders. By outlining the royal family's treachery and their plan to confiscate his holdings, the others would have realized that they, too, were vulnerable. The tribes would have banded together with Akbar in a display of outrage and self righteousness. The royals would not have dared to go against the wishes of all the sheiks. It was their Bedouin brothers who gave them the power to rule. Things would have been defused before reaching a critical point.

As his father asked, Mohammed attended the monthly audience held by the Crown Prince. After being ushered into the royal presence, he kissed both of the prince's cheeks and pressed his forehead to his leader's shoulder as a sign of allegiance. He then stood to one side. The room was filled with men from all social levels. The majlis was a Bedouin tradition. Each ruling sheik held a public audience in his region where every man was allowed to address their grievances to him and to ask for favors. A sheik could not deny any legitimate male Bedouin entrance to a majlis. Mohammed waited for his turn and then began his petition.

"Your Royal Highness, I thank you for seeing me." Mohammed's voice boomed as he bowed his head and waited for the prince to reply.

The prince looked past Mohammed and spoke with a bored and flat voice. "Speak quickly Fasheed. I have only a few minutes. The day is not long enough for all that I am expected to accomplish." He examined his newly manicured nails as he spoke.

Mohammed spoke again in an assertive voice. "Your Highness, I am here to protest the recent takeover of Fasheed International LTD by armed royal guards. Fasheed International is the most profitable business venture in the Kingdom. As you are well aware, for many generations my family has been successful in managing both of our family's investments and organizing them into profitable conglomerates. This business relationship was agreed upon decades ago by your brother, the King, and my father. It is the King's express wish that it continue." Mohammed's eyes never left the Crown Prince's face. He continued. "Fasheed International LTD is wholly owned by my family and......."

The prince had been staring at the floor, but began pacing up and down in front of Mohammed, signaling with his hand for quiet. He exploded with an angry voice that carried across the huge room.

"I do not need you to recount how long my family has carried yours financially!" His eyes blazed and dots of bright color appeared on his cheeks. "The royal family has always invested our money and risked our personal fortunes to back your family's business ventures, while you used banks for your investment share. You've risked nothing. Your family has forgotten their place and they have become too self important. The Fasheeds have become lazy and ungrateful. You are done!" The prince turned and stalked away. The audience was over.

Akbar's disappointment in his son's failure was evident as he growled, "I thought you would do better." The old man sighed and seemed to sink into his chair. "I am disappointed with you. Go back to America and continue your studies. You must apply yourself and acquire your MBA as quickly as possible. Your brothers and I will maintain our businesses until your return."

Mohammed jumped up from his chair, reacting angrily, raising his voice.

"I don't need more stupid college degrees to run our businesses. I am more than capable of taking control of our investments. Now."

"Sit down. Be silent!" His father hissed. "I promised the King you would have the proper education to manage our investments into the next century. I will keep my word. You will continue your degree and complete it as quickly as possible. Leave me now and do not disappoint me again." He waved toward the door.

Before he left, Mohammed met with his brothers and ordered them to communicate with him daily. If they did not talk to him about business decisions before any action was taken, he threatened to return and kill them. That night, on his flight to America, he used the long hours to finalize his personal plans. Arriving back in California, he contacted the al Qaeda leadership and invited to meet with them at a safe house in Malibu.

The two al Qaeda operatives greeted him with respect, well aware of his family's status. Mohammed did not recognize their names. They were not from families of consequence in Saudi Arabia but came from the untamed country of Yemen located on his country's southern border. The spokesman named Faisal addressed him.

"Mohammed bin Fasheed, we understand you are interested in sharing a plan you have devised to make our organization more successful. May I ask what you propose? Although you are a new convert, we are mindful of your influence in the world."

Mohammed bowed slightly from the waist. He was thinking of the untold millions of dollars still to be earned as he stated modestly, "I wish only to serve."

Faisal responded in amused tone. "Your family is one of the wealthiest and most important in the Middle East and has served the Saudi royal family for generations. Why should you now decide to serve us?"

Mohammed chose his words carefully. "My family is devout and we are honorable servants of the Word. We know Saudi Arabia must remain autonomous in order to grow in the grace of God and our faith, and yet the present royal family has allowed the Americans to have as much of our oil as they wish. We want the West to feel our country's power as custodians of the true faith. We know that they cannot maintain their economic status without our oil. It is my intention that, in the future, our help to them will not be measured in millions of gallons of oil a day but in small drops. We will bring them to their knees through their own selfish greed. This is the way I will be of assistance to you in accomplishing your goals as well as mine."

"Does your father Akbar bin Fasheed feel the same?" Faisal asked with hooded eyes. He had done his homework and documented the old man's allegiance to the royal family.

Mohammed shrugged. "My father has designated me his heir. He is unwell and will not be active in our businesses once I return home. He will retire. I can assure you I will be in control."

Mohammed then outlined his plan. He would continue in his role as a major fundraiser as well as a covert operative while he was in the United States, but, when he returned to Saudi Arabia and assumed leadership of his family's business empire, he would broaden his responsibilities with the terrorists. As one of his country's wealthiest businessmen and head of its most powerful family, he would have no trouble elevating al Qaeda's fundraising to the highest level. He would use his numerous contacts throughout the Middle East to massage large donors who wished to remain anonymous and yet punish America. He projected he could raise an additional 100 million dollars in the first year alone. In return for his efforts, he not only wanted his usual fifteen percent, but also command of all al Qaeda operations within Saudi Arabia.

"I know you have a plan for taking control of my country," he stated it flatly as if it was old news. The men stared blankly at him but made no comment. "I promise to speed up your timetable with the help of our

National Guard Army. As you know, the guard is comprised of Bedouin tribesmen, many of them my kinsmen. My men will hunt down and kill all foreign agents and will respond only to my orders. I will personally carry out the assassination of the Crown Prince, and depose the royal family. Once that is accomplished, the nation will be destabilized and you will be invited into the country to restore order. As a consequence of gaining control, we will have command of one of the best equipped military forces in the Middle East. The power of that force will allow us to control the export of oil to the West. From this new vantage point, we will engineer the economic destruction of America. Controlling the rest of the Middle East will come easily.

My payment for these services will be as follows. As soon as Saudi Arabia is within our control, the Fasheed family will be established as the new first family of the nation. Since I am a Saudi and respected by the tribal leadership within my country, as head of my family I will be named King. Saudi Arabia will be made available to you as a forward base for any other terrorist operations in the Middle East. The Saudi military will fight by your side. We will divide all oil revenues equally. Please forward my terms to your leadership. I expect an answer from you as soon as possible."

The men initially remained silent, overwhelmed by Mohammed's rhetoric. Faisal replied they would forward his proposal to their superiors.

That summer, the University in California conferred a Bachelor of Arts degree on Mohammed bin Fasheed in absentia. Two years later, as he was completing his Master's degree, he spotted Yasmina al Amar at an international student's mixer.

CHAPTER 4

Mohammed met Yasmina al Amar while she was volunteering as a translator at a foreign student's reception. He thought her very young and quite attractive in a slender, boyish way. Her dark shoulder length hair framed large eyes that were beautifully deep set and lively. Long legs developed upward into slim hips centered with a small waist. He watched closely as she moved around the room's perimeter with a natural athletic grace, smiling confidently as a professor introduced her to each new Middle Eastern student, eagerly shaking their hands in welcome. Speaking flawless Arabic she assured them of her help in improving their English speaking skills.

He momentarily felt himself stir with desire. He had hired a local prostitute the night before, but she had been an untalented slut who hadn't particularly satisfied him. He wanted another woman for tonight and he was only attending the mixer to pick up a girl for sexual entertainment. He thought college girls fun to seduce and considered many of them quite talented. There was always a pretty one who would trade her body for a free meal and a ride in a Porsche. He moved towards Yasi.

"Hello. My name is Mohammed bin Fasheed and I think you are the most beautiful girl in the room." He smiled down at her smelling the perfume in her hair.

She heard the velvet voice first and then looked up into a darkly handsome face. He had one of the most beautiful smiles she had ever seen.

"Hello. It's nice to meet you, too. My name is Yasi al Amar." She held out her hand to him. "Thank you for the compliment. You are most kind." She blushed and looked down.

"Are you blushing? I'm impressed." He looked surprised. "I've been in this country for years and I've never seen a woman blush before! Are you a foreign student?" He desired her and moved closer, her sweetness filling his senses.

"I'm American." She replied. She turned away from him in answer to the host professor's frantic waving from across the room. "Nice talking to you," she smiled over her shoulder.

He watched her walk away and felt his arousal continue. Frustrated with her disinterest, he began to walk around the room evaluating the rest of the women, deciding on whom to approach. He finally picked out a red-headed German girl with huge breasts and a high pitched giggle.

The following day Mohammed hired a private investigator to run a background check on Yasmina. The results were ordinary. Her father was a naturalized American, a Yemeni immigrant who owned an Arabic-English newspaper in Dearborn, Michigan. Her mother did not work, but volunteered at local charities. Yasmina had three brothers and had graduated with honors from high school. The al Amars seemed to be a typical upper middle-class American family. Yasmina was a freshman at Georgetown and lived in a tiny apartment within walking distance of the university. Her major was International Relations and she had a good GPA. She had no known boyfriends and a few girlfriends. The report included her telephone number. It was all he needed.

The effort graduate student Mohammed bin Fasheed expended toward winning freshman Yasmina al Amar's affection was overwhelming and continuous. The first time she agreed to go out with him he swept her off her feet. Arriving at her apartment with a huge bouquet of fresh flowers, he waited patiently while she put them in water, complimenting her on her small but tidy living space. Opening the door of his Porsche GT3, he saw her eyes widen at the sight of the luxurious car.

"Do you like Porsches?" He smiled at her.

"Oh, I guess so. I've never ridden in one though. It's beautiful."

They drove to the Kennedy center and sat in box seats at a Mozart concert. Afterward, they dined quietly at Citronelle in a private booth. During their date, Mohammed was both intrigued and annoyed by her. Although not well traveled, he noticed that she was well educated for someone so young. Over dinner their conversation ranged from international politics, to recent books they had read, and sports. She asked him intelligent and perceptive questions about his home country and seemed genuinely interested in his answers. She had a quick mind with a good sense of humor, but he was disappointed that she did not seem particularly intimidated by his long winded description of his family's position and net worth. Also, as an American woman she did not show any deference to him as a man, and inwardly he thought her too self assured. It was of no importance at the moment. She was unspoiled and refreshing. He could always instruct her in proper behavior later on, and decided to keep seeing her. Her sweetness was a welcome change from the women he was used to, and winning her would be a delightful diversion. He thought it would be interesting to see how long it would take him to seduce her.

It was a magical evening for Yasi, but she politely declined his invitation to go to his apartment for an after dinner drink, citing an early morning class. In reality, she had an unsettling feeling about him, but she did allow him to give her a small kiss at her front door. Mohammed left her doorstep whistling and arrived at one of his favorite brothels in downtown D.C. less than thirty minutes later.

Mohammed's efforts to capture Yasmina's affection were relentless. He called her in the mornings, tried to have lunch with her every afternoon and offered to take her to dinner every night. When she protested she had to study and do homework, he offered the name of a student who would do her research papers for free, explaining that the student had helped him get his assignments done. He appeared to have all the time in the world for her, placing her needs and interests before his own, and constantly telling her how beautiful she was. Yasi was overwhelmed. No one had ever made her feel this way. Just nineteen, she had never lived away from home and had only traveled occasionally. While she was educated and well read, she was completely naive and innocent when it came to interpersonal relationships. It was no surprise that she thought Mohammed sophisticated and erudite, having more in common with her father than with her. She was flattered and fascinated by the handsome and urbane graduate student and totally guileless in her feelings for him. The chemistry between them was obvious to anyone who saw them together. The girl was an ingénue, the man older, and practiced.

Outside of Georgetown, Mohammed's other life raced forward at breakneck speed. Besides attending his university classes, he coordinated daily with his brothers in Saudi Arabia on the family businesses. He traveled often, supervising the establishment of secret cells for the terrorists, and at the same time fundraising for covert operating costs by collecting charitable donations.

To accomplish his charitable goals he aligned himself with dissident American Muslim leaders who were unhappy with the role the United States was taking in the Middle East, as well as Middle Eastern businessmen who though him politically connected to pro Muslim, anti-Israeli American politicians. He collected guilt money from wealthy liberal Americans who feigned shock and indignation at their country's political posturing around the world. While he amassed millions of dollars for the al Qaeda treasury, he took his percentage and watched his personal fortune grow along with it.

Mohammed and Yasmina had been seeing each other for almost three months, when he grew impatient with the slow progress of her seduction. She had steadfastly refused his sexual advances in a firm, quiet manner that frustrated him, and voiced a desire instead, for a long term relationship. She did not respond positively to his lavish displays of opulence, returning gifts she thought inappropriate to their friendship. She told him she considered them good friends, at the start of what she hoped would grow into a significant relationship in the future. She asked that they proceed slowly, expressing difficulty with seeing him so often while trying to keep up with her studies. He offered to pay for a stand-in to go to her classes so they could have more time together. She seemed shocked and laughingly refused. The more she refused him the more determined he was to have her while she was still a virgin and to take her back home with him that summer and keep her. In order to get her there, he was prepared to propose marriage. Once she was in Saudi Arabia and under his control, he would decide what her future would be.

Having to redouble his efforts to finish his MBA on time, he silently swore at his father for forcing him to waste precious time in acquiring what he considered an unnecessary piece of paper. His brothers had relayed to him the old man had suffered another stroke and was now unable to speak. Akbar would be dead soon. It pleased Mohammed to know he would soon be running the Fasheed conglomerate and have the pleasure of outsmarting the inbred dolts of the Saudi royal family. For now, he would allow the appearance of status quo by keeping his father's promise to the king, while he maintained his student status in America as a cover for his al Qaeda activities.

While he was making extraordinary efforts to see Yasmina every day, Mohammed schemed on how to bring their relationship to a sexual conclusion. Her behavior continued to intrigue him, but her refusals to give in to his advances no longer amused him, and he grew more irritated with her each passing day. For the first time in his life he was adapting his behavior to a woman's demands. Aggravated by the feeling, he decided to end the farce of a platonic relationship. He would control Yasmina's mind and her body. The old familiar emotion of rage enveloped him as he sped along in his Porsche on one of Arlington, Virginia's residential streets on a warm spring afternoon. As he approached a deserted intersection he again felt the rejection of Yasmina's refusal to sleep with him, and banged his hand in frustration on the steering wheel, wanting to lash out at her for her disobedience to his will. Out of the corner of his eye he noticed the movements of a young boy across the road. The child was running awkwardly on the sidewalk, chasing a small yellow dog. Mohammed could hear the child crying the dog's name, begging the animal to come back. As the puppy ran out into the street in front of him the Saudi pushed the accelerator down, making sure of the kill. A sharp yelp and a crunching sound were accompanied by the feeling of a small bump in the road. Mohammed smiled at the sight of the crushed dog as screams of horror spewed from the young child's mouth. He cornered the Carrera expertly into the next turn and disappeared.

Yasi fell in love with Mohammed without knowing how it happened. It was her first serious relationship with a man. She had not had sex before, although she had experienced intimacy. She enjoyed petting and necking with her high school boyfriends and thought it was pleasant to have her body touched, but she chose not to allow those relationships to progress. Deep down, it pleased her to know that she could get boys excited with desire without feeling any passion herself, remaining detached and in control. If anyone had asked, she would have lectured them on her family's traditional values, and declared she would never compromise those mores or her body until marriage. In truth, she had not yet felt real desire.

Mohammed's seduction succeeded three months after their first meeting at the university mixer. They had eaten a casual dinner at Clyde's in Georgetown, absorbing the excitement of the crowded and popular restaurant, and Yasi could not get herself into the mood to return home and study. She leaned into Mohammed and hugged his neck.

"What a fun evening! I know I really do have to go home and study, but I've had a wonderful time with you. Would you like to come back to my place and have an espresso? It's the least I can do to repay you for this delicious dinner."

Mohammed eagerly accepted the invitation and entered her apartment. While she was making the espresso, he went out to his car and brought back what looked like a small bottle of brandy. Yasi did not drink hard liquor, but he was very insistent on her tasting the prize winning Napoleon he'd brought with him. She obediently took a few small sips. It tasted exotic, and the coffee was a good accompaniment to it. He coaxed her into emptying her glass and quickly refilled it. While snuggling close to each other on Yasi's small settee, they toasted their new romance and Mohammed finishing his Master's Degree.

"You are the most beautiful woman I have ever seen." Mohammed's voice was silken, his breathing heavy with desire, his eyes seemingly devouring her.

"Mohammed, you make me feel beautiful. I feel wonderful when I'm with you." She kissed him on the cheek and felt his arms instantly encircle her, pulling her close to him. They tightened around her waist, making her gasp.

"I can't breathe," she panted. "Not so tight."

She began to feel slightly breathless and a little woozy as he passionately kissed her, pulling her body even closer against him, rubbing his hands up and down her back and hips. She felt her muscles relax; her whole body seemed to go limp.

His hands caressed her breasts and nipples and then moved below her waist and started up into her skirt. She knew she should resist his advances but she was powerless. She was too weak to push him away. Besides, his hands felt wonderful on her. The sensations they caused raced through her body with electric pulsations that she had never experienced before. She felt hot and excited all at once, and for the first time, passionate in her need to have sex. Wet with her body's juices her breathing rapidly increased with each kiss until she panted out loud in his arms.

As their mouths locked in passion, she saw flashes of colors behind her eyes; her body remaining separate, moving to its own rhythm. Mohammed's face was next to her as his lips caressed her neck and shoulders. He talked to her, told her what he wanted her to do to him and what he was going to do to her. He was very close, but his voice sounded far away. She smiled to herself, thinking how physically beautiful he was. She wanted him more than she had ever wanted anything in her life.

She felt him pull her to her feet and steady her body against his. He guided her into the bedroom and began to undress her. When he had stripped off both their clothes, he looked at her naked body and proclaimed her an angel of beauty. Laying her on the bed he entered her expertly with one swift movement. She was barely conscious of her hymen being torn.

A strong powerful man, he rode her slim body with long sweeping strokes. Her hip movements instinctively encouraged him to go deeper inside of her and increase his stroking. She wrapped her legs around him tightly and ground her pelvis into his. Their rhythm became primal and she kept tempo with him as he moved faster with each stroke. Yasi felt as if he was in total possession of her. He spoke wildly in her ear, telling her she was his, would always be his and there was nothing that would ever change that. She felt a sensation of hot desire growing between her thighs, spreading itself throughout her core, driving her to pull him deeply inside of her. In response, he bit and tongued her nipples causing her to moan out loud with pleasure and thrash wildly beneath him. She had a vague awareness of climbing higher and higher within herself, approaching a physical and emotional edge. The hot sexual pulsing between her legs intensified and finally exploded into a wildly erotic rippling eruption that plunged her from a ragged cliff of desire into a pool of clear, intense pleasure. She arched her back and heard herself scream. Mohammed shuddered as he finished and collapsed on top of her. She slept for the entire night in his arms, and when she awoke, he began to caress her again and brought her to her second orgasm, this time with his mouth.

Yasi had never known her body could experience the intoxicating sensuality that Mohammed's lovemaking caused. The sex between them was addictive. He possessed her completely when they made love and although she wanted to be more of an equal partner, he always directed her actions. Mohammed was an insistent lover who never seemed satisfied. He would caress her body with his hands and lips until she quivered and begged him to take her. Yasmina knew she had no defenses against his lovemaking and yet felt unashamed by her desire. He possessed her with his sex and she had never felt more alive.

Each week Mohammed filled her tiny apartment with fresh flowers, and showered her with small gifts. He seemed to do everything in his power to make Yasmina happy. He called her two or three times a day and asked what she was doing, who she had seen, and where she was. They dined together almost every night, either at a restaurant or at Mohammed's sprawling Georgetown condo with his valet doubling as a cook.

Yasi was not a great cook, and had no interest in the kitchen, but occasionally she would indulge in her passion for desserts and prepare a crème brulee' and espresso for the two of them upon their return to her apartment from dining out. On those nights they played a game called "Dessert or Sex?" and it became their private joke. Which would be the first thing they would have when they arrived at Yasi's place? Dessert or sex? During dinner they would slyly tell each other that it didn't make a difference. As the debate would progress throughout the meal, it was decided that they would make up their minds on the ride home. The outcome was always automatic, as they feverishly groped each other on the car ride back to her apartment. Mohammed struggled to keep his Porsche in the correct traffic lane while kissing and petting Yasmina as she massaged his crotch and tongued his ear. Crème Brule' and coffee were always served last.

Occasionally, when Mohammed would not see Yasi for a few days, he told her it was because he had been called out of town to meet with one of his father's business partners. While traveling he would telephone her many times each day, ask what she was doing, and who she had seen. In April, after Mohammed had been gone for five days, her phone rang.

"Yasmina, it is your lover and most obedient servant, the man who misses you and desires you. I am lonely at night not having you in my arms. I want you, now." He murmured softly into the phone. She purred her approval. His tone shifted as he began to question her. "I called earlier, and you weren't home. Where were you? You were not at your apartment at 6:30 this morning and your car was gone."

"Mohammed! I miss you too." She replied. "I had an early tutoring session with one of my students. He couldn't make it at the normal time, so we got together at school this morning before class. Where are you now? Are you still in Boston? How did you know my car wasn't parked in front of the apartment this morning? Are you having someone watch me?" She laughed as she asked the last question. Mohammed responded quickly, a smile in his voice.

"Yasmina your safety is my only concern. I love you too much not to worry about your welfare. The city is not always safe. Marry me and let me protect you for always. I will be home later tonight and we can talk about our future."

That evening as he held her close to him, he teased that even though she was not a virgin, he would make her his first and only wife. She knew by custom he was allowed four wives and many wealthy Saudis took mistresses besides. She feigned anger and admonished him for discussing the possibility of having more than one wife, but he stroked her hair and whispered that she was more woman than he could ever wish for or desire. He called her his lovely Yasmina and caressed her doubts away.

She never met his family, but was not particularly concerned. He told her his father and brothers constantly traveled the world, overseeing their vast properties and businesses, never staying in one place long enough to take time off. When she asked about his mother he replied flatly that she was dead. She did not lobby for him to meet her parents, primarily because she had not told her mother and father about him. She knew they would immediately see the depth of her emotional involvement the moment they looked into her eyes and she did not want to have to explain her love affair to them. How could she? Even she didn't understand his power over her. It had taken all of her willpower not to move into his Georgetown condominium when he asked her. She could not acknowledge her betrayal of the moral upbringing she had received and face her parents' certain disapproval.

As their affair intensified, Yasmina teased that Mohammed seemed to be in a big hurry to put her in some sort of a secret harem. In truth, she felt flattered that he wanted to marry her, but she still had college and graduate school to complete. After that, she wanted to live in Europe. Her parents were loving, and caring people, but intense in their roles as her guardians and she knew that she needed some time away from them to taste the freedom of her own decisions. She would not trade their supervision for a husband's permission.

The intensity of their relationship had begun to wear Yasmina down. Mohammed seemed obsessed with knowing everything she did, every place she went, and everyone she spoke to. He discouraged her friends from visiting when he was not there, and listened in on her telephone conversations with her family. She began to feel edgy and ill at ease as he increased his scrutiny over her actions. When she tried to discuss her misgivings with him, he shrugged off her questions and told her he was only trying to protect her.

In the spring of 2001 before summer break, Mohammed formally proposed marriage to her. They were standing on the terrace of his spacious apartment overlooking the Potomac River when he placed her hands in his and spoke softly, staring into her eyes.

"Yasmina, I have wonderful news, I have spoken with my father and he has given me permission to marry you. You are to accompany me to Saudi Arabia this summer. We will be married in the fall when the weather is cooler, but until then we'll tour my country. I will take you to see the fabulous ruins at Mada'in Saleh. We will take a week of rest in the beautiful ocean side city of Jedda and dive in the Red Sea. When the summer is hottest we will travel to my family's cool mountain palace in lovely Asir, and you'll get to know all my relatives, all five dozen of them. I will introduce you to the Saudi royal family and someday when you return home to America for a visit, you will be able to brag to everyone that you have dined with princes! You will be my princess Yasmina bint Amar al Fasheed."

Before Yasi could speak, Mohammed dramatically got down on both knees and held out a small black velvet box to her. At first, the sight of him on the floor seemed so comical she thought he was teasing. When she realized he was serious she quickly tried to defuse the situation.

"Mohammed, please get up." She pulled him to his feet, ignoring the box in his hand. "I can't do this now. It's too much. It's not the right time. There are things….I…. I have to think. Please let me out of here." Her voice was shaking as she fled from the apartment and got into a taxi.

The next day the al Qaeda notified Mohammed that they had begun the final planning of a large covert operation. Attending a secret meeting in New York, he found out an initial attack on the United States would occur within the next months. He was issued an operations warning order and was tasked with immediately updating information about selected American targets, as well as insuring his team of operatives would be available to coordinate with other al Qaeda agents who would be leading the operation. He was directed to remain undercover where he was, and supervise his people from Washington. He sent Farouk coded instructions to disperse their operatives to pre-designated sites and to await further instructions. The easy going façade Mohammed presented to the world began to crack. An unforgiving calendar transformed him into an anxious man concerned with a myriad of tasks he had to accomplish before summer was over. There were too many loose ends for his liking.

One May afternoon as he stood behind Yasi, watching her prepare coffee, he suddenly demanded an answer to his marriage proposal.

"Yasmina, you must give my proposal the answer it deserves. I will not leave here until you have." He tugged at her elbow and turned her toward him, placing his arms lazily around her and nuzzling her neck.

"Mohammed, you know I'm honored by your proposal." She smiled softly and looked up into his face, touching his cheek. "But I can't accept at this time. We're still learning about each other. I love you but I think we need to give each other more time. You know I've just started my education and my goal is to finish my undergraduate work in three years to immediately begin graduate school. These are things I have promised myself that I must accomplish. You must understand. You do, don't you?"

Mohammed removed his arms from around her and stiffened. She searched his eyes looking for affection, but there was only blackness.

Disheartened, she continued speaking, her hands now folded in front of her, her eyes purposely averted.

"Also, I won't be able to go with you to Saudi Arabia this summer. It's a wonderful invitation, but my father has offered me an internship on his newspaper's International Desk as an associate editor. It's a unique opportunity for me to improve my Arabic, and learn more about Middle Eastern politics. It will be invaluable experience when I begin to study International Relations this fall. It is my father's heartfelt wish that I work with him. I can't refuse him. We have plenty of time to see Saudi together. Maybe we'll go next year." She touched his arm for reassurance.

Mohammed had backed away while she spoke, his body unbending, his face now frozen in a scowl. She reached toward him with outstretched arms, her voice barely audible.

"I'm sorry if I've upset you, but I need more time before I can commit to marriage. There are things I must do first. My education is very important to me and I would think that you would want me to...."

He reached out suddenly, roughly grabbing her upper arms, bruising her skin. Pulling her sharply toward him, he glowered. His voice was hoarse and hard.

"Your stupid female ideas of achievements are of no concern to me!" He pushed her away and stomped angrily out the door, slamming it hard behind him.

Yasi stood still. She was too stunned to move. She felt as if he had physically hit her. She leaned against the counter as tears streamed down her face, her body shaking. Didn't her dreams matter to him? He had been so cruel. She thought he loved her, but how could he love her and talk to her like this? They had only been together a few months. She didn't understand. What was his hurry to be married? She didn't want to live in Saudi Arabia. Her life was here, in the United States. Today, when he had grabbed her she had been afraid of him. She wept miserably, feeling confused and lost. It was as if she had done something terribly wrong, but did not know what it was.

She called Mohammed everyday begging him to talk with her, but he never answered. In the weeks that followed she remained inconsolable, and locked herself in her apartment. Her grades faltered. When her parents telephoned, they were alarmed at the depression in her voice and begged her to come home for a visit. She refused and kept to herself. Her friends lost interest in asking her to go out with them, and eventually left her alone. Time dragged by without any word from Mohammed until late one afternoon in mid June. He had called while she was at an afternoon class and left a message coolly asking her out to dinner. She felt her spirits soar when she heard his voice. She had missed him more than she ever imagined. She accepted his invitation immediately, leaving a message on his cell phone.

The night of their date he barely spoke to her during the ride to the restaurant and continued his sullen behavior throughout the beginning of dinner. He appeared tired, his dark eyes sunken and lined, his usually handsome face sallow. Yasi spoke first, seemingly concerned about his appearance.

"Mohammed, are you all right? You look very tired."

"I'm fine." He grumbled.

"Why did you finally call me after all these weeks? I can see it obviously wasn't to have a carefree dinner and talk over old times. Something is really bothering you. You're not happy, and I don't want to fight with you again. What do you want with me?" She searched his face, and rested her hand gently on his.

"I guess I'm tired of eating alone with my valet," he said. "Seriously, I wanted to talk to you." He stared at her face, as if he was studying it. He took her hand, kissed the back of it and stared deeply into her eyes.

"Yasmina, I am asking you once again to come with me to Saudi Arabia. I want you to become my wife. I will provide you with everything you could ever want or need. You will be my one love; you will be treated better than any princess in the history of the world. We will always be together. It is not safe here; you must understand that. You are in danger here, but, you will always be safe with me. Come with me to my homeland this summer. Let me take care of you and protect you."

She shook her head slowly. "Mohammed, this is America. Where could I be any safer?" She looked down at their joined hands and spoke carefully. Her voice was soft but firm. "Thank you for your proposal. You know I am honored. But, I can't marry you. Not now." She gently removed her hand from his and took a sip of wine.

His emotions remained cloaked for the rest of the evening and he made no other attempt to touch her or to lighten the evening with conversation, but continued to stare at her as if he was trying to memorize everything about her. On the drive back to her apartment, Yasi spoke again.

"Mohammed, I want to thank you for everything you've done for me. I truly enjoyed you spoiling me, and I want you know I will always love you in a special way. I hope your family's business continues its success and that we stay in touch with each other."

Mohammed didn't reply, but suddenly swerved the convertible to the nearest curb braking hard, the sports car rocking from the suddenness of the stop. He grabbed at Yasi, roughly pulling her close to him, his breath hot in her face, "You are a spoiled bitch! I could crush you with one hand if I wanted to. I have wasted too much time." She felt the raw power of his body hard against hers and tried to shrink back into the leather seat as he leaned across her, angrily opening the Porsche's passenger door. He shoved her violently onto the sidewalk with both hands, her own hands and knees scraping on the pavement. As the car peeled away, tires squealing, she found herself sprawled on the cement, bruised and crying, stunned by the violence of what had happened. The Carrera disappeared into the night. Yasi got up and pulled herself together. As she brushed herself off, still sniffling the tears away, she began to walk down the street and felt a sense of relief come over her. She hadn't been physically hurt tonight, not really. Oddly, it was as if an invisible burden had been lifted. She involuntarily shivered as she understood she had just survived a close encounter with something both dangerous and violent.

During the fall semester, she found out from mutual friends that Mohammed had finished his MBA and left for Saudi Arabia the day before the 9/11 attacks on the United States.

CHAPTER 5

Mark Harrison was born at 15:09 Hours Sunday, February 6th in Martin Army Hospital at Fort Benning, Georgia. His entry into the world was one of the many births logged in that day by the weary and irritable maternity staff on duty. The hospital's OB-GYN doctors were also tired and ill tempered, having been forced into working long shifts in the hospital's delivery rooms.

There was a reason for this. Soldiers assigned to the two Infantry divisions permanently based at Ft. Benning normally rotated through stateside and overseas tours at least twice a year assigned on temporary military duty orders (TDY). One sent them away for two to three months in order for them to participate in joint military exercises outside of the country. In addition to that, soldiers were further assigned to train at remote training posts throughout the United States. Arriving back home in Georgia with their families was always a reason for the young men to celebrate. As soldiers they did not have much money to spend but found other inventive ways to have a good time. The emotional hellos and goodbyes of their transient lifestyle caused the military hospital to be continually inundated with newborn babies.

At twenty-seven Mark's mother Carrie had been one of the oldest women treated at the hospital for prenatal care, and on February 6th she was the oldest woman in labor. Although she had never met the OB-GYN doctor who would be delivering her baby, she was not bothered by the lack of a social introduction. She had checked into the maternity ward at nine o'clock that morning after her water broke and the first labor pains began. Now, three hours later she was still having labor pains but nothing else seemed to have progressed. From time to time a nurse came into the labor room and sweetly patted her hand assuring her the doctors would examine her as soon as they possibly could. Carrie nodded that she understood but she could barely endure the frustration. She felt as if she wanted to punch someone.

Thirty minutes later a doctor entered the tiny room. He didn't bother to introduce himself but immediately began a pelvic examination.

Carrie began a tirade. "Doctor where have you been? I've been here for over three hours. What's the word, doc? How much more of this waiting is there?" She lifted her head from a sweat dampened pillow, her face flushed from the last waves of a strong labor pain. She was in no mood to be polite. She wanted her baby born.

The doctor had finished examining her. He turned away to wash his hands.

"You've got a ways to go, Mrs. Harrison. You need to be dilated a couple more centimeters and your body isn't cooperating. I'll send a nurse back with some PIT. It's a drug that will help you to increase your labor efforts." He exited the room brusquely without looking at her again, his bedside manner non-existent.

"Jerk," she muttered to no one. The labor room was bare except for the bed and a small black and white television that was showing an annoying NASA press conference. She was wondering why she should care about NASA's latest moon mission, today of all days. Fifteen minutes later a nurse entered. She wore a starched white uniform adorned with the insignia of the rank of Major.

"Here you go, honey." The white capped woman injected a syringe of fluid into Carrie's IV. "This will get you going to the finish line." She smiled, patted her patient on the head and bustled out.

Three hours later the resultant tsunami of labor pains cumulated in the birth of Mark Justis Harrison.

Mark's father John, a Captain in the Infantry, was not present at the birth of his son. Hospital regulations did not permit him to be in the labor or delivery rooms. Husbands were considered too much of a distraction to the hospital staff. The reality was that the battle hardened heroes who were about to become fathers were actually terrified of seeing their babies born. They either remained in a tiny smoke filled hospital waiting room, or at their homes. John Harrison opted to wait at his small set of quarters located across the Army post from the hospital. It was a two bedroom, one bathroom duplex, just off a busy road entering the main housing area. The telephone in his house rang at 3:30 p.m.

"We have a son." The soft female voice on the other end of the phone sounded exhausted but happy.

"Carrie, are you okay? How's the baby? Are you all right?"

"Come and see for yourself, John. We'll be waiting for you." The phone went quiet.

Because Mark's father was an officer, his mother was assigned to a hospital room with only one other new mother as a roommate. Enlisted soldiers wives recuperated in rooms that held four to six patients.

An hour later John walked into his wife's room with a huge bouquet of blue carnations. Although it was Sunday, he had been fortunate. The PX still had flowers left over from Friday afternoon's delivery. He even had a choice: red or blue carnations.

Carrie was sleeping soundly when he arrived. John thought that she looked frail and very pale. Her roommate, a woman who had delivered her baby the day before, smiled shyly at him. "She just dropped off to sleep. They took the baby to the nursery. Congratulations Captain Harrison."

"Thank you ma'am. If she wakes up tell her I'll be right back. Gotta go and see my boy." He smiled a huge grin at the woman and strode out.

"Did you see him?" Carrie looked hopefully at John's face when he returned.

"I did. He's a handsome devil, takes after his father. But, he seems a little small." He thrust the big blue floral bouquet in her arms and sat in a chair.

She struggled to sit upright. "Listen Bub, you try expelling eight-and-a-half pounds from your body and then tell me that it's a small thing!"

"What are these?" She stared down at the bouquet. "I mean, you brought me blue carnations? I don't believe it. Blue is the color of the Infantry. You're an Infantry officer. It's always the Infantry you think about first. I just ..."

"The flowers are blue because we had a boy." He smiled, his handsome face glowing with happiness.

Still scowling at him, she realized he was telling the truth, shook her head and laughed. "Oh God, you're right. We have a baby boy. Blue is for boy."

John got out of his chair walked to his wife's bedside and kissed her hard on the mouth. "You did great, honey. Really great! Now we're a family. We're the mighty Harrisons."

Three months later, Captain Harrison received orders to report to Washington, D.C. The family moved before Mark's first birthday. They spent two years in Washington and moved again every two years for the next twenty years. Carrie and John purposely kept close contact with their individual families providing their son with a strong sense of who he was and where he had come from. He traveled happily with his mother and father, secure in the knowledge he was an important part of something much greater than himself.

Carrie and John's families loved to see them as they traveled to new assignments. In return, both sets of Mark's grandparents journeyed to the Army posts where their children were assigned, maintaining the family's closeness. The deep friendships the Harrisons formed over the years with other officers families were a unique stabilizing force in their lives. These friends shared in their extraordinary experience of being part of a military family and their friendship provided a taste of the familiar, even at remote postings.

While a junior in high school Mark made up his mind to try for an appointment to the United States Military Academy at West Point. His father was a graduate, but the academy did not give preferential treatment to children of graduates. In order to be eligible all applicants had to have an excellent high school GPA, extracurricular activities and solid recommendations from their community leaders. The President of the United States and members of Congress appointed youngsters to vacancies at the service academies. Each year thousands applied for a few hundred vacancies. It was one of the most competitive selection processes in the world.

Mark had superb extracurricular activities and strong support from community leaders, but was rejected for admission because his high school GPA was not high enough. As a consolation he received an appointment to the United States Military Academy Preparatory School. The Academy felt he needed a year of tutoring in college preparation courses in order to survive the rigorous academic atmosphere of West Point. He would be reconsidered for another appointment at the end of the prep school year. If he quit the program, or didn't qualify, he would owe the army two years service as a soldier. Mark accepted the challenge and never looked back.

He was finishing the first week of summer training for new cadets when a senior cadet who was part of the cadre spotted him and yelled his name from across the cadet area.

"Mister Harrison! Get your sorry butt over here on the double." The upperclassman barked the order. Mark double timed over to the senior cadet, stopped in front of him and stood at attention. As a new cadet he was expected to stand with his shoulders back, his neck painfully braced in rigid alignment with his spine, his chin tightly tucked in to his chest.

Mark focused his eyes on the far wall. "Yes Sir!" He answered strongly. The first classman leaned in toward him, his face inches way.

"Mister Harrison do you know who I am?" The man's spittle spattered on Mark's cheek.

"Yes Sir!" Mark responded, frozen in place. This particular cadet had gone out of his way to terrorize the new class. A first generation Asian American, his parents had emigrated from South Korea twenty years before, succeeding in business and admonishing their son to excel. Now, as a senior at West Point he considered himself all-powerful.

"What is my name?" the senior yelled.

"Mr. Chou, Sir," responded Mark smartly.

"Then why is it I don't know who you are?" The older cadet became enraged. "Why is it that I had to find out from the Tactical Officer that your daddy is an O-6? A Colonel in the Infantry. Why is it that in a few months after I am a Second Lieutenant in the United States Army I may have to serve under your father the Colonel? Why did you hide that fact? Are you trying to get me? Answer me you screw up!" He screamed the last order so loudly that his voice broke.

"No excuse Sir." Mark wanted to disappear.

The man leaned closer to Mark, the stench of his breath causing Mark to try and hold his own breath. "You're going to write daddy that I'm just the best guy you ever saw. You're going to be my biggest fan. Come to my room tonight at eight o'clock and I'll dictate what you will write. Now get away from me, you little fag," he snarled. The upper classman turned and sauntered away.

Mark turned away quickly and double timed across the area, his face and neck glowing bright pink. "Ah, Mr. Chou," he thought. "I'll write my dad for you. You're damned right I will, and then I'm going to call him and tell him what a bastard you really are, you North Korean prick. If I had my choice I'd knock you on your ass."

Four years at the Academy passed quickly and Second Lieutenant Mark Harrison found himself commissioned in The Infantry and eagerly volunteered for Airborne and Ranger Schools. Being an Army Ranger was the most fun he ever had, and he couldn't wait to deploy to his first assignment in Special Operations Command. At the completion of that assignment he was selected by the Army to attend post graduate school at Georgetown University.

The night he first saw Yasmina al Amar, Mark finally knew what the cliché "love at first sight" meant. He was one of a few dozen students who had remained behind after a lecture by the Commanding General of CENTCOM. The audience had moved to the front of the lecture hall and students were standing around the General genially asking him questions. As Mark listened to his responses he felt a light weight brush the top of his foot. He stepped back and became aware a dark haired girl who had been making her way through the crowd had inadvertently stepped on his boot. As she touched his arm apologetically he smelled the soft scent of sandalwood. She was one of the most beautiful women he had ever seen.

CHAPTER 6

Sept021 11, 2001 exploded into history as America gasped in agony. Yasi was in her second year at Georgetown, and since the terrorist attack her parents had been frantic with worry for her safety. At first, they demanded that she leave Washington and return to Michigan. She refused and argued successfully she stay at school, to prove the terrorists could not succeed in dictating how she lived her life. Her small act of defiance gave her the satisfaction that she would not give in to their brutal intimidation. Al Qaeda had attacked her country and vowed to destroy her freedom, but that would not happen.

Most students remained at school, and everyone seemed to draw comfort from staying in close proximity to each other. Campus life continued normally, and Yasi felt renewed purpose. A degree in International Relations had never seemed more important to her than it did now. She knew she would be doing something truly relevant with her life. She was disgusted by the slaughter of innocent Americans who had no chance to defend themselves by terrorists who spewed Fundamentalist dogma as an excuse for vicious butchery.

By the end of the previous summer she had been successful in locking away the painful memories of her affair with Mohammed but was jolted into thinking about him again after the attack. The media identified fifteen of the 9/11 terrorists as Saudi Arabian. Watching the news she felt both curious and frightened. Were these men the same as Mohammed? They looked like him, but he had acted differently. During the time they had been together he had been apolitical. Any discussion of politics bored him. He immediately changed the subject. Was he lying? Why had these men attacked the U.S.? What was their motivation? Did they truly want to annihilate her way of life? She didn't know, but whatever the answers, they would affect her life and her nation's future.

By the middle of the semester the university settled back into familiar academic routines. Yasi began to concentrate on her studies, bringing her grade point average up to a new level. By spring she was training for local marathon races and playing in a coed soccer league, her life again full and boisterous. Her emotions stabilized.

Although she dated from time to time, she did not allow relationships to develop. She was content to go to class, pursue sports and debate the world's situation with her fellow students. At her father's request, she volunteered a few hours each week translating documents written in Arabic for the newly formed Department of Home Security. The remaining months of her sophomore year raced by in happiness and fulfillment and when she had completed the early summer semester, she once again took two weeks off to work with her father. The next academic year sped by uneventfully. As planned, she received her Baccalaureate degree in three years with academic honors. Already accepted into the Middle Eastern Political Studies Program, she began her first Master's degree classes that summer.

Georgetown University is an integral part of a city known around the world as a crucible of power. Washington, D.C. has some of the greatest political minds of the century residing in the suburbs surrounding it and within close proximity to the college itself. The university's advanced degree programs benefit from these intellectual resources and invite their worldly wise neighbors to become a part of the curriculum by lecturing in their area of expertise. Because of this, monthly guest lectures were always well attended by students and faculty.

The first year of Yasi's Master's program was passing as quickly as her undergraduate years. Her classes were peppered with new analytical assessments of Middle Eastern political theories, and comparative studies of political histories of the region. Cultural diversities and historical trends were dissected, discussed and examined. Since 9/11, students studying International Relations had evolved into dedicated classroom participants and complained they did not have enough hours in the day for all the necessary reading and research they wanted to do.

In addition to her academic workload, Yasi added to her volunteer duties by translating Arabic television broadcasts from Al Jazeera and scanning Arab newspapers for references to al Qaeda and the United States. It was both fulfilling and educational. She was astounded at the amount of misinformation disseminated about America and the negative feelings about her country in the Arab world. For a diversion, she began to study Arabic poetry and found it intriguing. Within some poems she found the rhythmic patterns more important than the words themselves. Arabic poetry, especially when read aloud had an almost hypnotic effect on listeners. She now understood how whole populations were mesmerized by a poem's cadence while they absorbed its cultural message.

That summer she interned once again with her father, working as

"Sadeek's" International Editor's assistant. When vacation ended she reflected back and felt the satisfaction that came from having learned and accomplished new things. Her proudest moments were her contribution to the success of her family's business, and working again with her father. To Yasi, her father was a true patriot, who was untiring and passionate in his efforts to defeat terrorism while protecting his adopted country. She would help him every way she could.

Adel had procured a government security clearance for Yasmina and welcomed her valuable assistance in completing a seemingly endless list of translations. She eagerly helped, and through her efforts became more expert in understanding and speaking Arabic, along with the language's lesser known dialects. She now spoke textbook Arabic, along with her father's Yemeni dialect, and four other Saudi dialects. During rest breaks she and her father debated as to where they thought al Qaeda would strike next, and what the West must do to defeat them. Adel listened intently to his daughter's opinions and sadly agreed she, her children and their children would have to fight this war. Both of them knew there were no easy answers and no quick fixes. It would take generations to defeat the Islamic terrorist infestation of hate and violence that now held the world hostage.

The last day of Yasi's vacation Adel summoned her to his office, took her hands in his and kissed them, thanking her for all her hard work.

"I am very proud of you Yasmina. No man could ask for a more beautiful or brilliant daughter. With you, and young people like you, I know we will be successful in the long difficult war we are now embroiled in." He continued to speak, his eyes growing moist, his voice quavering. "I thank God everyday for all of his blessings, but you need to know that I thank him most for the very special blessing you have been given."

She looked at him, not quite understanding. "I have seen that you carry a unique gift from our ancestors deep within your heart. Endurance and strength from our ancient tribes will always be intermingled within you along with your love for our country. Don't ever forget that you are a direct descendent of one of the most ancient of all Arab cultures. When the time is appropriate the power of this inheritance will partner with your Western knowledge and make you invincible." He hugged her close to him and sighed.

During the second year of her Master's program Yasi made it a point to join with other students and participate in after hours discussions on topics that had been addressed by the university guest lecturers. Occasionally, a speaker would remain and mingle with them, answering questions. She found being a part of these exchanges both educational and exhilarating.

She met Mark Harrison after attending a guest lecture given by a high ranking U.S. Army General. He had gloomily outlined the threat of a future land war with North Korea. After his presentation ended, a large group of students remained behind and surrounded him, intent on asking questions. Yasi was trying to inch closer within the crowd to hear what was being discussed when she inadvertently stepped on a young man's foot. He whimpered loudly, causing heads to turn. When she reached out and touched his arm in an apologetic gesture he flashed a huge smile and said in a sotto voice, "It's okay, I was faking." She smiled wryly and shook her head.

After the informal give and take session was over, students slowly left the hall. Mark limped dramatically to Yasi's side favoring the foot she had inadvertently stepped upon. She gave him a dazzling smile. "You're a faker. Go away. I honestly thought I had hurt you."

"Madam, you have found me out. You're right. My foot is fine." He held out his hand and said, "Mark Harrison, known malingerer."

"Yasi al Amar," she placed her hand in his and asked with interest. "I saw the General pat you on the back. Do you know him?"

"Yes. He and my father served together in Europe. He was my dad's boss. His daughter used to be my babysitter." He chuckled and looked toward the exit doors. "Can I buy you a cup of coffee?" he asked.

Yasi felt attracted to him. She thought he was wonderfully handsome, and she liked his forthright manner.

"Yes," she heard herself answer. They talked over coffee, chatting easily for over an hour. Neither wanted the conversation to end.

"Are you studying for your Master's?" She asked.

"Yes. Conflict Resolution. You?"

She smiled. "International Relations. I'm from a family where politics is passed around the dinner table as often as the salt. It's in my blood, I guess."

Mark thought her eyes were lovely.

"Yeah, I know what you mean. I'm an Army Captain on temporary duty as a student. My dad was in the Army and just retired after thirty years, so I guess the military's in my blood. Besides, the college where I did my undergraduate work sort of encourages you toward a military career," he laughed.

"Where did you do your undergraduate work?" Yasi thought him to be very open and easy to talk to.

"West Point." He said quickly. He found himself rattling on, enchanted by her beauty. "In exchange for this degree, I'll owe the Army four more years of active duty in addition to the six years I already owe them for my undergraduate time. Hell, I'm halfway to a twenty year retirement!" he laughed.

"Oh, so that's why you're studying Conflict Resolution. But does it make sense for a soldier not to want to go to war?" She flashed him an inquisitive smile, turning her head a little, waiting for his reaction.

Mark's blue eyes leveled at her and he spoke with feeling, "More than anyone else." He became upbeat again. "I'm on orders to be posted to Afghanistan as a liaison officer with the new Afghan army. I'm going there to help them build their military infrastructure. You know, design their command structure and teach them how to equip their troops. All the good stuff. We know that if their army becomes a force to be reckoned with they'll eventually be able to wrest power from the country's warlords and there will be a greater chance for peace. I can make a contribution to that end."

They talked quietly about the terrorist threat and the way their world had changed since 9/11. Mark listened closely to what she had to say, and marveled at her grasp of world politics. She was as intelligent as she was beautiful. Swallowing hard to summon up his courage, he asked her for her phone number and if she would go out with him. When she said, "Yes," he felt on top of the world.

He called her that weekend to ask if she would be interested in going to the Smithsonian with him to see an exhibition of airplanes depicting the history of flight in the United States. The Smithsonian was one of her favorite places to visit, but this exhibit would be in the Stephen Udvar-Hazy Center in Chantilly, Virginia. She had not been to that particular museum and accepted eagerly. Mark suggested they bring a picnic lunch and eat in the country. Before picking her up he went to Sutton Place Gourmet and got them a basket of food and a bottle of wine.

The exhibition turned out to be fascinating. Afterward, they drove to a county park and picnicked on the food treasures they had brought with them, chatting easily while sitting on a blanket. It had been a perfect day from beginning to end. They genuinely liked each other's company and felt a mutual attraction. Soon, talk began about growing up and their families. Yasi sat on the blanket, her legs crossed, her hands folded in her lap. She leaned forward toward Mark.

"My father and mother are immigrants from Yemen. They arrived here over twenty-five years ago with nothing but the clothes on their backs. As I've told you, my father is the publisher of an Arab/English newspaper in Dearborn, and my mother volunteers as an English language teacher. I've lived in Michigan my whole life. It was a wonderful place to grow up. I have three brothers. My older brother, Fahd is married and teaches mathematics in a middle school. My twin brothers, Yosef and Ibrahim are seniors in high school. I think my family is amazing, chiefly because of my parents. The values they taught us and how they raised us was wonderful. Maybe I haven't said it right. My parents are more than what I've just described; they are the best people I've ever known. They're kind, caring and more patriotic than anyone I've ever met. After the happiness of our family, the welfare of America is their passion. 9/11 devastated them. My father has worked tirelessly trying to get the Arab American community mobilized to help in the search for possible al Qaeda cells here in America and has endlessly volunteered for Homeland Security. To sum it up, if they weren't my parents I would want to be their protégé so that I could learn from them. I would also want to be their friend."

Mark reached out for her hand. "That's impressive Yasmina. It's a wonderful accolade. Not many kids would want to be friends with their parents. Your folks sound like wonderful people." He looked deeply into her eyes. "I'd like to meet them someday."

When it was his turn, Mark made her laugh by telling stories about his cadet days at West Point and how he had gone to war with the Tactical Department. They were in charge of the Academy's day to day regulations, and Mark had spent hours on punishment tours for breaking the rules. He turned a bit more serious as he related his family background.

"I'm an Army brat, an only child. My dad graduated from West Point and was a career Army officer. I've already told you that he's retired now, but he served thirty years on active duty. I was brought up on army posts across the country and in Europe. My dad was away from home a lot on temporary duty, so my mom raised me almost single-handedly. She was a strict disciplinarian and let me tell you, when I had done something wrong I never heard her say, 'Wait until your father comes home.' She would spank me. But, both of my folks have always been there for me since the first day, and I love them. They are good, solid people, and I too, would want be their friend if I wasn't their son. Also, I can't imagine anything better than being in the Army. I was born to be in the Army. I loved growing up in it, and I am looking forward to being one of its leaders. I am excited about my new assignment, and I can't wait to start. It's a real way to contribute to the fight." He reached out and put his arm around her shoulder. They finished their day with a lingering kiss. When she arrived back home at her apartment it seemed to Yasi she had known Mark Harrison all her life.

As was her practice, Yasi ran not just for exercise but for the joy and pleasure it gave her. To her, the physical act of running was more than a work out. It freed her soul from the earth. She had felt the need to run since she was a child. For Yasi it was essential to feel her lungs expand with air, the muscles in her legs stretch out and propel her body forward. The elation of feeling her heart pumping like a well maintained machine filled her with pure adrenalin. Her mind focused more clearly when she ran. It gave her time to think and prepared her for the rest of the day. It was a personal catharsis. She tried to run at least five miles everyday. When she could not she'd feel let down physically and mentally.

For additional physical conditioning she enthusiastically pursued her hobby of Judo. She had begun taking lessons after her summer at the outdoor achievement training camp, when she discovered she could make her body serve and obey her mind. She earned her black belt and participated in matches at a local dojo every month. While a freshman in college, the total force concept of Tai Chi intrigued her with its combination of yoga and meditation and she added those disciplines to her repertoire. She practiced often at one of the university clubs, continuously raising her level of expertise along with her core strength.

Mark ran because he knew it was a cardio vascular discipline that his body needed to stay in shape. His daily regimen began at dawn and included a five mile run followed by a workout doing weight resistance training. He participated in additional hand to hand combat drills once a week. As a Special Operations soldier, he was required by the Army to travel to Quantico on alternate weekends for more extensive military field training. In his profession there was no such thing as too much physical conditioning. He was expected to arrive at his new overseas assignment in top physical shape, ready to fight.

Most mornings Mark would pick Yasi up and they would drive to places around the city where they could run their miles. Sometimes it was Rock Creek Park, at other times the Pentagon and Arlington Cemetery, across the Memorial Bridge to the Kennedy Center or around the Tidal Basin and the Lincoln Memorial. On occasion, they competed against each other in local marathon races. Yasi always finished at Mark's side. Some evenings, they worked out separately at their particular gyms and met afterward for a bite to eat.

Yasi was a few months away from finishing her Master's degree when her father called and offered her the permanent position of Editor of International News at his newspaper. Although "Sadeek" was published locally in Dearborn, the paper had important American and international subscribers. She knew many prominent Middle Eastern politicians thought it was the true voice of the Arab American community in the United States. As "Sadeek's" publisher, her father was revered and respected, not only for his grasp of international politics but his views on the growing threat of Muslim Fundamentalism. Because he offered her the job, she knew he respected her as a colleague. He would not have offered his most important editorial post to her because she was his daughter, or if he wasn't certain she could do it. She was pleased beyond expectation that he thought her qualified to work and travel with him in the future. She would have the opportunity to witness world leaders' discussions on the global expansion of al Qaeda and plans on how to defeat them. There was no question of her not accepting the job.

At seventy years old, Hunter Farrington was a Senior National Security Advisor to the President of the United States. He should have retired years earlier, but his vast experience within the Foreign Service and the Middle East had proven invaluable, and he had become indispensable to presidents. The present American president was no different, and he had asked Hunter to remain in the NSA's multifaceted job as a special favor.

Hunter was an expert on Middle Eastern politics but since the carnage of 9/11 he found himself embroiled in an extremely dangerous situation. He and other senior advisors to the president were tasked with making global decisions on how to fight terrorism, but often did not have hard intelligence to make those decisions. America was a country that had few human intelligence or "HUMINT" resources available to gather information in the Middle East. One of the intelligence community's greatest needs was native Arabic speakers. The United States desperately needed people who were fluent in the Arabic language and knowledgeable about the Middle East. Recruitment of overseas agents was slow and difficult, and any attempt to use non-native speaking Arabic Americans to infiltrate foreign countries was not feasible. Arabic was not a language that someone could learn to speak fluently in a short period of time, and even the most talented linguists needed intensive instruction. America's three letter services (FBI, CIA, NSA) had a severe deficit of trained agents. Because of that, they were facing the reality of having to close down a number of important operations. All agencies had been trying to operate without reliable intelligence, and that was perilous. The Israeli intelligence service Mossad had generously shared what information they had but it was not enough. Ominously, even translations of terrorist transmissions were severely backlogged.

Hunter called his old friend Adel al Amar to discuss this, as well as any ideas he might have to help solve the country's gathering problems. Over the years the two men kept a close professional bond that had blossomed into a warm personal friendship. Hunter had often consulted Adel and greatly valued his opinion on Middle Eastern issues. Because of his extended Yemeni family and uncounted Arab friends in many countries he offered a unique perspective. Adel had close ties within his own native country as well as Saudi Arabia and Jordan.

Speaking with each other they used an ancient Yemeni dialect from Adel's home village, reflecting the thirty year long history they had with each other. Hunter's phone was secure as was any transmission spoken over its network, but using the old dialect had the additional benefit that no one who accidentally overheard Adel's conversation would be able to understand what they were saying. They chatted casually for a few minutes catching up on personal matters until the conversation shifted to the real reason why Hunter had called. The diplomat kept his voice low as he spoke.

"Adel, how can we mobilize our Arabic speaking citizens to help us with our translation needs? And, more importantly, recruit citizens within our Arab American communities to volunteer for service within our intelligence agencies? I know that in some Middle Eastern families, there is a struggle between being a newly sworn American citizen and keeping loyal to old country ties and relatives."

Hunter leaned back in his chair and listened as Adel began his long and eloquent answer. His friend had long since emphasized that all Americans, especially those of Arabic descent had a sacred obligation to assist their new country in the war against terrorism.

"We must get the government to begin an intensive recruitment program that will target Arabic speaking Americans for basic translation needs, not espionage agents. You don't need a top security clearance just to translate an overseas newspaper. I think if you appealed to our people's love of freedom and family this could be accomplished within a short period of time. As far as newly naturalized Arab Americans working for any of our agencies, this will be more difficult. We must convince them of their value to America and reward their volunteerism. The program should become a national priority with strong Presidential and bipartisan endorsement. America had a seven year program to put a man on the moon, and from what I've read in international newspapers we need that type of government dedication to upgrade our intelligence capabilities. You know I will work within my community to help accomplish this and will do everything in my power to see that America is kept safe."

Hunter thanked him. He waited a long moment and added quietly, "Congratulations on Yasmina having completed her Master's degree program."

"Thank you." Adel's voice was filled with pride.

Hunter continued speaking, a smile in his voice. "I understand she completed both undergraduate and graduate programs within five years. What a brilliant accomplishment. You and Suhair must be very proud." He suddenly paused, and began again in a somber tone. "I know you are aware that Yasmina has volunteered and acted as a translator for Homeland Security. She is both a talented and dedicated volunteer, and has contributed a great deal. My colleagues tell me she is one of the best they have ever worked with. Adel, do I have your permission to call her, to recruit her to help our country…to work for us?"

Adel's heart skipped a beat. He pictured Yasmina years ago as a little girl with long dark hair and laughing eyes, and the beautiful young woman she was today. All the things he owed to his new country sparkled emotionally within his memory; he and his wife's love of America, his children's futures, his successes as a man. He heard once more the whoosh of the helicopter rotor from a dark night long ago in Yemen, and remembered strong American arms lifting him up to safety and freedom.

"Hunter you will ask her about working for us now? As soon as she graduates from Georgetown?" He stumbled over the words. "I mean, are you aware, I have already hired her as an important editor for Sadeek and she has accepted? She would be my right arm."

Hunter replied. "No Adel. I didn't know about your offer, but I understand. I will not call her if you do not wish it. Even if you give me permission tonight, I'll only ask her one time to help us. There will be no pressure. I will make sure she can easily refuse without losing face. However, if she says yes, I will have someone contact her from one of the agencies. You know, she is most uniquely qualified to help." He paused. "Our country's problem is acute at the moment. But then, you know that." He stopped talking and waited.

Tears filled Adel's eyes and he blinked the droplets onto his shirt front. He wavered for a moment, took a deep breath and then replied in a steady, even voice, "Old friend, you have my permission to ask her. God will guide her decision. Enshallah."

A day later, Yasi's father called her, this time from his office instead of from home, and although he tried to sound unemotional, there was an underlying sadness in his voice. He told her that she was going to receive a call from an old acquaintance of his, a man he had known years before he had come to America. They met in Yemen when the man had served in the Diplomatic Service. He explained the man was now a high ranking member of the present administration and a patriot. He was also an honorable and trustworthy friend to the Yemeni people. He said although he did not know specifically what the man wanted to talk to her about, it probably had to do with government service. He told her that whatever it was, the position would be extremely important, and that she was to think things through before she made a decision. He gave her Hunter's name, but when she began ask him questions, he begged off and told her he would call her again in a few days.

At the end of a couple of months Mark and Yasi had become romantically involved, and were falling in love. Unfortunately, both had professional commitments that would not allow them the luxury of being together in the future. Their relationship would be temporary at best with Mark already scheduled to leave in a few weeks, and Yasi supposedly getting ready to move back to Michigan. Mark already had his orders to leave in two weeks and report to Afghanistan for a two year tour of duty. Yasi had secretly made her own life changing commitment. Time raced by as their passion for each other glowed more deeply with each day.

Extraordinary things had happened after Yasi answered the telephone call from Hunter Farrington at eight o'clock one evening. A man's soft cultured voice asked if he might speak to Ms. Yasmina al Amar.

"This is she," Yasi answered quickly, guessing correctly who the caller was.

"Yasmina, I hope you will permit me to call you by your first name. My name is Hunter Farrington. I am an old friend of your father's. I would like to speak with you about an important matter, if this is a good time." The silken voice paused. "Are you alone?"

She spoke with quiet eloquence. "Yes to both, Mr. Farrington. I know who you are. You are the National Security Advisor to the President. It is an honor to speak with you. My father told me that you might call. He has always spoken of you with great respect and considers you a friend. What may I help you with?"

Hunter's voice brightened. "First of all, I want to thank you for all the hours you have generously volunteered to Homeland Security. You have been an immeasurable help to our country. I only wish we had a million more like you."

"Thank you, sir," Yasi said proudly.

"Yasmina, I would like you to listen carefully to me for a moment and consider what I am about reveal to you. As we speak your telephone transmission is being scrambled to block anyone from listening to us, and I am sure I can rely on you to keep what I'm about to tell you close hold. It is not widely known yet, but our country is having difficulty conducting the war on terror. We do not have enough people who are fluent in Arabic or who have knowledge of Middle Eastern politics helping us with the fight. It is imperative that we bolster our forces in our struggle with al Qaeda as soon as humanly possible in order to prevent any future catastrophic attacks such as 9/11. We know al Qaeda will continue to attack all over the world, and are waiting for the next opportunity to wound us again. "

His voice suddenly sounded weary. "Yasmina, I know how intelligent you are. I have been told by your professors that your Master's thesis was a brilliant piece of work. I also know how talented you are. Your translations of Al Jazeera broadcasts were timely and accurate and our analysts tell me they helped us immeasurably in our planning. You speak Arabic, as well as numerous other dialects fluently, and you have a professional's grasp of Middle Eastern politics. I'm aware you are now about to begin a new life and career, and will be working with your father, but I am going to offer you an alternative choice. I am asking you to consider joining our government by working for one of our information gathering agencies. Our people will train you and utilize your talents where they are most needed."

"Where would that be? What would I be doing?" She interrupted, her heart racing.

"At this moment I don't have the answer to those questions. I do know you would be instructed and evaluated by people who are specially trained to decide where to place you. I promise that if you accept, you will be made aware how valuable an asset you are, and that your talents will be used wisely. I want you to take your time and consider what I have said. We would be proud to have you join us, but I will understand if you refuse. I know you would also contribute to our national security as an editor at Sadeek, working with your father. Thank you for taking the time to speak with me." He finished, giving Yasi a private number to call when she had made her decision.

Yasmina felt as if a jolt of electricity had entered her veins and was soaring through every capillary in her body. There was no doubt about her accepting the challenge of working for the United States. After a sleepless night, she eagerly called the number she had been given and offered her services.

She was ordered to begin her Agency training the next month. As part of the cover story created by her and her Agency handler she told Mark that her father had hired her as his new International News Editor and she would begin traveling extensively with him both in the United States and overseas immediately after graduation. At the moment, only weekend travel might be required. Mark congratulated her on her new position and accepted her story without question.

While Mark trained in the field with the Army at posts throughout the United States, Yasi traveled to locations in Virginia to begin training with the Agency. In a short a time they would be living thousands of miles away from each other. There was no turning back for either of them. On an unconscious level, their need for each other intensified pushing them forward to a natural physical conclusion.

They made love for the first time on a weekday night after watching the movie "Casablanca." They had been drinking a bottle of Schweiger Vineyards 1997 Cabernet Sauvignon that Mark's father sent to him for his birthday and when the film was over, they laughed and bantered while trying to recite the dialogue of the movie's famous scenes out loud to each other. Suddenly, they began to kiss and touch and they both knew that it was time.

They came together as caring equals, intently curious of each other, hungry for the intimacy that sex would finally allow. They took their time exploring, and as they discovered each other, rejoiced in the physical act of making love. Mark was a gentle lover, who moved slowly and carefully. He waited for Yasi to catch up with his excitement, and then propelled her forward into new waves of desire. He seemed to envelop her within his aroused body, breathe his being into hers, and become one with her. Yasi's passion matched his, and she became the aggressor demanding to take him upward, pulling him into her, her pelvis undulating with eagerness and in movements of desire and intensity. Her body responded move for move to his, with eagerness and intensity she had no control over. There was a rhythm between them, a sharing in their lovemaking. One of them would take and the other would give, alternating dominance with submissiveness. Yasi felt that this physical act with Mark was the most wonderful thing she had ever done. It was joyful. It was right. Her heart rocketed with every kiss and caress her body received. She was not only being possessed, she was possessing. She was not being taken, she was giving. She had never felt so alive. When they were finished they collapsed in each other's arms and laughed out loud, hugging like two children who had just had the most wonderful adventure.

The joy of making love with Mark was similar to the freedom and joy she felt when she ran. It was natural, intense and life giving. He made her feel whole. She would always want to be a part of him and hoped he would be a part of her. They made love every night after that and tried to memorize their bodies with their eyes and hands. Time raced away and soon they were living their last days together. Mark finished his thesis early and the Army moved up his reporting date. He promised he would try to call her as often as he could, and would take leave as soon as it was possible, but he had no idea when that might be. Yasi said she would fly overseas and meet him for a holiday in Europe, but admitted that it might be months before she could join him. They clung tightly to the thought of being together again and drew solace from the fact that they would be able to email each other.

Mark left on a rainy Saturday. There was sadness and resignation the morning of his departure, and they made love one last time with a determined slowness that underlined their loss. Both of them cried as they said their goodbyes and agreed that it wasn't fair, they had just found each other and now they would be forced apart. Mark didn't want Yasi to go to the airport, and she agreed. She did not want to be with strangers when he walked away from her. They held each other for one long moment until he turned away and walked quickly out of the apartment and down the stairs. She ran to the window following him with her eyes until he got into a cab. He never looked back.

Three months later she found herself in the Kingdom of Saudi Arabia, beginning the most important job she would ever be asked to do.

CHAPTER 7

I t was only because the water tanker was almost empty that Yasi was able to cruise along at fifty-five miles per hour. She sipped constantly from the water bladder, swallowing slowly, swishing water around her teeth and letting it soak into the membranes of her mouth. She reached into her pocket, took the greasy butter from the goat meat and rubbed it onto her tongue and teeth. She had seen the Bedouins put it in their camel's water before a long trek across the desert. It would help protect the delicate tissues of her mouth from drying out later on. While she drove, she searched the cab for anything that might be of help to her, but found nothing except for a disposable cigarette lighter. She put it in her pocket and pushed the truck's accelerator down to the floor. There were no other vehicles. The desolate roadside sped by as a brownish blur and the highway looked as straight as a hallway carpet runner.

As she drove, her emotions swung from solid determination to grim desolation. She remembered the headlines about her parent's murder. "Ah, my God," she moaned. Her parents died because of her, not just because she failed to complete the mission she was sent to do, but because she allowed herself to be uncovered as an operative. She had no doubt that the news article had been genuine. The bastard Mohammed told her the night in Riyadh when he tortured her, that he had a surprise for her. He viciously doled out retribution for what he perceived as a personal betrayal. How had she allowed herself to become infatuated with him, and his Goddamned rich-boy lifestyle? How had she allowed herself to be distracted from what was important? What an idiot she had been to be seduced by his ornate displays of hospitality and tradition, his privileges of wealth and power.

She wondered how he had become a trusted friend of the Western diplomats and gotten access to their embassies and classified information? She knew his success at international business had been one of the reasons. Profitable business deals between his conglomerate and Western countries had given diplomats an excuse to be sloppy about security. Profit, like politics, made strange bedfellows. She had been duped into trusting him, but she above all, should have known better. She knew what he was like.

"Son of a bitch, of course!" She shouted out loud in the truck cab. Mohammed bin Fasheed was not just an operative, but possibly the man in charge. He could be the commander controlling al Qaeda operations in Saudi Arabia. With security contacts placed within all the embassies and his ability to glean information from the high ranking diplomats his network was far more sophisticated than anything the Americans had conceived. He had not been uncovered because no one was looking in the right places.

She remembered when he threw her out of his car onto the sidewalk in Washington, D.C. on a spring night years before. She felt something dangerous had been close to her then, and now she knew why. He was the man the Agency was looking for, the butcher who had not only wrecked their information network, but murdered their agents. She remembered, too, he had left the United States right before the attack on America occurred, obsessed about taking her home with him to Saudi Arabia. Was he also part of the al Qaeda group involved in 9/11? "My God," she shuddered. Had she slept with one of the murderers that attacked the United States? "I will kill you." She declared to no one.

She failed her parents, failed the Agency and almost committed suicide by stupidity. As her Marine buddies would say, "She had fucked up to the max." She swore at herself again, banging on the truck's steering wheel with her palm, glaring at the tattooed fingers of her right hand. A cold chill raced through her, causing her to shiver. There was an old cliché that claimed when a chill ran down your spine in hot weather someone had accidentally stepped over your grave. If it was true, Mohammed had probably not only stepped over her grave site, but already had it dug and waiting for her.

She clenched the wheel with tight fists and blinked away the tears that fell heavily onto her shirt front. "Dimwit," she said to herself. She pictured him laughing at her. How naïve she had been. She recalled they had met while she was a freshman at Georgetown and he was a graduate student finishing his MBA. After their meeting at a reception for foreign students, Mohammed had proceeded to sweep her off her feet. All Yasi could remember was a blur of sex and conflicted feelings. Thankfully, she had found the common sense to refuse to marry him and accompany him to Saudi Arabia. She had not seen him again until six months ago, when he appeared at an American Embassy party in Riyadh and kissed her hand warmly. Even then, she hadn't connected the dots. As she pictured the infamous Fasheed smile, she once again swore out loud.

Furious with the remembered pain of her brutalization and torture and flushed with anger at the intimate memories of his body possessing hers, she forced herself to concentrate on the highway, overriding waves of self loathing that engulfed her. Her mind revisited the times she had been with him. She tried to understand why their relationship flourished for a second time, and it all came down to one thing. She was fascinated by the thought he was in love with her. She was actually flattered that he might love her. What an egotistical cow. The reality of how he abused her sent her into another spasm of swearing as she strangled the steering wheel.

She directed her thoughts to Mark and tried to recall the feeling of love the two of them shared before he'd left for Afghanistan. Apart for almost a year, she remembered his caring and gentle way, and how good she felt when she was with him. Mark was her rock and her future. How could she have forgotten that? Pushing negative feelings aside, she recalled the first days of her assignment in Riyadh, and how she had enthusiastically taken on her new job.

When people are trained as covert operatives they are studied and evaluated by their instructors as to how and where they will be most useful to the Agency. Some are earmarked for intelligence gathering or HUMINT, and some are chosen as combat assets. The selection is done with the immediate requirements of the service as the only consideration. Technically, Yasi had been one of the most talented combat trained assets that the Agency had ever produced. Although she was slightly built, she was strong and competed well because of her agility and core strength. Her insatiable will to win was complemented by an indomitable stubborn streak that would not allow her to accept defeat.

The Agency weapons training phase had intrigued her and she quickly became proficient in its technology and techniques. With an intensity that impressed her instructors, she focused on the mastery and use of each of the Agency's preferred weapons until she became one of their most proficient assassins, lethally adept with rifle, pistol, or knife.

Although she completed the physical training phase as an honor graduate, her instructors did not recommend her as a combat asset. Her psychological profile didn't support it. Her background had been too moderate, her personality too balanced. She had been raised in a loving, secure family and never experienced hardship. Every test revealed her to be a well adjusted individual. Her instructors felt she was competent, but had "no edge" and determined she wasn't predator material. As a fluent Arabic speaker, she would be more useful to the Agency as a human intelligence asset. Ultimately, she was assigned to Riyadh, Saudi Arabia to gather information using her language skills and cultural knowledge.

As required, she maintained her combat skills. She loved the physical challenge that hand to hand combat necessitated, and strenuous daily workouts with the Marine guards at the American Embassy in Riyadh offered her a unique opportunity. She remembered the first time she met the Marine sergeant in charge, watching him smirk as she approached a group of Marines in the gym.

"Yes ma'am? Miss al Amar isn't it?" He nodded to her and spoke with an easy Okie/Texan drawl that belied the intensity of his personality. He knew she was new to the embassy staff. He didn't know what she did, and didn't care. He supposed she was probably one of innumerable paper pushers who processed passport and visa applications.

"Gunnery Sergeant Baser," she greeted him with a smile and held out her hand. "Nice to meet you. I would like to work out with the team." She motioned toward the dozen or so sweating men who were grunting and pummeling each other on gym mats.

The sergeant gave her a grin as slow as his drawl. "Er, ma'am, no disrespect meant, but the guys here don't do well with beginners. I mean, you wouldn't like to get yerself a pulled muscle, or break a nail, or something? Why don't you jes' join the squad for the five mile run we're going to do after this? The men tell me you're a good roadrunner. You could give them a real chase that way."

She scowled at the older man. "Gunny, I have black belts in both Taekwando and Judo. I'm expert in Nagewasa. My basic strength however, is in Yang Taijiquan. I think I can hold my own with the fellas, and I don't give a shit about my nails." She jerked her head in the soldiers' direction and almost scorched the sergeant with her eyes. Bazer stood up straight, and squinted hard at her for a few seconds. He suddenly knew she wasn't any sort of candy-assed clerk. "Martinez," he bellowed out. "Get your bee-hind over here. Ms. al Amar..."

"Call me Yasi."

"Miss Yasi is going to whup your young ass," the sergeant chuckled.

Corporal Martinez was a head taller than she was, and built like a muscle bound fire hydrant. They shook hands and began to circle each other. It only took Yasi ten seconds to do an Ippon Seoinage arm throw slamming him hard to the mat. When he got up she followed it with a leg throw. She was in a killing stance on the third move. Two more Marines worked out with her, and she earned their respect. In the ensuing weeks they accepted her unorthodox approach to combat training, watching respectfully as she practiced Tai Chi to center herself before beginning to fight. Technically and physically, they had come to consider her their equal. She ran with them every morning, dressed in Marine issue desert cami's, tee shirt, and boots. With her long dark hair tucked up in a cap and her boyish long legged body, she looked like just another Jarhead to the Saudi soldiers guarding the Diplomatic Quarter's perimeters. The Marines admired her but didn't necessarily share her passion for what they considered a necessity of physical fitness, and laughingly referred to her as a running fool. Memories of Riyadh faded from her mind as quickly as they had come. She once again concentrated hard on the highway in front of her.

She had been driving south for almost three hours when the old Bedouin's cell phone in her pocket gave off a jarring metallic tone that made her jump violently, almost running the tanker off the highway. She reached into her trousers fumbling for it, finally checking the caller I.D. It showed a Riyadh number had called and left a message. She pulled the truck over to the side of the road and let the engine idle, as she pushed the requisite buttons on the cell until she could hear the message. A cultured Arabic male voice spoke, "Abdul, do not let the girl live for one more day. I have changed my plans. Kill her immediately and save the head for proof. You will be paid the full amount by messenger. He is on the way to you." She quickly turned the phone off with shaking hands.

It was Mohammed. The hair on her head felt as if it was standing straight up. Her mind raced. He said his messenger was on the way. She had been driving for three hours and was approximately 170 miles away from where she had started. If Mohammed's messenger arrived at the Bedouin's camp now, he would call in an alarm and a helicopter could be dispatched to search for her. They would find out she had driven south and would have time to begin a grid search. There were two more hours of light left until sunset. She had to get the truck off the highway and headed in a different direction immediately. She engaged the engine, turned the wheel east, and drove off the road into the desert. She would head south again after an hour or so, and try to navigate at night through the countryside.

At the end of a grueling two hour drive over rough terrain, one of the truck's tires blew. Keeping a hard grip on the steering wheel, she managed to wrestle the rig to a stop without flipping over in the soft sand. Shards of shale had shredded one of the rear tires, leaving only a small amount of rubber on the rim. The setting sun framed the western edge of the sky behind her with brilliant shades of bronze and gold, and turning her head to the right, she saw the hazy outline of the distant mountains of Yemen in the south.

It was time to rethink her escape. First, she stripped off her clothes, including socks and boots. Standing barefoot, she turned the spigot of the truck's water tank to high filling the goatskin completely with water. As she poured it over her head she sucked in small sips, swishing the water in her mouth, and spitting it out. She refilled the goatskin and continued to run the water over her head and down her body a dozen times. Using the gutra and loose sand she scrubbed the dried blood and sweat off her skin and rinsed her body and hair. The water was warm from the sun and felt wonderful. She used her shirt to dry, and then pulled her trousers and boots back on. She pulled the old man's shirt over her head and tied the gutra headscarf around her neck. Cinching the belt around her waist she placed the revolver and dagger securely at her middle and put the cell phone, the box of ammunition and the old lighter back in her pockets. Biting hungrily at the piece of dried goat meat and butter she had taken, she shoved what was left into the top of her boot. She filled the goat bladder until it was bursting with water and slung it over her back. After two more long drinks from the truck spigot she felt new energy begin to flow into her body.

Starting up the tanker's engine, she positioned the truck to head directly into the eastern desert and tied the steering wheel to the door handle with strips from her shirt. She set the engine idle high enough so that the rpms would keep the vehicle moving forward. The desert was flat as a board for as far as she could see, and when she released the hand brake, the tanker ambled off into the gathering eastern twilight. There was no way to know how far it would travel before it stopped, but if anyone was looking for her, the tracks from the highway led away from the south, and the inference would be that she had headed east, toward Riyadh. She looked up at the sky, checked the stars, flipped the cell phone on, and noted the time. She turned the cell off, and started to jog southward.

The moon rose slowly and with each minute illuminated more of the desert floor, enabling Yasi to easily navigate the terrain. After jogging for about two miles, she stopped to rest and turned on the cell phone to check the time.

The cell's electronic voicemail signal sounded with a deafening clamor in the silent desert night. Her hands were unsteady as she flipped the phone open and pushed down the "listen" key.

"Yasmina," the whispery voice purred. "You have killed and killed surprisingly well. Who are you, my little desert flower? I thought I knew you as an amateur. Now, I have my doubts. I have new admiration for you. When I find you, and I will find you, I will have you killed in a more interesting way than my previous plan had called for. You have earned a stunning death, and it will be yours. I am coming for you."

She clumsily turned off the phone, her body involuntarily shaking. It was as if Mohammed had reached out and touched her core with a piece of ice. She shook off the fear and vowed she would make sure that he would not find her until she was ready for him. "Fuck you!" She spat out the bravado. It was time for him to figure out that she was on her way to get him.

Calculating she had completed only half of the cross country trek necessary for that night, she still had time to run until dawn. It was important to widen the distance between her and the truck, and she focused her mind on the challenge ahead. Starting off at a full lope she hoped her body would produce enough adrenalin to keep her stamina level where it needed to be in order to finish this run. On the old man's orders, Armallah had barely fed her, but Yasi secretly kept herself nourished by stealing milk from the goats and eating locusts and grubs she found on the salt bushes. As she ran she let her body go, relying on old instincts. After a few minutes she relaxed in the sheer exhilaration of feeling free, letting the warm desert air flow evenly in and out of her lungs, enjoying the pure act of breathing. Powerful muscles in her legs drove her body forward.

Her mind drifted back to memories of her parents. She could smell her mother's perfume; hear the sound of her voice and her laughter. She saw her father's gentle smile and soft eyes and remembered their love for each other, their family, and America. Her parents' ancestors lived in the Middle East for centuries and two of Yemen's most powerful tribal families were joined with their union. Her mother's family, the al Jouf, were from South Yemen, and her father's family, the Maerb, were from North Yemen. Both were ferocious warrior tribes who traced their lineage to ancient kings and queens. Over the centuries they had evolved with the times, becoming wealthy traders.

As great as her parents' love had been for their native Yemen, it paled in comparison for the love they felt for their new home. They were forever grateful for the opportunities their adopted country offered them and their children. They became American loyalists.

Yasmina knew her mother and father were proud of the work she chose to do and yet that was the reason they were dead. By allowing her identity to be uncovered, she failed to keep her family safe. Now, she would never see them again, and she took full responsibility, realizing it was her fault. They never hurt anyone, nor had they done anything wrong, but were tortured and murdered in response to a terrorist's revenge. Mohammed ordered their murder in retaliation for Yasi's crime of being an Agency operative, and attempting to infiltrate his organization. He did not want her to die immediately; he wanted her to suffer first. Killing her parents would be the beginning of her suffering. Enslaving her and having someone cut off one of her fingers every month would be the midpoint. Hacking off her head would be the agonizing end.

Her reverie was broken by the sight of a dozen shooting stars overhead in the night sky. She suddenly felt new hope, as if God had sent her a sign. She knew she would survive and get out of this place. She would secure her brothers' future, and exact revenge that was due her parents and other victims of the bastard terrorist Mohammed. She would find him, and his life would be forfeit. Mohammed bin Fasheed was a dead man walking.

Tears streamed down her face. She roughly brushed them aside, not slowing her pace. She ran until she saw the moon grow pale, and the eastern edge of the horizon lighten.

Each dawn, the sun dazzlingly explodes in the eastern quadrant of the Saudi Arabian sky, heating the desert's surface like a far away blow torch. Yasi knew she only had a short time to find a hiding spot before full light. The airport at Khamis Mushayt was one hundred eighty miles away and a helicopter taking off at dawn could easily scan the desert for her. She had to find a place to rest where she would be protected from the 100 degree temperatures as well as sky trackers. She discovered what she needed in a wide, thick outcropping of flat strata rock. She pulled the revolver and the dagger out of her belt and climbed up into the space between two flat boulders, easing herself into the deep gap between them. The rock felt cool and, when she stretched out, she realized she was completely hidden from above, protected by a foot or more of stone. She pushed her body backward into the crevasse as far as she could, and faced outward into the desert. She untied the gutra, wadded it into a pillow, and swallowed a mouthful of water from the goat skin. Something scuttled into the dark recesses of the crevasse behind her but she didn't care. She placed the revolver and dagger in front of her on the rock and fell instantly asleep.

The desert sun had only been twelve inches away from her all afternoon, but inside the tiny cave where she slept, it remained cool. The slabs were thick enough to act as a shield, not just from the elements, but from twenty-first century technology. No helicopter picked up her life signs. Her body fell into a deep, healing sleep using time to heal and gather its resources. She started wide awake at sunset, having slept for the entire day. She remembered she tried to arouse herself earlier, but her father's image appeared and told her to remain where she was.

She slid slowly out of her hiding place and leaned against the warm rocks. Raising her eyes to the darkening heavens, she warily scanned the sky and the terrain around her for any sign of movement. Both were still. She held her breath for a minute and listened, but the only sound she heard was the soft rustling of the wind as it moved grains of loose sand. Nothing seemed unusual or out of place. She relaxed. Her mouth was sore and she gingerly sipped a few drops of water from the goatskin avoiding her cracked lips. Her back still ached as a result of Armallah's beatings and when she tried to walk the muscles in her legs cramped up. She stretched rubbing her legs and arms vigorously, kneading out the knots.

After swallowing another drink of water, she waited for the effect of it to diffuse throughout her body. Her stomach growled its message of hunger. She took out the piece of goat meat from inside her right boot, and ate it hungrily. It was rancid from the enzymes in her sweat, but the meat had softened, so it was easier to chew. After drinking a few more sips of water she took the last of the goat butter and gently coated the inside and outside of her mouth and lips with her finger. She sat and breathed deeply a few more times, feeling energy return to her core.

The long shadows of the setting sun created a kaleidoscope of colors and shapes, and Yasi knew that in a few minutes everything would be engulfed in darkness. As fast as the sun rose at dawn, it seemed to disappear faster at dusk. Soon, she would be able to see the constellations and calculate the rest of her route. She ruffled her hair, pulled off her boots and gingerly rubbed her feet. They were blistered and bloody, but she could move her toes. The pain seemed to go down into her bones, but the old man's boots had enabled her to cross the desert. The slipper shoes that Bedouin women traditionally wore would have been useless.

As she took the cell phone out of her pocket she felt reassured by its smooth plastic shape sitting in the palm of her hand. It was the key to all her hopes of being found. She based her plan on classic escape and evasion techniques learned during her training. Use initiative, surprise, and overwhelming force. Do the unexpected. Back at the Bedouin encampment she had found her weapon in the mica beds and created a stone dagger, transforming the rage of her own brutalization and her parents' murder into calculated action. She killed her torturers skillfully and unemotionally, gaining confidence and strength from their deaths and successfully fled from her pursuers by going in the opposite direction they predicted she would go. Moving at night, she made it difficult for Mohammed's men to detect her in the barren vastness of the desert. As training had taught her, because she had acted in an unexpected way, the bad guys had been unable to capture her. Ingenuity abetted by resourcefulness were the actions that brought her freedom. Now she understood what seemed to be an intellectual exercise during her Agency training. The core tenet of survival and the control of her own destiny was centered in her, not in external forces. She smirked, imagining the depth of Mohammed's anger at his loss of face in front of his men. By now, he would have gathered an army to hunt her down and bring her back to him. He would want her to beg for her life, but that wasn't going to happen. He was going to have to beg for his.

Time was essential to success. Tomorrow, her water would be gone and by now, Mohammed's trackers were scouring the desert. There would be no more rest. It was a straight run for the foothills of Yemen and extraction by friendly forces. Looking up in the southern sky, she saw familiar constellations and was elated at being close to her goal. She could reach the Yemeni mountains before dawn. She pulled her boots back on and dressed, stuffing the weapons into her belt. The goatskin bladder rested across her back, the water in it bobbling reassuringly.

At first her pace was no faster than a slow dog trot, but as her body began to respond the adrenalin her heart was pumping into her she let her legs stretch out and her body go free.

CHAPTER 8

At first, it sounded like a loser assignment. Travel to Detroit to find out who killed a local Arab newspaper publisher and his wife, and then find out who hired them to do it. As a senior operative, Joe Bridges ordinarily would be offended that he was assigned to such a routine mission until he and his partner, Ron Boreal were briefed by their boss. Oddly, the murder had the highest State Department and White House priority. Their supervisor grumpily shared that he had been personally summoned to the White House that morning at dawn. He would not tell them anything else, except they would have all the FBI and Detroit Police Department cooperation they needed, and the Agency's jet was waiting to fly them to Detroit, ASAP.

Sitting at a conference table their boss dictated the facts to them as he knew them:

"Deceased male: Adel al Amar fifty years old. Naturalized American. Emigrated from Yemen twenty-five years ago. Publisher of the Arabic-English newspaper, "Sadeek," in Dearborn, Michigan. Model citizen. Local politician and VIP. Father of four. Fiscally responsible.

No warrants or history of warrants. Cause of death: Execution style murder. Bullet in head. Body beaten and burned.

Deceased female: Suhair al Amar forty-eight years old. Naturalized American. Emigrated from Yemen twenty-five years ago. Homemaker, mother of four, volunteer. Model citizen. No warrants or history of warrants. Cause of death: Heart attack. Body beaten and burned."

He continued on in a monotone, perusing from an official file. "The al Amars were supposed to have driven to a fundraiser in downtown Detroit and wound up murdered in the middle of the city's main drug war zone." He looked up at Joe and Ron. "Local PD thinks it was a 'strayed off the main road' random drug killing for money and wrote it off. Your first question should be how could they get lost going downtown in a city they lived in for the past twenty-five years? Anyway, the White House picked up on the murders and called in the FBI. FBI Forensics found the fingerprint of the perpetrator, Jerome Al Hussein on the leather seatback of the driver's side. Al Hussein is African American, a local enforcer with a Detroit gang called The Brotherhood. Has a reputation as a real sick-o. He's into sadomasochistic torture. Rumor has it that he loves to see his victims beg for their lives before he beats them to death with his fists. Has a long and strong history of masochism and is said to have such a high threshold for pain that he once cooked his hand with a cigarette lighter rather than admit he felt any pain."

"Rare or medium? I mean, how did he cook his flesh?" Quipped Ron, looking up from his notepad. "It might make a difference. You know, cooking temperature versus time to cook."

"What?" Snapped the supervisor. "Get started tomorrow and find out what happened. Stay until the job is done," he growled. "And do it fast! I don't need to lose any more sleep over this."

The two agents went over the file again. Everything about the deceased was within norms. There was nothing unusual about the two al Amars except for the fact that people in the State Department and the White House were personally interested in finding out why they were murdered. Putting that mystery aside, the agents both focused on the coroner's report. Mrs. al Amar had initially died of a heart attack. Her dead body was then beaten to a bloody pulp, soaked with gasoline and set on fire. Mr. al Amar was shot in the head first, and then died from the head wound. He too, was beaten and burned.

Ron spoke first. "Joe, I just don't get it. The old woman crumped first, but her husband died a few minutes later, after being shot in the head. Why did the perp keep on trying to kill the both of them when they were already dead?"

"I know what you mean," responded Joe. "The second and third attacks were a waste of time and energy. Could have been ritualistic maybe, or rage induced. But in reality, totally unnecessary."

As they studied the file, they saw that statistics and information from the FBI on Jerome was sparse. They scanned the list.

Jerome al Hussein:

African American male, thirty years old, six foot five inches tall

Three hundred pounds

Physically fit male specimen trained in combat disciplines

Mentally unbalanced with hair trigger temper

Specializes in torture and execution of victims selected by a local gang, The Brotherhood.

Joe knew The Brotherhood was an all black gang that specialized in drugs, gun running and prostitution. Noted in the comments column: It is the opinion of the Bureau that Jerome Al Hussein will not be intimidated by use of weaponry or force.

Joe smiled to himself. In other words, you could point a gun at him, but you had better kill him, or he will kill you. That in itself wasn't particularly impressive. Joe knew the right caliber could bring an elephant down, and if there wasn't a big enough gun to use, there were always explosives. The tougher he was, the dumber he'd be.

Ron and Joe came to the conclusion they would have to find a way to have Jerome volunteer to tell them why and how he murdered the al Amars. This wasn't going to be easy, but it was going to be interesting. The gang leader of The Brotherhood was presently in jail awaiting sentencing on a federal gun charge. They would start with him. A pre-sentencing jailhouse interview was always fertile ground for negotiations.

The two agents returned home and told their families that they would be gone for a few days on a business trip, but could be reached on their cell phones. The flight to Detroit gave them time to plan and they spoke with both the FBI and Detroit police. They made arrangements to meet with the patrolmen who had found the al Amars' bodies and police who had past dealings with Jerome.

Their first stop was the Federal Detention Center in Detroit to meet with the jailed leader of The Brotherhood. A short, slight man Mustafa Kabul more than made up for his unimpressive physical presence with a reputation for brutality and murder.

Mustafa was laid back and in a talkative mood. They sat at a metal table and offered him a smoke.

"Hell man, I don't tell him who to murder, just who to discipline. He freelances most of the time. It's cool. Saves us money, you know. The man makes enough to give hisself a bonus." Mustafa shrugged, the cigarette dangling from his fingers. "We don't give a shit who he kills," he chuckled. "He's psycho anyway."

Joe leaned across the interrogation table toward the prisoner.

"Mustafa, we want you to do us a favor. We want you to make a phone call to him. Our agents will tell you when."

"Me? Call Jerome? Why? Why should I help you, pigs?" Mustafa looked at the floor in disgust and shook his head negatively. "Like I give a fuck about doing you a favor. Fuck you!"

Ron jumped up, leapt across the table, and grabbed the prisoner by the neck, violently propelling him across the room. He slammed Mustafa into the concrete wall, holding him up against it. Mustafa dangled a few inches off the floor, his face pushed sideways against the rough cinderblock. He was gasping and drooling.

"Listen you no good piece of street shit. You have given me no reason to not file a report that you attacked me, right here in the interrogation room. That should be good for at least sixty days in solitary not to mention other discipline the guards will come up with. You will make the call, asshole. Comprende?" Ron held him in place.

"Mustafa, we know you requested to do your time in the federal facility in Mississippi, so you can be close to your mother. We could help to expedite that request if you cooperate with us." Joe motioned for Ron to let go, then pulled out a chair for the prisoner to sit down.

"Man's a lunatic!" Mustafa peeled himself off the wall pointing excitedly at Ron, making gang hand signals for self protection while he carefully edged his way back to the chair.

"Okay, okay. I'll make the call if you get me close to home. I got to do at least three years hard time, and my mama will be dead before then. I want to be close to her. You fix it to happen."

Joe nodded.

Meeting with the Detroit patrolmen had not been much help. All Ron and Joe learned was local cops preferred to leave Jerome alone and most had only seen him at a distance or worse, the remains of one of his victims. They did get his present address, a list of his favorite hangouts and the names of his favorite whores. Afterward, they reviewed his rap sheet and sat down to study his personal file.

Because he had never served time, the official file on him was thin. Born to a crack addict mother, he and his three siblings spent their early childhood begging for food while living in rat infested apartments. Filthy and sick, the children were in and out of Child Protective Services numerous times. Medical notes showed they had been treated for malnutrition, infected rat bites and cigarette burns. Placed with foster families numerous times, they were always returned to their mother by social workers. At nine years old, Jerome went onto the streets and began purse snatching. At ten years old he joined a neighborhood gang. At twelve he killed his first man. His mother and brothers died from their crack addiction before he was eighteen. When he was twenty years old his sister was found beaten to death by a jealous boyfriend while she was hooking on the streets. He had no living relatives and no friends. As the top enforcer of The Brotherhood, he had earned his position by volunteering for the bloodiest assignments. He beat his victims to death with his bare hands.

It was rumored among gang members when he was a Brotherhood apprentice he had held a cigarette lighter underneath his palm for over a minute while he recited the hip hop lyrics of the gang leader's favorite song, "Fuck Tha Police," not putting the flame out until ordered to do so. People had smelled his flesh burning. The resultant scar in his palm was an inch deep and three inches wide. Jerome was seen to constantly open and close his fist to keep it from stiffening. It became his favorite punching hand when he had a disciplinary "problem" to deal with.

A sociopath, he was the ideal enforcer for The Brotherhood. Obsessed with physique and body fitness, he pushed himself through hours of grueling physical training every week. Sparring viciously with gang members, he fine tuned killing techniques. When summoned by gang leadership and given an assignment, he accepted each assassination without question and affirmed the jumbled dogma of The Brotherhood. He was intimidating because his presence and innate cruelty could make anyone admit to anything. Before he tortured his captives he described in detail exactly what he was going to do to them. One look at Jerome's gleeful pre-execution face made grown men weep.

His personal quest for physical perfection included satisfying himself both professionally and sexually at the highest levels. The sexual part was easy; the gang supplied him with prostitutes. Most of the women were addicts who would do anything for a free score. After servicing him, they told everyone mind boggling stories about the size of his penis and his prowess in using it. Most claimed he was the most magnificent stallion they had ever had. Brotherhood members wondered if the effusive flattery given by the whores was honest admiration, or just fear triggered histrionics. They knew when it came to his reputation, Jerome had an ego the size of the state of Texas, and no sense of humor. He would have killed any prostitute who did not speak about him in wondrous terms.

When they finished reading Jerome's file Joe and Ron began to formulate their plan. First, they had to protect themselves from Jerome, and then protect Jerome from himself. Next, they had to make him insanely afraid. They agreed it was a "cocktail" case and they would use the most potent mix available to them. Coordinating their movements with the FBI and Detroit P.D. they put everything into place.

Joe and Ron found him lounging over the bar at the Tip Top, a dumpy joint locked in a seedy pocket of downtown Detroit, just off Woodward Avenue. His file did not lie. He was a huge man, with an intimidating arrogance about him, and he looked the part of a dangerous dude. Watching at a distance, the two agents saw that he wasn't completely stoned, but had obviously already swallowed his gift of a triple ladder of Xannies. The drug was beginning to work. Jerome's voice echoed off the walls of the bar, loud and demanding. The attractive woman with him was a local pro who usually worked the street nearby, but she was acting as his girlfriend tonight. There would be no charge if Jerome wanted her. He whispered a lewd joke in the prostitute's ear and rubbed his hands familiarly over her buttocks.

"Hey baby, after I get you in bed, you're never going to volunteer to work the fire department because I'm going to hose you better than they ever could!" The hooker threw her head back and laughed. His cell phone rang, and he answered it. Putting the phone in his pocket he kissed the woman on the neck.

"I'll be back in an hour baby. You stay here with that magnificent ass of yours and wait for me." He locked onto her eyes. "I mean it, you stay here, bitch. I don't want to have to look for you." She nodded vehemently as he left the bar.

Following the tracking device they planted under his car, the two agents easily kept Jerome's vehicle in sight. Traveling on the Ford Expressway, they were crossing the downtown area when they saw his car begin to weave slightly in the right hand traffic lane. Quickly positioning their car on his left, they edged forward staying just behind him, in his blind spot.

Detroit police officer Sam Johnson saw Jerome weaving in and out of his driving lane and thought he would get the drunken guy off the road before he killed himself or somebody else. A rookie, Sam was eager to make a difference. Initially feeling disappointed to be assigned to traffic patrol during the midnight to 6 a.m. (dead shift) he knew tonight's DUI arrest would look good on his record. He dutifully followed police procedure calling dispatch with the license plate of the errant SUV and the code for a DUI stop.

As he sped up his cruiser in pursuit he noticed a dark sedan shadowing the SUV, but thought they were following behind because they were afraid to take a chance and go around. Putting on the cruiser's lights and siren, he pulled up in the lane next to the SUV and motioned for Jerome to pull over. The police dispatcher's excited voice blasted over his radio. "Blue 14, cease and desist. Blue 14, repeat. Cease and desist apprehension of SUV plate RF1143. Over. Code 7. Repeat, code 7. Do you read?"

At that moment the sedan behind the SUV accelerated and put itself dangerously between the police cruiser and SUV. The SUV raced ahead. Someone in the sedan rolled down the left rear window and aimed the business end of a double barreled shotgun directly at the police car.

"Shit!" Sam's reflexes were immediate. He hit the brakes on the cruiser and lurched back into the interstate's middle lane until he was a quarter of a mile behind both the sedan and the SUV. The dispatcher was still transmitting Code 7 when he took the first exit that led back to downtown.

"Stupid Detroit uniform!" Ron spat. "What the fuck is he doing out here at this hour. It's the only fucking time the fucking traffic moves in this ghetto! I wanted to shoot his stupid face off for almost spooking Jerome. I hope he pees his pants. Let's catch up Joe."

"Shit! Goddamn it! What the hell was that?" Sam knew a transmitted code 7 meant it was not his jurisdiction. Not his jurisdiction? What the hell was that all about? His whole body shook uncontrollably as he hyperventilated with anger. No sir, you're Goddamn right. It isn't my jurisdiction. That was a Goddamned 12 gauge shotgun someone shoved in my face. Jesus! I'm supposed to be a traffic officer. I am not a fucked up SWAT team gomer. What just happened? As he was driving off the freeway he realized he had wet himself.

Pacing themselves for about a mile, Joe and Ron raced the sedan into Jerome's line of vision. Seeing them suddenly appear on his left, he swerved his vehicle onto the highway service road that would eventually lead down into an abandoned automobile warehousing area. It was exactly as planned.

Jerome had trouble keeping his car under control on the service road and wove crazily across both lanes, crisscrossing back and forth. He blinked hard but his eyes wouldn't focus. He saw two roads. Actually, he saw two of everything. It was impossible to know what was real and what wasn't. He realized the bitch in the bar put something in his drink. He would deal with her later, but right now he had to stop driving. He slowed down. What was wrong with his body? He tried to use the brake but realized he could barely move his legs. His foot fell off the pedal. Everything was moving fast forward and then stopping. He could not make the car go where he wanted it to. It would start forward, lurch for a few feet and then stop. Finally, he pushed down hard with both feet and felt the SUV stall out.

The agents were close when they saw the SUV come to an abrupt halt in the middle of a parking lot. Jerome struggled with the driver's door. He was trying to get out of the car. They sped up to the driver's side with Tazers drawn and watched as Jerome forced his body out of the vehicle. As he tried to propel himself toward them he reached into his jacket for his weapon. Drunkenly, he fell forward onto his hands and knees, his weapon still in its holster. Panting, he rested his forehead on the tarmac. The agents noted that he couldn't hold up his head. Drool oozed from the sides of his mouth. As Joe and Ron approached him with their weapons drawn, he passed out.

An International DT 466Navistar tow truck, the kind used for towing semis, appeared out of the darkened warehouse area and stopped next to the unconscious man. The driver and a helper got out and stripped the giant of his clothing. They put chains around the man's waist, legs and hands and joined them together with steel snap-locks. A tow hook caught at where the man's hands and feet were joined together and began to lift Jerome into the air. He was winched up onto the back of the truck and driven into one of the deserted warehouses' huge bays. The agents followed in the two cars.

Jerome came to with an ache in his head that was blasting at a jackhammer's pace inside his skull. His eyes burned as if they were on fire. His mouth was dry and cottony, his lips cracked and bleeding. He felt as if something or someone had hit him repeatedly on the top of his head. When he tried to touch his head with his hand, he realized his arms were bound above his head with chains. His chest was chained as well, as was his waist and legs. The chains were all bolted onto the back of some sort of a truck.

He was naked. He tried to flex his muscles, to use his powerful chest to force the chain's metal links, but he could not move. His tree sized legs were splayed apart and individually chained. The only thing he could move was his head. There was some sort of IV tube stuck into his arm with a drip bag attached to it. He flexed again and felt the chains tighten and bite into his body. The world spun in a wave of agony and he passed out again.

A soft voice entered Jerome's dreamscape. He was floating in a boat on the ocean, thirsty and in desperate need of water. As he reached for a cool glass, a voice took him away.

"Jerome, wake up. It's time to talk."

He slowly lifted his head and tried to clear his vision. He saw there were two of them. They looked like stinking FBI all polished and neat. So, it was the puking pigs that had him. He began to grimace at them, his huge mouth opening and closing in what looked like a silent laugh as he spat words in their direction.

"Fucking Feds!"

The two men laughed out loud, honestly amused.

Joe spoke. "No Jerome, you're not even close. We're not police. We need information from you and are hoping that you will be able to help us. We are businessmen, in need of help."

"Blow me mothers." Jerome let his head hang down again and stared at the floor. The chains didn't give an inch and the pain hammered unabated on top of his head. His eyes felt like hot pokers were sticking in them. He felt someone pull his head back and shove a plastic cup in his mouth, holding his nose shut.

"Drink this, asshole." A nasty voice ordered

He started to choke as the liquid ran down his throat. He couldn't breathe. He tried not to drink the stuff, but it tasted like water and he needed water. He swallowed. He could breathe again. He wanted more.

"Jerome we've given you water. It will be easier for you to talk to us."

Joe's voice crooned. Ron approached him with another plastic cup and growled. "Drink some more." Jerome swallowed eagerly, the contents ran down his throat. This time, the liquid tasted bitter.

"Who are you?" He drooled the words, trying to keep his head up.

"We told you Jerome. We're businessmen," Ron snapped.

"What fucking business?" He looked at them with his huge head, his eyes rapidly blinking, trying to focus.

"The information business." Joe looked at Jerome squarely. He saw his captive's pupils were the size of golf balls. "We want information."

"Fuck you! When I get outta here I'm gonna find you mothers and rip your arms and legs off with my bare hands. I'm gonna...."

Jerome's head fell forward. As he struggled to lift it again he looked across the room and saw a square table in the corner. There was something black lying on top of it, but before he could tell what it was, he fell back into unconsciousness.

A 12 volt truck battery sat on the top of a small rolling table. There was a delicatessen sized kielbasa sausage, twelve inches long and three inches wide positioned next to it. The kielbasa had two wires coming out of it, one at each end. There was a pair of pliers lying on the opposite side of the battery. Jumper cables were placed next to a folded white cloth. Ron and Joe had set up the table after Jerome was chained to the truck and rendered unconscious.

"Jerome," the soothing voice woke him again. "We know you murdered two people last week. We really don't care that you did, but we do need to find out who ordered you to do it. You see, it's really important that we find out who gave you the order." It was Joe again.

"Go fuck yourself!" was what Jerome wanted to say, but it came out "Go fugg yoursff." His head was heavy, his body limp and weak. He was confused about not being able to talk clearly and felt his heartbeat racing. Suddenly, he felt something brush across the top of his feet and saw a large rat run into the shadows. He tried to jump out of the way, but couldn't move. "Wha...?" he shouted, his pulse increasing.

"Jerome, Jerome," Joe's voice purred. "We have a time table we have to keep. Right now we only have an hour to talk with you before we have to leave, so it would really help us if you would cooperate."

A loud voice boomed. "Jerome, you big stupid pig, know that I will hurt you." It was the nasty voice again. "I will kill you! I will cut your body up in such small pieces that they'll wash down a kitchen drain." Ron was doing a little body dance while he ranted, slashing at the air with an imaginary knife.

Jerome wanted to spit at them, but couldn't. He lifted his head and started to say something but was stricken with fear when he saw nasty voice push the table in his direction. What was he going to do with that? His eyes darted to the corners of the room and he saw rats gathering in the gloom. There seemed to be dozens of them, their bright yellow eyes glowing with malevolence. He knew they were waiting to get him, just like they did when he was a baby. They were going to bite him and eat him if they could. He saw his mother and brother sitting on the floor with the rats, laughing at him. They were smoking their crack shit, stoned out of their minds. He exerted all his bodily strength on the chains, but nothing moved. He wasn't going to get loose. The rats sat back, watching and waiting, tasting their tongues. His heart hammered faster in his massive chest.

The table rolled in front of him. He saw a large truck battery, and a sausage of some kind with things sticking out of it. Pliers and jumper cables were placed alongside the battery, beside a small white rag. Ron sneered at the captive murderer. "What we have here Jerome is the reason you will talk to us. You see, we know how much you enjoy pain. Torture will not impress you. Hell, you'd just enjoy yourself." Ron stomped toward the table and made himself busy, purposely blocking Jerome's view.

Joe walked close to Jerome and whispered. "Jerome the information we need is extremely important. You will be free to go as soon as you tell us who hired you to kill Adel and Suhair al Amar. We know you take

great pride in your body, especially a certain special part of your body."
Joe looked down at Jerome's huge limp penis. "We want you to know if
you cooperate with us we will respect your concern, if you know what
I mean."

Jerome could feel the most brazen of the rats standing on his feet,
rubbing up against his ankles, smelling him, wanting to bite him. They
were trying to climb up his legs and he bellowed for them to get off of
him.

"Offen me! Get offen me! You devils off of me!" He screamed.

Although he could not move he started to twist his head from side
to side, his eyes rolling in their sockets, his heart hammering at a killing
tempo.

"Oh fuck this!" swore Ron.

Jerome's eyes seemed to bug out of his head as he watched Ron's
actions.

"I haven't had anything to eat in almost ten hours and I'm starving."
He hefted the large kielbasa sausage off the table with both his hands,
looked at it and then stared hard at Jerome's penis. Shrugging, he
attached the wire from the one end of the kielbasa to a battery terminal
and then did the same with the other wire. He placed the sausage back
on the table top. Immediately, a dull crackling sound could be heard.

Jerome could smell the sausage cooking. The rats smelled it too.
Their noses twitched back and forth in anticipation, their movements
becoming more agitated. More of them tried to climb up Jerome's legs.
He tried to jump up and down and began screaming.

"Mama, mama, ohheeeeyeeei!" The chains held tightly. "Off me,
eeeeyyyeei!"

The soft voice came close to him and whispered in his ear. "Tell me
about the murder of the al Amars. You'll be set free after you tell me

about the al Amars."

The sausage was bubbling now, its skin blistering, the fat running out of it, dripping off the table top onto the floor. The room stunk of garlic and cooking meat. Jerome saw rats jump up on top of the table and inch toward the sausage, while others lapped at the juices on the floor.

He had to get out. His heart hammered in his chest, his breath in ragged gasps. His head felt as if it would explode. Suddenly, he was in full panic mode. Straining against the chains with all his strength he howled in fury and then sobbed as he told the voice everything he remembered about the old Arab and his wife.

"I'd been hired to kill them, to make them suffer, but they got over on me. When she saw me point the gun at her husband the old lady had a heart attack or something. She checked out immediately, holding her chest. The old man saw her die and grabbed my gun, trying to pull it away. It went off in his forehead. He died instantly, too. I was paid to beat them to death. I had to beat them to fulfill my contract. Afterward, I drove their car to the drug zone and set it on fire so that no one would know. Sweet Jesus, let me go!" He screamed at the two men.

He saw the rats swarming now, their numbers filling every inch of the warehouse floor, making it undulate with their panting bodies.

"Nice Islamic prayer Jerome. I'm disappointed in you." The nasty voice chuckled.

"Who paid you?" The soft voice asked.

"Hassan Jabar. Hassan Jabar!" He kept yelling the name louder and louder.

"Who is Hassan Jabar?' the voice purred. "Tell me."

The rats were up to his knees now, trying to claw their way up his thighs. They were staring at his penis, licking their lips, their awful mouths parted in anticipation. They fought with each other to get closer to him. He could hear their jaws snapping.

"I don't know. Some guy, just a guy. I don't know. Get me out of here. Yeow!"

Jerome was jumping up and down in place, his eyes bugging out, his body straining to get free.

The nasty voice cut into his brain. "Lunchtime." Jerome stared terror stricken at the fully cooked kielbasa in front of him. The wires had been removed. He saw nasty voice lift up the small white cloth on the table and take out a fork and knife. He cut into the greasy sausage, put a large piece in his mouth and began to chew it noisily.

"Yeeoooew!" Jerome yowled. The rats were going to bite him now. They were going to eat his dick! He was screaming at the top of his lungs, his huge chest heaving up and down like pistons in a race car, his body's muscles cramping spastically.

"He's a car dealer in Ann Arbor. Arab guy. Mercedes. Ann Arbor, Ann Ar....!" His heart was hammering and his blood pressure close to blowing out the walls of his arteries when he passed out.

"That's it," said Joe. He picked up his cell phone and murmured instructions. Ron was still munching on the kielbasa as he quipped, "You know, I always wonder what they're honestly seeing and hearing with that mescaline/amphetamine mixture we give them. What a beautiful, mind blowing hallucinogenic martini it is! Sort of makes me want to drink one after a hard week with the wife."

Jerome awoke at dawn sitting propped against his car, his clothes piled neatly beside him. Still naked, his body was covered with bruises from where the chains had held him, but he was a complete man. There were no rat bites anywhere on his body, but he shivered uncontrollably remembering the nightmare he had been put through. His head still ached and as he dressed he vowed he would find the two Feds who kept him prisoner, and he would kill them and their families.

He turned his SUV off the Ford Expressway onto Interstate 696 headed home to his apartment. Behind him a forty-two wheel steel hauler was moving up rapidly and changing lanes. Investigators never determined why the experienced truck driver lost control and rammed the rear of Jerome's Navigator, crushing the SUV into the concrete retaining wall of the highway, killing Jerome instantly.

The name that Joe and Ron wrested from Jerome was Hassan L. Jabar, a Jordanian born naturalized American. His name was put into an Agency database. His car dealership's name was added, as was his corporate name, his wife's name and all his relatives' names. United States Government and international databases instantly correlated, and began searching for data.

The corporation that owned his dealership and paid Hassan his one million dollar salary was traced to a larger holding company in Bermuda. The Bermuda holding company owned companies in the Caymans and Lichtenstein. The Lichtenstein company was co-owned by a California based corporation named Aleisha Data Controls, or ADC. The principal owner of ADC was a man named Abu Ahmed, a Saudi national.

Abu Ahmed was a well known international trader, a multi millionaire who owned dozens of companies in as many countries. Interpol had collected data on him for years, and at various times had closely watched his intricate business dealings, but never found anything illegal. He seemed to trade equally between east and west and had survived dealings with the North Koreans.

The Saudi Internal Security Police had minimal information on him, but they did have a memo in his file noting that he was held in high regard by the royal family through his Saudi Arabian business holdings with a man named Mohammed bin Fasheed. They owned a dozen or so businesses together and were also on the board of directors of two of the largest charities in the Kingdom of Saudi Arabia.

The name of Mohammed bin Fasheed was added to a list of names and input into databases for further investigation.

C H A P T E R 9

As she entered the elegant outdoor patio area of the embassy, John Brewer, the Chief Consular Officer turned to greet her. His right hand cradled the elbow of a handsome man with a goatee. The Saudi was attired in a traditional long white robe that ended at his ankles called a thobe, and his head was covered with a red checked Bedouin headdress, or gutra. As her colleague formally presented the man to Yasi she absentmindedly held out her right hand while she looked around the room. The Saudi gently took her hand, brushed the back of it with soft lips and murmured, "Yasmina, you are more beautiful than ever."

The man's silky voice made the short hairs on her body stand up and she felt herself sway toward him involuntarily. Her knees felt as if they were going to give way, and she dared not move. It was Mohammed. She looked up into his eyes as he smiled warmly at her. "My God," she thought. "He's more handsome than ever."

The consular officer wandered off to mingle with other guests. Yasi hesitated for a second, gathering herself. She turned away briskly, desperate to escape Mohammed's gaze. He spoke to her quickly from behind in a pleading voice.

"Yasmina, please wait a moment."

She turned, leveled her eyes at him and said evenly, "What is it?"

"I had resigned myself to never seeing you again, and now it is wonderful that you are finally in my country." He grinned broadly. "You are actually living in my country. I understand you're a member of the diplomatic team. How wonderful this is." A smile transformed his face while his dark eyes watched her.

She spoke softly looking straight at him, "Mohammed, you ended our relationship a long time ago in Virginia. Let's leave it at that." She stepped away feeling better, but felt his eyes burn into her back as she walked across the patio and into the embassy's main hall. She left the party and returned to her apartment. She needed a drink.

Mohammed had been a difficult lesson for her. For weeks after he pushed her out of his car on a wet Georgetown sidewalk, Yasi was distraught. He was the first man she loved, and she had been lost without him. She remembered thinking she was the one who caused his rage and blamed herself for destroying their relationship. The summer after her freshman year she was back at home with her family. Signs of her deep depression worried them and although they did not know what caused it, all of them worked determinedly to cheer her up. At the end of her short vacation she was back on the road to her old self. The accomplishments at her father's newspaper gave her great self satisfaction and pleasure, and the time with her family had been healing. All of them had made a special effort to care for her, and she loved them for it.

The years passed incredibly fast, and when Yasi met Mark Harrison she was finishing her Master's degree. They fell headlong into a wonderful relationship that quickly developed into love, but their career obligations forced them apart. Six months after they met she was halfway around the world from Virginia, and Mark was assigned to Afghanistan. Geographically, they were not far apart but in reality they might as well have been on different planets.

The area in Riyadh designated for diplomats to live is the Diplomatic Quarter, or DQ. Saudi architects duplicated the shapes and structures of ancient Arabian cities and incorporated the ochre based colors of the desert in their designs. The result is a series of beautiful buildings and complexes for embassy personnel to live and work in. Thousands of trees and flowers are planted within the five square miles of the quarter giving it the appearance of an oasis. Charming and beautiful, the compound is heavily guarded by specially trained Saudi security police. No one is allowed access to the area unless they have the correct identification or paperwork. It is supposed to be one of the safest places in Riyadh.

Ambassadors are housed on the main grounds of their embassies in separate residences from the administrative offices. Staffers like Yasi are given apartments within specified residential areas of the DQ. From their exterior, the resident's buildings retain the ancient look of mud stucco facades, but the interiors are ultra modern and beautifully furnished with Western comforts.

Each complex of apartments has small shops nearby to accommodate the needs of residents. For residents use there is a women's center, male and female athletic complexes, tennis courts and restaurants. It is a lovely island of luxury located outside of an otherwise dusty and bustling city.

Yasi was pleased with her small apartment. She had been given a one bedroom unit with a balcony that overlooked a green quadrangle planted with date palms and jasmine. There was a gas fireplace, a

Western kitchen and large bath. Laundry was sent out and returned the next day. The furnishings she had chosen from the diplomatic warehouse were traditional and comfortable. She had forwarded her personal belongings from home, and now had her pictures and books spread comfortably around her. To the world she looked like the perfect junior attaché.

Riyadh had been selected as her first assignment as an agent. She was ordered to assist the senior agency operative responsible for managing and maintaining the local HUMINT network. Its mission was to gather information on all known local al Qaeda operatives.

The day before she arrived, the senior operative had been killed by a hit and run driver in Riyadh, and her orders changed. She was instructed to move cautiously and quickly, contact the remaining operatives, and warn them of a possible security breach. She was directed to coordinate with the ambassador's personal security team, and temporarily close down the intelligence net. An experienced operative was being sought as a priority replacement for the senior agent. Until then, important sources must be protected. Time was critical as it was supposed that al Qaeda had infiltrated the highest levels of Saudi intelligence.

Her cover as a junior consular officer offered her the perfect way to move about the city of Riyadh. The Agency flashed a coded list of operatives and the locations of previously used drop sites. She designed a plan on how to quickly pass a warning to the now compromised agents. While she mapped the location of each old drop site, she chose alternative locations for new drops that would be activated in the future. The information was left at the old sites during the times she was sightseeing and shopping. Returning to the embassy, she updated her handlers in Washington.

Yasi was chauffeured around Riyadh by Jake Morris, in an armored embassy SUV. Jake was an experienced member of the Ambassador's personal protection team and a veteran Middle East hand. Jake stood six feet four inches tall and had shaggy brown hair that crept over his collar. He was graceful for a large man, and moved with quiet confidence. Yasi had no doubt he was well trained and was armed. It was his job to protect her when she worked the drop sites.

Although local custom did not normally allow unmarried men and women to be together, Jake would be permitted to accompany Yasi because he was her driver. Saudi law dictated that women were not permitted to drive, so chauffeurs were a necessity for the upper class Saudi woman. On their first ride into downtown Riyadh, an attentive Yasi listened carefully as Jake explained Saudi customs to her.

"By law, women in Saudi Arabia are not allowed to drive. Until the first Gulf War, it was only traditional that women didn't drive. During Desert Storm, in preparation for the defense of their ally, American soldiers had been sent to Riyadh. Saudi women watched American women soldiers drive heavy vehicles, including tankers, trucks and cars. The women soldiers contributed valuable assistance to their army, and walked proudly beside their male counterparts. A few educated Saudi women from prominent families decided to show solidarity with the American women they admired, and quietly drove their own private automobiles through the streets of Riyadh. They were immediately arrested. Religious leaders from the Fundamentalist Left demanded their execution. Realizing world opinion would be passionately negative, a high ranking Saudi prince intervened and put the women under his protection while he kept them under house arrest. It was only because of this intervention that they weren't physically harmed. Most of the women's families disowned them." Yasi shook her head sadly. Jake continued his lecture, catching her eyes in the rear view mirror.

"I'm sure you've read in your briefing book that Saudi women are required by custom to wear a black robe called an abaya that covers their entire body whenever they appear in public. Their heads are covered with black scarves, and in addition, many women wear black mask-like coverings over their faces, with everything but their eyes hidden from view. Some even go shopping wearing black gloves, shoes and socks. The soldiers who were stationed here during the war referred to them as BMOs, or Black Moving Objects. They are truly weird looking. I've seen some women with their entire faces covered with such a thick cloth that they can't see, and walk into walls."

Jake continued his educational discourse. "Miss Amar, you know I will be right beside you when you are on the streets, but it is in your best interest to be aware of your surroundings at all times." Yasi leaned forward, fascinated by the private tutorial she was receiving.

"Mutawas, or religious police are easy to spot. They look as if they've been leased from Hollywood's central casting. They dress in traditional Arab garb. You know, the long white nightshirt looking thing called a thobe but theirs is shorter than ordinary ones. They also sport scraggily facial beards sometimes dyed red with henna. Their mission is to prevent vice and lewdness within the Kingdom, according to their strict religious interpretation of the definition. They eagerly patrol the city's public areas looking for anyone who might not be adhering to the dictatorial laws of Saudi Arabia's interpretation of Islam, called Wahabism. Traveling in pairs or groups, they arm themselves with long sticks and or whips. They are prepared to accost anyone they consider to be breaking the law. If a municipal policeman accompanies them they have the power to arrest people and put them in jail. Powerful leaders within the country are known to be sympathetic to the Fundamentalist Movement and often secretly endorse and finance the actions of the

Mutawaein. They are a nasty reminder of the power of religious zealotry. Watch out for them."

Yasi remembered reading her briefing books. As a foreigner, she was not required by religious law to cover her body, but female American Embassy personnel were strongly advised by their Protocol Officer to wear an abaya over their Western clothes so as not to instigate an incident with the religious police. Now she knew why.

She learned from her cultural briefing that al Riyadh meant, 'The Garden' in Arabic. The Saudis had transformed and modernized their capital city, spending millions to bring it into the modern age. Initially, it had been designed to be one of the newest and most beautiful cities on the Arabian Peninsula, but it never developed the charm of Jedda, the beautiful old city on the Red Sea. Riyadh's buildings were modern, its avenues modeled after Western freeways but above all, it was a working city. Traffic choked the main roads each day, heaviest at rush hours and prayer times. One of the few excuses permitted to not be at prayer is to be driving an automobile.

Jake rattled on continuing to weave his colorful tapestry of information.

"Thousands of foreign nationals from dozens of nations roam Riyadh everyday, shopping alongside the locals. They have a choice of spending their money in modern malls, or in dozens of smaller shopping areas called "souqs" that are concentrated in neighborhoods throughout the city. Most people consider strolling through the souqs an idle pastime. Local men often sit on the sidewalks outside the shops and visit with each other, sipping tea or coffee. The size of a souq depends on the number of small shops gathered together that create it. All souqs are specialized as to what type of goods they sell, and range in size from a section of one street, to dozens of blocks. One of the most famous,

the Dira Souq, is located at the Riyadh Clock Tower in a replicated part
of the old city. It's located adjacent to what the Saudi government refers
to as Justice Square. We expatriates refer to it as "Chop Chop" Square.
It's the place where the Saudis carry out the executions of people who
have been convicted of capital crimes by publicly beheading them. As
you are well aware, Saudi Arabia is a Muslim nation and Friday is their
religious day as well as their day of rest. The authorities often schedule
executions on Fridays, immediately after the noon prayer call when the
greatest number of men will be leaving the mosques. Any Westerner
who gets too curious to see what is happening might be pushed to the
front of the crowd and forced to watch the execution from the first
row, sometimes getting spattered with blood from a newly beheaded
corpse."

"Ugh. Have you seen a beheading?"

Jake responded. "Yeah, it's not a pretty sight. The last one I saw
the head didn't come off after the first two blows of the executioner's
scimitar. They had to cut the neck skin to remove it."

"Jesus Christ!" She swore.

"That's the wrong curse for this country," Jake laughed into the rear
view mirror.

He made a right turn off of the main road and headed for a large
parking lot in front of the clock tower he had just described. Pointing
to the left front he motioned her to look.

"The Altamari Gold Souq is located just a short distance from here.
It's a conglomerate of over 100 shops selling gold jewelry and precious
stones."

Directing her attention over his shoulder he continued. "A mile or so
away, the Pakistani Souq houses tiny shops stacked floor to ceiling with
fabrics imported from around the world. There are silk saris and cottons

from Egypt as well as British woolens and synthetics from China. We'll visit that another time. Also, we have ritzy Olaya Street with its designer boutiques, and smart department stores. It's on the other side of town. I guess you could say that Riyadh is a thriving, vibrant place to visit. Unfortunately, it's also a city where people sometime disappear, so stay close."

Yasi smiled to herself. Jake was like having your very own guard dog to protect you. They got out of the vehicle and walked side by side along the main street. Jake kept up his chatter and pointed out different shops to her as they walked by them.

"Remember, in the morning the downtown streets are jammed with thousands of people trying to get their shopping done before the noon prayer call. Shops are forced to close before noon and don't reopen again until after evening prayer. If you don't get what you need in the morning, you have to come back in the evening. Therefore, it's not going to be unusual for you to make more than one visit a day to the downtown area." She nodded in agreement, knowing she had just received valuable information.

Jake drove her along a different route each time they made the drive downtown as she scouted out future drop sites. She slowly walked the streets and browsed in the shops, familiarizing herself with the souqs. On the drives back to the embassy she took note of each different route they used and discussed with Jake the formulation of a standard evasion plan.

She had chosen what she thought was a good area for the new drop sites to be used by the network's surviving operatives. It was the old general merchandize souq located in the Ba'atha area of the city. The Ba'atha was always filled to overflowing with a roiling mixture of men, women and children, all browsing the busy catacombs of the city's largest market, looking for bargains. The main entrance was located underneath a dilapidated building that housed a decrepit hotel named the Cairo Hotel. To a newcomer the Ba'atha was a confusing maze of block-long vendor stalls, blind alleys and switchbacks all located beneath Riyadh's streets, while occasionally spilling upward above ground into various neighborhoods. For Riyadh's poorly paid third world laborers it was a place they could find affordable goods manufactured all over the world. Shopping beside the poor were wealthy Western businessmen's wives and international embassy staffers looking for bargains for their luxurious apartments and villas. It was a conglomeration of all levels of Riyadh society, and although Yasi would not be able to spot someone following her, it would be difficult for someone to single her out. She confidently dropped the first messages a short way into the Ba'atha, at sites she had chosen by calculating a progression code devised by her and her case officer. Second and third locations had also been chosen with the same calculations and would be used at a later time. The operatives had been taught to visit a new drop site no more than once to look for a message. If there was no information on their first visit, they were instructed to go immediately to the next designated drop site.

The flowers appeared the day after the embassy reception. Yasi had been out with Jake mapping future drop sites and upon returning to her apartment found a dozen or more floral bouquets in her living room. There were no gift cards except for one. It read, "You are most welcome in my country, beautiful Yasmina." She immediately called building security and was told an employee of a Saudi corporation delivered them to her. She knew they were from Mohammed. She was furious that he had been able to have one of his men walk freely into her apartment without security stopping him. She would report the Saudi guard's security breech to the American Embassy.

When she relayed her concern to the American Embassy security officer, he dutifully entered it into the daily log, but was well aware Mohammed bin Fasheed was a trusted ally as well as fabulously wealthy. He sat at the American Ambassador's private dinner table at least once a month. Hell, he sat at the British and French tables as often. If Mr. Fasheed had been overzealous in his pursuit of a beautiful girl, it was understandable. The security officer knew the Saudi building guard had been bribed to allow the flowers to be put in the apartment, and wrote up the man, recommending he be replaced. Mohammed bin Fasheed however, was never mentioned by name in the security officer's report to Washington.

Her apartment phone rang that evening.

"Yasmina, my lovely friend. Did you receive my flowers?" His voice was bright and charming. "They are but a small bouquet next to your beauty."

She answered. Her voice had an edge to it. "I received them Mohammed. I did not however, appreciate the invasion of my privacy. I must inform you that no one is permitted to enter an embassy staff member's apartment without permission. The guard who allowed your messenger to enter my apartment has been reprimanded, and your messenger could have been arrested." Mohammed smiled to himself but made no comment.

"Yasmina have you managed to get away and see our beautiful city? I know you have been working hard, but have you been to the souqs or out to Gucci's on Olaya Street?" Mohammed prattled on in a charming way, acting like a playful, inquisitive child, asking what she had seen and liked most. He enthusiastically offered to take her on a private tour and told her there were wonderful things he could show to her that would make her time in Saudi the most memorable of her life.

"Ah, Yasmina I have been working so hard the last years that I feel like an old man," he laughed. "Just talking with you again makes me remember our wonderful days together in Washington, and I feel young. What a fool I was to lose you."

Changing the subject, she politely inquired about his father and Mohammed informed her that he had died. He was now the head of the family and the Chief Operating Officer of his family's conglomerate. He listed his responsibilities with a bored cadence. He also volunteered that he had not married. His voice was sincere as the words flowed easily.

"Yasmina please listen, I know we didn't part well in Washington and I'm entirely to blame for that. I apologize for what was inexcusable behavior. I hope you will forgive me. There was no possible excuse for my actions, but now I can tell you I was under terrible duress at the time. I......"

"I thought you were angry because I wouldn't give in to your plans. I wouldn't marry you and accompany you to Saudi Arabia," she snapped.

"Yes, yes of course." He quickly brushed away her annoyance. "I was devastated you wouldn't marry me. My heart was broken. But the day you refused my proposal the last time, my father sent word that he lost control of one of our family's most lucrative businesses. He summoned me to return home to resurrect the damage. The pressure was horrendous. I was not myself."

Yasmina did not respond.

He broke the silence and asked quietly, "Will you give an old friend another chance and join me for a reconciliation dinner next week?"

She sighed. "I don't think that's a good idea Mohammed. Let's leave things the way they are. You're one of the Ambassador's closest advisors and I'm a junior embassy officer. I think as a new arrival I should keep a low profile. Besides, how could we dine together when the religious police would see us and beat us?" Mohammed laughed heartily. "Yasmina, men and women of means have always found a way around the rules. Please let me call you again?"

She tentatively agreed.

They ended their conversation on a much friendlier note than she had thought possible, and shrugged away a feeling of uneasiness. What would be the harm in having Mohammed show her the city? She had already checked him out with embassy security, and the report showed that he had been personally cleared by the Ambassador.

She reviewed her notes from the day's foray around Riyadh. One of the HUMINT operatives had left a distress code at an old drop site. Yasi received it and redirected the operative to a new drop site. She would check the new site tomorrow to see if it had been used. She debated whether or not to include this information in her report to Washington, but decided to wait and see what developed. Her report was too incomplete at the moment.

Her thoughts wandered to Mark and what he must be going through. She missed him more every day but had not been able to speak to him. During the first weeks he was in Afghanistan she did not hear from him at all. After that, his calls were sporadic. When he did call he sounded tired and distracted, barely able to hear her. Her emails to him went unanswered. The night she recited her cover story about becoming a Junior Consular Officer at the American Embassy in Riyadh to him, she knew he did not believe her. It was only after telling him her parents approved of her taking the job that she felt he began to accept her lie. She told him her father not only approved, but thought the experience would give her some needed depth in future business. She felt guilty about lying, but her orders were specific.

She knew Mark was training and living with Afghani soldiers. He was often in danger, not able to make telephone calls or use a computer. Because his job was so critical to the defeat of the Taliban, he was on every terrorist assassination list. Once the Afghan army was refitted and trained to protect its country, Afghanistan could be kept from being used as an al Qaeda terrorist base and the Taliban would disappear. If anyone could accomplish this, Mark would. She felt afraid but also immensely proud of what he was doing.

She realized her life had changed drastically since the day in Virginia when Mark was ordered away from her. Now, it seemed they were inhabitants of different universes. If there had been time, she would have felt the pain of their separation more acutely, but Agency training didn't allow for that. Her training was so intensely demanding that she had barely been able to complete her Master's thesis on schedule. The government did not give you the luxury of extra time.

After finishing her thesis, she flew to her parents' house in Dearborn, to say goodbye. When she first told her father and mother her well practiced cover story of taking a State Department job in Saudi Arabia, both of them seemed tentative and unsure. Now, after spending time with her they were supportive. Neither of them complained when Yasi told them she would have to report to her new posting immediately and would be unable to take any vacation. Instead, they told her how proud they were of her accomplishments and that they loved her.

The night before she was due to leave her father sat across the room from her, his face serious, his lips pursed. Her mother had left the room to get some hors d'oeuvres. Yasi was studying a map of Riyadh she brought with her to show her parents.

"You are sure of your path, Yasmina?" Her father asked the question gravely, looking at her with moist eyes. She got up and walked over to him. Sitting down, she held his hands in hers. As she looked into his eyes she saw deep concern mixed with sadness. "I am doing the absolute best thing I have ever done in my life, father. I am sure of it. Your old friend and my new mentor have placed me where I can contribute to the downfall of al Qaeda. I can fight back for all of us. Trust me."

Adel's eyes filled with tears as he whispered. "Enshallah."

When she left her parents the next evening, she did not leave the country as she had told them. Her phone call to them would actually be made from her first assignment, an Agency training school in Virginia. Training took place in the middle of the country at what was euphemistically called "The Farm." Earlier, she had spent weekends going to the Marine Corps Base at Quantico learning hand to hand combat, weapons training and escape and evasion procedures. Now, she was going to learn the basics of espionage from the most experienced operatives that the Agency had to offer. She was eager to begin.

The superb small group training she received at The Farm was one of the reasons Yasi had no concern about becoming the newest Agency operative in Saudi Arabia. Her instructors were excellent and the training extensive. Some lessons were intentionally bizarre, designed to make students improvise in order to survive. One scenario had an assassin attempt to murder an unarmed agent with a hidden dagger during a formal dinner party at a foreign embassy. When it was Yasi's turn to be the target she survived by breaking the stem off of her heavy crystal wine goblet and pretending to stab her attacker in the carotid artery with it. Her fellow students thought the act ingenious, and broke a dozen glasses in her honor.

Before she departed overseas, she was briefed about the senior agent's hit and run murder in Riyadh. She asked she be permitted to begin her own investigation upon arrival in country, but was denied. A priority replacement agent would arrive within the month and assume command. Until then, as an inexperienced operative she was ordered to shut down the network and pass information forward warning the other operatives. She accepted her orders without question. Yasi trusted the dogma she had been taught and innately understood the strength of the brotherhood that she had been privileged to join. During her assignments someone would always be watching out for her, but her first priority was to take care of herself.

CHAPTER 10

Operative Carlita Vasquez left a coded message at the new drop site in the Ba'atha Souq asking for a meeting as soon as possible. Jake and Yasi planned for Yasi to meet her the next day at a popular Riyadh family restaurant before the noon prayer. Jake dropped Yasi at the restaurant's door and returned to the SUV to wait.

Restaurants in Saudi Arabia are divided in two separate areas to accommodate the strict cultural code of women not being permitted alone in the presence of any man who is not related to them. One part of each restaurant is designated for men, the other part for families and women. One door allows men and their families, as well as unescorted women to enter. The other door is for single men only. Unescorted women can enter the family side, but not the men's side. The women's chauffeurs remain outside with their vehicles. Because all food servers are non-Saudi men they are allowed to work in both sides of the restaurant. The windows are covered on the family side of the restaurant to keep anyone outside from looking in. Many of the Saudi women still keep their faces covered while they eat; only lifting their veils away from their mouths to take bites of their food.

Yasi arrived at the restaurant first and sat with her back to the blacked-out window facing the entrance door. She had on her abaya, but her head and face were uncovered, indicating she was a Western woman. She ordered from the waiter. Carlita Vasquez came in the restaurant's door and nodded slightly at Yasi. She sat at the adjacent table to her, with her back to the front door. She was a small Philipino woman about forty years old, slightly chubby with a pleasant but tired looking face. She wore an abaya and her head was covered by a black scarf. The waiter appeared, took her order and disappeared.

"You are a fan of the Yankees?" Carlita whispered.

"I am a Red Sox fan," Yasi answered softly.

"Who are you?" The Philipino woman leaned forward curiously.

"I am Abacus," Yasi replied.

"You must forward information about what is happening now." Carlita urgently whispered to Yasi. "There is a man high up in terrorist al Qaeda who is gathering his forces and will take over this country."

"How do you know this?" Yasi asked, and then sat up straight and stopped talking. The waiter approached her table with the food. She nodded a thank you.

Carlita continued. "My mistress is very wealthy. She is a divorced Saudi with many important friends. She's a famous photographer. She visits with the royal princesses every day and gossips with them and other friends. The royal family is very afraid of this man. No one seems to know who he is, or what he looks like, but he travels in the highest circles and is very powerful.

They have heard he will kill all of them and al Qaeda will run the country. One of the royal cousins was found murdered at his desert camp, his throat slit like a sheep. No one saw anything."

Yasi leaned in toward her. "Who do they think it might be?"

A soft whisper came from Carlita. "They think he might be a Syrian, maybe an Iranian."

Yasi flashed Carlita a warning look with her eyes. The waiter appeared at the woman's side, placed a plate of food at her elbow and left. Carlita continued. "All I know is that he is a terrorist and I am frightened. I want the money I am owed and I want to be returned to my country as was promised." Her voice shook as she took a bite of her food.

Yasi looked down at her plate pretending to cut her meat.

"Carlita, whatever promises were made to you will be kept, but first you must help get more information for us. We must find this man. No one will be safe until then. We cannot move you right away, but I will tell my superiors what you have said. Begin by watching your mistress's actions more closely. I want the name of all of her friends and everyone she sees. Include the royals."

Carlita talked with her head down. "My mistress does not speak to me. I am only a maid, but I listen and I watch. She has a lover, a wealthy Saudi who comes by the estate and stays for hours. She goes away with him, often. Sometimes, I overhear her on her cell phone gossiping with him and her girl friends. I will talk with her chauffer to find out where she goes this week. He is my boyfriend."

"Good," said Yasi. "Start a list of all her calls, with time and date, and if you can, the length of the call. Also, find out everywhere she goes. If she has a preset schedule that she suddenly changes, find out why. She probably knows more than she's willing to tell the royal family. Communicate with me by using the drops dictated by the new code you received. I am by your side. We will find this man." Yasi stood up. "I must go now. Don't worry." Yasi gave Carlita a quick smile, placed some Riyals on the table and left.

Mohammed was pleased with the evening's telephone conversation with Yasmina. Perhaps she agreed to speak with him again because she remembered their past relationship with fondness. He smiled to himself. He hadn't recalled much about her except for two important details. He'd taken her virginity and then pretended to ask her to marry him in order to get her to Saudi Arabia and under his control. Sadly, his plan had not succeeded. She would have been a delicious morsel to educate in the decadent ways of the world.

Anticipation rose within him as he remembered how quickly the date rape drug GHB (Gamma Hydroxybutyric Acid) had released Yasi's sexual energy, but faded when he recalled her childlike refusal of his proposal of marriage. If he had not been distracted by planning the 9/11 attack on the United States he would have kidnapped her and flown her to Saudi on his private plane. Once there, she would be under his control forever. No one would have ever seen her again. Her refusal to accompany him that summer had been unfortunate. There wasn't any time to retaliate against her; he had more important things to do at the time.

He was curious about how she would perform in his bed now. Obviously, she would not be as innocent as she once was, but she might even be more appealing. She still possessed a special quality, a boyish beauty that intrigued him. He decided to make an effort to bed her again. It would be a delightful diversion to begin the chase. Besides, a change in women would do him good. He was getting bored with his latest mistress and his wives were both pregnant and misshapen, disgusting in their appearance.

It was hard for Mohammed to find sexual satisfaction. He was only able to become truly sexually excited by the molestation and rape of children. He had been a voracious collector of child pornography for years, but now he had only to click his cursor and order the images of tiny victims sent directly to him from the internet. Children were bought in Africa, Europe and Asia, and shipped around the world. If they survived, they would live their lives as sex slaves in brothels. Buying and selling children was only a small sideline to his main fortune, but it pleased him that he made a profit. He picked up the telephone and called Yasmina's apartment.

He met Yasi at the American Embassy garden cocktail lounge. It was a strict rule that American personnel would not drink alcohol within the country of Saudi Arabia, but the American Embassy was considered sovereign soil. The Ambassador joked to his staff that he operated the best bar in Riyadh. Most embassy personnel as well as a few select foreigners were often seen at day's end sipping their favorite alcoholic libations at the rooftop bar. Because Mohammed was a personal friend of the Ambassador's, with a special security clearance, he was included on the list of Saudis who were permitted to drink on the premises.

"You are always beautiful, Yasmina. I am made to feel fortunate when I am in your presence. You bring me joy." He smiled broadly, his white teeth contrasting against his dark skin.

Yasi sighed. "Mohammed, let's be honest. It is nice to see you again, but I have no interest in beginning a romantic relationship with you." She looked away and waved at a woman she knew.

He shook his head slowly as he smiled. "Yasmina, you and I spent all those wonderful months together in Washington and you don't remember how deeply hospitality is ingrained within a Saudi Arabian? It is part of our culture to make our guests as comfortable as possible, even if it causes us personal discomfort or denies us things we need. I cannot allow you to live as a guest in my country and not take responsibility for showing you the things that make us unique as a people. I consider it a wonderful obligation to be your guide while you are here and if you allow it, your friend."

He looked directly into her eyes but did not move to touch her.

"I know the embassy has a program of familiarization tours of Riyadh and the surrounding areas, but I wish you to allow me to show you more than just things. For example, I think you would enjoy visiting an encampment that has just recently been set up in the desert far from the city. It reflects an important part of our ancient customs and traditions." She arched her eyebrows questioningly.

Mohammed continued. "There is a site approximately 100 miles from here where one of my brothers is hunting, but he is neither using guns nor man made weapons."

"How is he hunting without weapons? And what is he hunting?" She seemed interested.

"He is hunting using an ancient technique called falconry. Falcons have been used by tribal sheiks for centuries as hunters in a sport that teaches patience and endurance. He is also using Salukis, the breed of dog that Bedouins have favored for hunting gazelles and hares. The hunt is more than just the killing of animals. It is a structured series of customs and celebrations that culminate with songs and poetry around the camp's fire pit as well as the feasting on the day's prey."

"A hundred miles away? How could we just visit?" He could tell she was hooked.

"Ah, that's where I can show off my extraordinary friendship! We will fly in my helicopter in the morning and return after dark. I guarantee you a once in a lifetime experience and in return I will hope for your friendship!" He gestured with his palms upward and a large smile.

Mohammed had not lied to her. The trip had been a fantastic experience and Yasmina felt seemingly familiar things stir within her as she watched the ritualistic hunting and the celebratory feasts. It was as if she had seen it all before, even though she had not. She would never forget the beauty and the savagery of the desert. Since then, Mohammed had escorted her around Riyadh many times. His black Mercedes whisked them from the souqs to private art galleries and hotels. He showed her the old areas of the city, and told her stories about them. They shopped together at the gold souqs, visited private artists, and dined at the best hotels. He was always enthusiastic, cheerful and fun. Riyadh began to turn into a fascinating place to live and Yasi started to like her new friend.

Mark had called and left a voicemail on her apartment phone. His tired voice was a monotone. He would be unable to communicate for a few weeks, maneuvering with the army and would call her as soon as he got back. He told her he loved her and missed her, and to be careful. The call was only thirty seconds long, and the message left her feeling empty and sad. She looked at the calendar. Months had passed since they had seen each other. She was so lonely for him her body ached.

The next morning Yasi checked the drop sites in the Ba'atha Souq looking for information from Carlita, as well as confirmation from other operatives that they received her warning. Carlita left a message requesting an emergency meeting. She inserted a code word indicating she was in danger. Yasi and Jake quickly set up a meet for the next morning back in the Ba'atha and decided to hold it in a bustling corridor in front of the Pakistani goods vendor. The vendor occupied a large space and his counters were always crowded with dozens of customers. The two women could easily stand side by side and pretend to examine shawls and robes while they talked. The crowds would provide excellent cover. That afternoon Yasi took the encrypted meeting instructions and placed them at Carlita's new drop site.

The next morning Yasi arrived at the Ba'atha exactly at the designated time and spent thirty minutes at the Pakistani vendor patiently examining scarves and cloths. Carlita never appeared.

CHAPTER 11

The small woman's face was covered in blood, her nose and teeth broken, her eyes blinded by vicious beatings. She shuddered from time to time, her naked body shivering uncontrollably on the metal table she was shackled to. Her captors noted there were only a few minutes of life left in her. Her skin was already blue.

Once the two men had begun their torture Carlita had screamed out everything she knew, and even invented information in an effort to try to stop the unbearable pain. They knew how she had been recruited, as well as the American system of drops and codes she used. She volunteered that she forwarded her information to a woman agent she knew as Abacus and told them of the appointment she had for the next morning. She then prayed for her life, begging for mercy from her captors. In the end, the al Qaeda butchers had been gleefully brutal, hacking at her neck with knives until her screaming head fell sideways off of her shoulders and onto the floor.

The next morning an al Qaeda operative was sent to the Pakistani vendor's stall in the Ba'atha Souq, the meeting place Carlita confessed to them. The agent remained in the souq for the entire morning and secretly videotaped every person who approached.

Reviewing the tape Farouk noticed one woman shopper who arrived at mid morning and seemed inordinately interested in a specific selection of shawls. She remained at the booth for over thirty minutes and occasionally looked around, as if searching for someone in the crowd. She was young and dark haired, but not Saudi Arabian. Although she wore an abaya, she was a Western woman.

Mohammed received a call from an excited Farouk on his scrambler phone. Farouk related the latest news about the American agent they had captured and questioned. The artist Noor bint Taleed had found her Philippine maid listening in to her telephone calls and had complained to her housekeeper. The housekeeper was an al Qaeda employee who related the information to one of Farouk's men. Farouk authorized his agent to follow the maid on her evening shopping trip downtown where he observed her taking something from a basket display at the Ba'atha Souq. He immediately called Farouk for further instructions and was told to intercept her.

"We captured her after she left the souq last night. She still had the coded message in her hand. She was easily broken and confessed to working for the Americans. She gave us her latest codes and the name of her American contact," Farouk sounded very pleased.

"What was the name of the American?" Mohammed questioned.

"Abacus," responded Farouk. "She also told us where and when the next meeting would take place. It was this morning, at the Pakistani shawl vendor in the Ba'atha. My man videotaped everyone who came within 50 feet of the vendor's stall. The video is being analyzed now. We think we've found a woman of interest who was there. She left after waiting for a half hour. She was wearing an expensive abaya, and she was a Westerner. When she left the souq she got into an American

Embassy SUV."

Farouk related how they had executed the Philipino woman after they felt she told them all she knew. Mohammed wasn't interested. "Did you follow the American car?" Mohammed asked as if he already knew the answer.

"Yes, we had one of our men verify that it drove through the Diplomatic Quarter's gate thirty minutes later. The car drove into the American embassy underground garage," Farouk answered.

"Drop a copy of the film off to our embassy contact and see if he can put a name with the face. Have the rest of the American intelligence agents been identified yet?" Mohammed sounded bored.

"No. Not yet. We think there are probably three or four more. Once they discover we have their codes they'll have to realign their entire organization. Hopefully until then, they'll make another mistake. Are we still on line for the royal family?" Farouk eagerly asked.

"Yes. But not on the phone. Come see me in Riyadh tomorrow and we will go over the plan. Keep me updated on the woman." Mohammed hung up.

Yasi was bone tired. She had been locked in the embassy's safe room all day. Because it was the most secure room available she and the Agency handler assigned to her could communicate freely with no concern that anyone could either listen to, or intercept any transmissions emanating from them. The two agents had been piecing together a design for a new information network that would be put in place of the old one. Many American agents had been identified and killed, so the previous design was no longer workable. Yasi spent the day describing each new drop site she chose and why she had chosen it. She included her suggestions of new timing sequences to be used. If her superior gave his approval, the new codes would be issued and integrated into the network. It was careful and tedious work.

One hour after not showing up at the prearranged meeting point, Carlita Vasquez was considered "compromised" by the Agency. All codes and drop sites that she used were immediately discarded and all evidence of them destroyed. As a normal precaution, each agent was given their own encapsulated information system so any possible leak ended with them, and information flow from the network would not be contaminated. Yasi still had five agents in place and, as far as she knew, they had received her warning. They were ordered to keep low profiles and operate at condition red.

She sighed, rubbing the back of her stiff neck. Tomorrow was Friday, a religious holiday as well as a day of rest throughout the Kingdom. Tonight, she would have a luxurious hot bath and go to sleep. Tomorrow morning she planned to come into the embassy and work for a short time, work out a little, and then go for a long run. Afterward, she was going to sit on her terrace and read a book. She needed a break. She quickly secured her paperwork, grabbed her things and turned off the office light. Getting off the elevator, she stopped at the security desk to sign out, smiling at the middle aged man who was the duty officer.

"Have a nice weekend Jack. I hope you have the day off tomorrow. I'm going home to bed. If I'm lucky, I'll be asleep in an hour. Wish me luck."

She yawned widely and waved a lazy goodbye.

"Goodnight, Miss al Amar. See you on Saturday." The digital clock showed the time to be 8:00 pm local, Thursday. The Saudi Arabian weekend was just beginning.

Mohammed's meeting with the Venezuelan Oil Minister had been fruitful as usual, and he was on his way out of the DQ when he saw Yasmina walking on the sidewalk toward her apartment building. He told the driver to intercept her at the next street. He called his mistress and cancelled their evening, citing work related responsibilities. The woman sounded sullen at first, but then acquiesced, and he told himself to remember to send her a piece of jewelry in the morning. The limo slowly approached Yasi from behind. She looked at it questioningly as Mohammed leapt out of the backseat onto the sidewalk.

"Oh, it's you! Wow. Mohammed, you frightened me." She held her hand to her chest, her eyes wide.

"Yasmina, it is kismet to find you at this moment. I have just finished the dreariest meeting in the world with the Venezuelan Oil Minister and I am desperately in need of human companionship and sustenance. Please come with me and join me for a late supper!"

She shook her head. "No, Mohammed. I'm afraid not. Not tonight. I'm too tired. I also had the dreariest day. But thanks, anyway." She started to move away. He stood in front of her blocking her path.

"But it's the weekend! I won't take 'no' for an answer. The Hyatt has just received a shipment of huge prawns and lobsters and they're holding some for me. I promise to have you back home in three hours and you'll be so full of delicious seafood that you will sleep like a baby." He pulled her gently toward the car.

As Yasi hesitated she realized although she was tired, the thought of not being alone seemed more attractive than going home to an empty apartment. Mark probably wouldn't call tonight anyway, and she was concerned about Carlita Vasquez's disappearance. Going out and enjoying herself would be good for a change. She was not officially due to work tomorrow so she could take her time getting to her office in the morning. She smiled. "Okay, but I must be home early. I'll turn into a pumpkin if you keep me out too late."

Mohammed was elated and fawned over her as if she was some sort of precious prize he'd won. "Ah, my beautiful Yasmina, you have made my horrible day disappear. I am so happy!" She allowed herself to be seated in the rear of the limousine and was driven through the gates of the Diplomatic Quarter.

Mohammed previously arranged for the evening's supper to be served in the sumptuous ten room Sheik's Suite atop the Hyatt Hotel. The menu was already selected, the wines chosen, and the flowers put in place. The only thing that changed was the name of the woman he would dine with. The chauffer called the hotel manager notifying him of the limo's pending arrival. After entering the sumptuous suite via private elevator, Yasi asked to freshen up and was shown to a large, elegant bathroom. There were a half dozen porcelain boxes filled with expensive perfumes and cosmetics scattered across the bathroom's exquisite marble countertops.

She flipped open her cell phone and frowned when she saw there was no signal. She would not be able to notify the embassy watch officer that she had changed locations. She was breaking a cardinal rule of security, but she shook off feelings of apprehension by telling herself she was in a very public hotel with a personal friend of the Ambassador of the United States. Mohammed had been investigated and received the highest security clearance the embassy could issue for a foreign national. Hell, she heard he had even been to the White House for dinner! She would be back at her apartment in a few hours. The call to the security desk was not a big deal. Even though she had no interest in an emotional involvement with Mohammed, he was good company. Always entertaining to talk to, he would make her laugh and flatter her shamelessly. As she told herself to relax, she opened one of the gift boxes and dabbed some Hermes perfume behind her ears.

Mohammed was not going to take any chances with the opportunity that had just been given him. He remembered Yasmina was not a woman easily won over, and he would not wait for permission to have sex with her again. He opened a bottle of 1994 Haut Brion Blanc. Putting the familiar white powder of GHB into her goblet, he watched it instantly dissolve. The date rape drug had worked with her before, and it would again. It would either rekindle passionate feelings of sexuality in her, or render her unconscious. Either way was okay with him.

The dinner's first course was delicious. Mohammed kept up an interesting and teasing banter, making Yasmina laugh out loud, relating the latest diplomatic tidbits of outrageous gossip. His attentive and charming manner worked its magic as she relaxed and sipped her wine. She was glad she had not gone home. It was nice to be the focus of a man's attention and to feel pampered again. She'd forgotten how much fun it was to laugh.

The main course of lobster was being served when Mohammed's chauffer appeared and bowed to his employer. Mohammed excused himself and went to a corner of the room conversing in low tones with the man. He nodded affirmatively and then returned to the table. Yasi held a large lobster claw in one hand and a lobster cracker in the other.

"A small business matter my lovely Yasmina. It's really nothing to speak of, but when the Crown Prince requests me to call him I have no choice. I must insist that you remain comfortably hand in hand with your lobster. I am going to call him back on the secure limo phone and will return momentarily." He quickly kissed her hand and disappeared into the elevator.

She took another drink of white wine and began to feel lightheaded and nauseous. Reaching for a glass of ice water, she fought off a sudden wave of fatigue. She had to lie down. As soon as the waiters left the suite, she wandered unsteadily into the living room and curled up on the sofa.

Reaching the limo Mohammed picked up the scrambler phone and dialed Farouk. "What is it?" He growled, annoyed to have left Yasmina. "Why did you bother me?"

"Our man in the American Embassy couldn't identify the woman from the photos taken at the Ba'atha. He says she must be new. He will begin to search for her after the holy day." Farouk stuttered, frightened he had angered his chief.

Mohammed raised his eyebrows, suddenly fascinated in seeing what the woman looked like. "Email me her photo, immediately!" His voice snapped the order. Hanging up the telephone he opened the laptop computer that he kept in the car.

Yasi felt herself purring. She was floating on air, not really asleep. Her body felt deliciously warm, totally adrift. It was delightful, and she stretched out lazily on the large divan.

Mohammed jumped on the sofa next to her, his breath hot in her face. Shaken, she tried to pull away, but he crushed her body against him. He kissed her fiercely, bruising her mouth with his teeth. She ordered him to stop as he moved his mouth to her neck, his teeth biting into her flesh. What the hell was he doing? Crying out in pain, she tried to hit him, but he pinned her down on the couch. He rubbed his body against hers while he ripped her dress. She managed to squirm up into a sitting position and tried to swing her fist at his face but missed. He hit her hard on the jaw, stunning her. She fell backward onto the pillows panting heavily, trying to clear her vision.

Mohammed was screaming she was a lying bitch and whore. He tore off the rest of her clothing while she strained to get away from him. She knew she had to find a place to get her balance, so that she could defend herself. She tried to wrestle with him, but her body wouldn't respond. She couldn't get her breath. What was happening to her? Instinct told her to run, but she could not move. Her brain did not function. She pushed away a surge of panic.

Mohammed was yelling at her again. He dragged her onto the floor and was now sitting astride her, slapping her across the face, pummeling her body with his fists, pulling her hair. Yasi fought to stay conscious, but couldn't get any air into her lungs. She was suffocating, able only to limply kick her legs while she twisted from side to side. Mohammed pulled her legs apart and rammed himself inside her, tearing her fragile vaginal wall. Insane with rage, he drove himself into her multiple times, biting her neck and breasts while screaming obscenities in both Arabic and English. She was conscious of unbearable pain deep inside of her, turning and tearing her insides. The pain increased in its ferocity and lengthened in duration. She had no escape from it.

After Mohammed finished his attack he left Yasi's badly beaten and unconscious body on the floor. He then left the room. After showering and dressing in a fresh thobe he made two phone calls. One was to Abu Ahmed, a colleague and wealthy businessman who had al Qaeda contacts in the United States. The second was to his private pilot.

Yasi moaned softly as she regained consciousness. She was naked, lying on her back on the floor of the suite. Her eyes were already swollen shut. Her teeth were chipped, her lips split open and caked with dried blood. She tried to sit up and groaned in pain. Her insides were torn to shreds and a bloody lymph-like fluid oozed down her legs. She remembered Mohammed both raped and sodomized her while viciously beating her. Her face felt warm and wet, the blood sticky on her fingers. She tried to rub her aching head, but when she touched it she discovered her hair was gone. She had only patches of blood soaked stubble left, interspersed with numerous scalp slashes. More blood dripped down onto her shoulders and her back. She began to shiver uncontrollably and reached out to pull herself up to the level of the furniture.

Mohammed was fully dressed, sitting a few feet away in a chair, sipping a cognac. He seemed amused by her pain.

"Yasmina al Amar, daughter of Adel al Amar of the great Maerb. Daughter of Yemeni swine. Do not attempt to get up. Stay down where you belong, you stupid American bitch! Look at you. My, my. You are neither pretty nor sweet anymore, I have guaranteed that. I raped you, you bungling whore, and when I'm finished with you, you will wish for my gentle touch. So, you are a covert agent for America. How stupid of them to try and use a brainless woman against me, and an amateur to boot. You thought you could use affection to entrap me? You will pay with all that is dearest to you." He spat at her head in disgust. His spittle hung on her cheek.

"Look at me!" He ordered.

Yasmina lifted her head and looked at him with bloodied, swollen eyes. She saw only the outline of a blurred figure.

"You could have had the life of a princess as one of my women. But now you'll have the short and hard life of a Bedouin slave. You will not die quickly. That is too easy. It is my wish that you suffer before you are killed. I am taking you to the desert where I have arranged for you to work as a slave for each day of the life that is left to you, with no hope of escape. While you are struggling to keep alive, and you will struggle, I have made arrangements for a little surprise to be delivered to you. It is my personal payback for what you have tried to do. I will keep that secret to myself until the right moment when it is revealed to you."

He approached her quickly and before she could react plunged a hypodermic needle into her shoulder. She blinked a few times and fell over sideways drooling, blood and lymph oozing onto the carpet. The last thing she remembered hearing was the whirring of what sounded like a small motor.

The Cessna Citation X touched down at Khamis Mushayt two hours after take off from Riyadh. A helicopter was already waiting at the edge of the tarmac with its rotor turning. It was nearly dawn when Mohammed stepped down onto the airstrip and climbed up into the Bell 407. Two men followed behind him and placed a rolled up tarpaulin into the rear seat of the helicopter before jumping in beside it. The pilot immediately lifted off. The sun had just cleared the horizon as the Bell set down ninety miles away, next to a Bedouin campsite. A Toyota truck headed away from the camp toward the still rotating copter and stopped close to it.

Mohammed loped down the helicopter's stairs toward the truck as an elderly Bedouin eased out of the driver's seat.

"Peace be upon you, my friend," he said to the old man.

"And upon you, young master." They shook hands and then began to walk back toward the encampment.

"I have brought you a special treasure old man. Something I want you to take care of, and to personally watch over, very carefully."

"Have you brought me gold to care for?" The old man's toothless grin widened from cheek to cheek.

"I have brought you a prisoner. A foreign woman…."

"A woman in my camp is not good! I don't want her here!" The Bedouin spat on the ground.

Mohammed stopped walking. "Silence! Do not interrupt me with your insolence. You will speak only when I am finished. You forget, I pay dearly so that you can still be the leader of your family. You don't think raising your stinking goats pays for your upkeep, do you? You owe me and our brothers in al Qaeda everything. We killed the tribal leader that murdered your sons; we gave you his herds and grazing rights, as well as most of his wealth. It cost us the lives of two good men. Now, it is time for you to repay us." He motioned to the men standing by the helicopter to come forward.

"Forgive me master. I only know that women are always trouble and I want no more trouble in my life. I have two wives and my sister to live with and I am miserable." The Bedu hung his head dejectedly.

Two guards carried the canvas wrapped object from the helicopter and dropped it at Mohammed's feet. He pushed it hard with his foot and motioned the men to remove the tarp. Yasi's unconscious and beaten body rolled out. She had pieces of what had been the dress she had worn the previous night stuck to the dried blood on her body. Her face was grotesquely swollen, her head appearing monstrous because of her slashed and bloody scalp. She moaned and began to regain consciousness.

"This woman is to be treated as a slave. She is a traitor and a whore. Work her as hard as you wish but I do not want her immediately killed. It is your job to make sure that she remains alive for at least five months. After that time I won't care if you kill her or let her die. It will be your decision."

Mohammed reached down, violently yanking Yasmina's right hand upward, motioning for the old man to come closer. Her swollen eyes tried to follow his actions, but her head spun dizzily as the sunlight burned her eyes.

"Here, I want you to see this. Each finger on her right hand is permanently tattooed with the name of a month, beginning with next month. You will cut off one finger on that hand at the beginning of each month and you will be paid gold at the time you do the amputation. One of my men will act as a witness to the punishment, and bring each severed finger to me. When all of the fingers on her right hand are cut off, you may kill her or wait for her to die. Since she will no longer be allowed to eat from the communal food bowl using her left hand, she will hopefully starve on her own."

Mohammed gestured for a wooden box one of the guards had been carrying, to be opened, and watched the greed in the old man's eyes grow as the glimmer of the gold coins became visible. "There are fifty Saudi Sovereigns in this box. They are yours today. As each amputation is verified, you will be paid another ten Sovereigns. At the end of our little exercise, after all five fingers have been severed; you will receive another fifty Sovereigns." He could see the old man struggling with the numbers in his head. "You will have one hundred fifty pieces of gold when our dealing is done. It is enough for you to retire with many young wives."

"It will be as you wish." The old man bowed low while reaching out for the box with both hands.

CHAPTER 12

Yasi had been running and walking cross country for two hours when she finally stopped. She was breathing heavily, in desperate need of a rest. The moonlight once again illuminated the desert floor providing ample light for her to avoid obstacles in her path. Taking a small sip from the goatskin, she let the water sit in her mouth, swishing it through her teeth, letting it rest at the back of her throat, purposely swallowing slowly.

She estimated she needed another two hours to make it to the first ridge line of the Yemeni mountains. They were close now, and she could see the jagged edges of the foothills smudged against the dark night sky. If she could keep to her previous pace, she would have enough time to find a hiding place in the rocks before full light. Her water was almost gone and she would have to be brutal with herself in regulating her body's ceaseless demand for it.

Closing her eyes, she mentally mapped out the route she would take to the caves. Once safely in the hills, she would turn on the cell phone and send a pre-established emergency signal. Her heart jumped at the thought of being extracted and returned to friendly hands. She sat down wearily on top of a pile of flat rocks, placing her hands behind her for support, letting her body relax. Flashes from the last weeks flowed through her mind.

After being kidnapped in Riyadh, she regained consciousness while still tied and blindfolded, wrapped in a tarp in the back of the helicopter. At that point, she had no idea how many days she had been held, or how long she had been traveling. Her wounds felt fresh and she supposed it was only a matter of hours since she had been captured. She was groggy and still under the effects of the drugs. It was hard for her to breath. Every breath felt as if there was a knife point in her side. She fought to control the pain and to remain calm. She remembered the desolate Bedouin camp. The encampment she had been delivered to was located in the middle of what appeared to be a vast wasteland with no discernable landmarks. The ground was hard scrabble and scattered with boulders. Her memory of the meeting between Mohammed and the Bedouin sheik was hazy, but her first days as a captive were locked within vivid memories of shock and pain. Disoriented and half dead from the beatings and torture she endured in Riyadh, she was barely able to survive the vicious beatings her Bedouin captors subjected her to. It had taken all of her force of will to stay alive.

At night, after working in the blazing sun all day, her jailer, Armallah tied her to a camel post outside of the women's tent. The desert breeze carried the old women's voices to her and enabled her to eavesdrop on their conversations. They did not know about her fluency in Arabic, and were not aware that she could understand their local dialect. She learned the camp was approximately two hours south of the western Saudi city of Khamis Mushayt. After drugging her, Mohammed had flown both of them there. Keeping her prisoner at the camp lessened the probability of the Americans discovering where she had been taken.

She wondered how she had made so many mistakes and was still alive. The night she met Mohammed on the sidewalk came to mind. Normally, she would have followed the strict embassy procedures required when leaving the Diplomatic Quarter, but she allowed Mohammed to pick her up off the street in front of her apartment. Before she had gotten into Mohammed's limousine, she had already signed herself out of the embassy security net with her destination listed as her apartment. As far as embassy security was concerned, she was safe and at home in the DQ. Friday was a day off from work, so the watch officer would not have known she was missing until Saturday. By then, she would have seemed to have vanished off the face of the earth. After handing her over to the Bedouins, Mohammed had time to fly back to Riyadh and appear to never have left the city.

She shook her head back and forth, feeling angry at everything she had done wrong. If only she had not gotten into his car without telling someone, or called from the hotel room telephone, but there was no going back. She was the only one who could get her out of the mess she was in. No one else knew where she was, or if she was alive.

At the start of every new covert assignment, agents are given specific countries designated as safe havens for them if their cover has been compromised and they must immediately escape. These countries have Agency resources available to aid and assist agents in getting back to friendly control. During her Saudi Arabian escape and evasion indoctrination, Yasi had been briefed there were Agency assets available to her in both Jordan and Yemen. Because of the myriad of escape routes from Riyadh to the northeast, Jordan was to be her primary evasion site and Yemen her alternate. As a result of her kidnapping, she was now hundreds of miles away from Jordan with no hope of reaching that country. Her only chance was to get to whatever friendly assets there were in the country of Yemen.

When she shifted her left hand behind her for support, she did not see the small black scorpion dart out from between the rocks she was sitting on. He began to dance sideways toward her and then struck. She jumped up as a jolt of hot pain seared the back of her hand. Yelping loudly, she waved her hand back and forth, trying to fan out the unseen fire that was already starting to move upward toward her wrist. The scorpion held on to the back of her hand tightly with his pinchers and stung her again. This time, she managed to shake him off. As the arthropod scurried away into the shadows, she realized it was a black scorpion, local to the area, and highly venomous.

Never take anything for granted, be aware of your surroundings at all times. It was textbook shit. Goddamn it! She had made another stupid mistake and ignored a basic directive. She hadn't checked out the rock pile before she sat down. Because of that, she was now a victim of one of the desert's most poisonous inhabitants. She recalled the data about scorpions she had read in an area study paper:

"Black scorpion, Scorpionidae Order: Aggressive, neurotoxin poison. Sting can kill a child or small adult. Survival is probable for most adults after painful muscle spasms, high fever, and incapacitation. Administer anti-venom serum ASAP."

She looked down at her burning hand, now throbbing and pulsing with pain and saw that it was also swelling quickly. Pulling the disposable lighter from her pocket, she flicked it open, holding it close to the bite area. It illuminated two small red sting marks on the back of her hand. The scorpion had been small, probably a juvenile, and that was in her favor. If it had been a large adult with full venom sacs, she was in danger of becoming comatose for the next twenty-four hours. Even so, without anti-venom serum, the neurotoxin would quickly travel up to her arm and cause high fever and pain.

Letting her gaze drift upward toward the sky she saw the constellations glittering, waiting to guide her to freedom. There was another ten miles to go cross country before dawn, with only a few hours left to do it in. She had to buy herself some time.

She took the dagger from her belt and heated the tip of it in the lighter's flame until it glowed. Stabbing the weapon into the back of her hand, she sliced open the flesh at the point of each sting mark. The pain made her moan and her stomach heaved but she placed her mouth over the bloody holes and sucked as hard as she could until she had a mouthful of blood and lymph. She spat out the fluid and repeated the procedure. Sweat ran down her face and neck. She continued to suck at the wounds until she could not taste anything but blood. Rinsing out her mouth with a sip of water, she cut cloth strips from her gutra and tied the wounds as snugly as she could with one hand. Her hand burned like hell, but her arm was only slightly swollen. She knew fever and muscle spasms would follow and that she had to get moving. She turned on the cell phone, noted the time, and took off at a slow jog.

Two hours later, barely able to walk, she tripped over her own feet, stumbling to a halt. She had not been able to keep moving in a straight line for the last half hour, zigzagging back and forth, barely making headway. It was costing her precious time and energy.

Looking left, she saw the eastern sky was beginning to lighten and stared with watering eyes at the ridge line of Yemen laid out in front of her. She had less than an hour before sunrise and, at the rate she was traveling, she would not reach the mountain caves before then. Her vulnerability in the vast openness of the desert was overwhelming and once it was light she could be spotted from any direction. The sun and heat would hinder her ability to move, and she was not sure how long she could survive in high temperatures. She forced herself to start walking again.

Her wounded hand was now dark black and swollen to twice its normal size. She was unable to move her fingers or wrist and her forearm throbbed. The venom attacked her whole body. She had a fever combined with a hammering headache that caused every muscle in her body to scream for relief. Her balance was affected and she couldn't walk a straight line. Laboring to breathe, she guessed she was in the beginning stages of respiratory distress. She squeezed the goatskin as hard as she could with her good hand and let a trickle of water drip into her mouth. It didn't seem to make any difference to her thirst. The fever was drawing all the moisture out of her body and, although she couldn't feel herself sweating, she was aware she was losing body fluids at a high rate.

There was not enough water left in the goatskin to get her to the mountains. Her body sagged and she hunched over, almost falling to her knees. She wanted to lie down on the desert floor and rest for a while, but instinct told her she would die if she stopped moving. She drank another drop of water and slung the empty goatskin back over her shoulder. The leather would have moisture left in it, and she would need it later on. She put her head down on her chest and willed herself to walk toward the mountains, cradling her swollen hand with her good arm. She aimed her body straight at the far off ridge line and tried to shut out the pain by forcing herself to review the intricate Agency procedures for an emergency extraction.

An hour passed. The sun began to bake the top her head, sending spasms of pain shooting down her neck. Delirium set in and she thought she was back in Dearborn, in her parents' backyard. Everything was cool and green and she heard the branches of the big backyard oak trees swooshing in the summer breeze. She mumbled Adel and Suhair's names and prayed to them and to God to help her. Blinking grit from her eyes her parents suddenly appeared directly in front of her, reaching out to her.

They were together, smiling reassuringly, their faces awash in love and adoration for her. They walked by her side while they whispered in her ear telling her not to stop, to keep moving forward and everything would be okay. They touched her with their fingertips, crooned into her face with joyful tears that she was their daughter, their prize. Yasi noticed there were dozens of ethnic looking people surrounding them, strangely dressed in clothing she didn't recognize. The strangers came toward her, chanting in a vaguely familiar dialect, rubbing her arms and shoulders in encouragement. Their energy was palpable and although she did not understand the words they were saying, she heard the victory trills of the women urging her on. The spirits pulled on her clothes, dragging her toward the mountains, forcing her forward. Her parents stood proudly to one side as the ghostly assemblage washed over her with their presence, caressing both her body and mind. When she tried to touch them, they remained just out of reach, and beckoned her forward again. She felt she was being pulled along a unique dimensional longitude, receiving energy from the beings. She willed her body to keep moving, the intense pain making her whimper, but she had no moisture left for tears. Instead, soft animal mewing sounds emanated from her nose and mouth as she shuffled her feet toward the sight of her parents' and her ancestors' reassuring voices. Each time she thought she had reached them, they moved further from her and closer to Yemen.

Another hour passed and her visitors faded away. Her own consciousness left her, hovering above her body as she neared her goal.

It was full light when she watched herself, bloody and delirious, climb falteringly into the foothills of the country of Yemen.

Her eyes caught the outline of a dark shadow between two boulders located a short way above the rocks she had chosen to rest on. With the last of her strength, she pulled herself up toward it. Crawling through the opening of a small cave, she lay face down on the rock floor, panting heavily. After a few moments, she pushed herself into a sitting position, her back resting against the rough stone. She unwrapped the gutra from her head and used it to rub the sand from her eyes. She took the phone out of her pocket and turned it on. Hearing it beep, a surge of excitement spiked through her. She squinted at the LCD display. The signal strength was stronger than it had been at the Bedouin encampment and there were still power bars showing. She had made it to the mountains!

As a covert agent on assignment, she had been issued a code that was known only to her and the most secure sections of the Agency. It was a personal doomsday code to be used if she was in imminent danger and needed to be extracted immediately. Comprised of a specifically sequenced combination of numbers, letters and symbols, the code had to be entered into a digital phone only after a special communications line had been accessed. The data would be uploaded by satellite and her location determined by the phone's digital ID. At the signal's recognition all available assets would immediately be diverted for an emergency extraction. The satellite was so accurate the Agency could determine within one square foot where the digital signal emanated from. It was imperative that Yasi find a safe hiding place before she transmitted. Once the code was sent, she had to keep the connection open for as long as possible to enable the Agency to verify her location. Unfortunately, Mohammed would also be monitoring the cell phone's use, planning to find her when she used it.

Carefully holding the telephone she dialed the first series of numbers. Listening, she breathed with a sigh of relief when she heard the audio prompt, "Enter." Her heart raced as she nervously cradled the phone with her injured hand and fumbled with the keyboard, being careful to punch in the correct symbols and numbers with her good hand. The code had to be entered in an exact sequence and within a specified number of seconds. She would not have a second chance. She carefully counted the seconds in her head and entered the first symbols deftly. When she was done, she depressed the green colored "call" key. The phone beeped once and then went quiet. Nothing more was audible. As instructed, she kept the power on so that the connection would not be broken. She placed the phone down on the floor of the cave next to her pistol. Then she grabbed the dagger and sliced the goatskin open. The inside of it was still wet. Slicing off a piece, she placed it in her mouth and began to chew. At first the wet leather barely made any difference, but as she sliced off more she began to feel some moisture on her tongue and the inside of her mouth. There wasn't enough to quench her thirst, but it helped. Her hand and arm were still painfully swollen, but her hand was not as black, and she could now move her fingers and wrist a little. Although her eyes were still irritated and sore, her head throbbed less.

She knew she had received supernatural assistance in making it to the safety of the cave. She silently thanked God and her parents. At the beginning of her escape, rage had been her only motivation but now she felt solid resolve and rededication to her mission. She would find Mohammed and make him pay for what he had done to her and her family. She owed it to everyone he had murdered and to all he wanted to murder in the future. The ancient blood flowing through her veins and the voices of her dead ancestors had spoken clearly today. Her tribe was an invisible ally in her struggle against evil. They would take her part in helping destroy the hydra of al Qaeda. Success of the mission was now the most important thing in her life. Until that was accomplished, she would keep herself alive and ready to fight.

The cave was dark and cool, the dim light easing the pain in her swollen eyes. During the last miles of her trek, her eyes had filled with grit and sweat and became badly irritated. While she walked she tried to keep them closed, but now she needed to be able see if anyone was following her. Earlier, when she had tried to look out the cave's opening into the glaring light, she couldn't see. She cut two more strips from the damp goatskin and placed one over each eyelid to ease the irritation. The damp leather was soothing and she immediately felt relief. Her body relaxed, and exhaustion did the rest.

A rumbling sound caused Yasi to jolt awake. She had fallen into a deep sleep, her back braced against the cave's stone wall, her head resting against an outcropping in the rock. She looked toward the direction of the sound and then back at the open cell phone, trying to understand what was happening. The phone's power bars indicated it was just about out of juice and the LCD clock showed two hours had passed. My God! How could she have slept when she was supposed to keep watch?

She inched her body over to the cave's opening and peered out over the valley below her. It took a few seconds for her to recognize what had caused the distant noise. It was a military style Humvee racing toward the foothills, closing in on her position. She could not tell how many men were in it, but it had camouflage coloration and large military antennas. Her coded mayday message had gotten through. The military had come to get her and, in a few minutes, she would be out of here. She laughed, her body suddenly feeling lighter. Pulling herself to her feet, she stood in the cave's opening and began to wave her arms frantically at the vehicle below.

CHAPTER 13

U nited States satellites were used by America's covert agencies for a wide range of intelligence gathering. All "Three Letter Agencies" used them and shared information. Not only could the National Geo-Spatial Intelligence Agency, or NGA, data be uploaded from selected points around the globe, but, given coordinates, they could also send messages to specific targets. Satellites could be repositioned in order to search for something of special interest in a specific area while they gathered photographic, digital and electronic information. It was a simple task for a programmer to reroute a satellite's orbit and to have it "fly" over different terrain. They could instruct it to search for a specific piece of data or to concentrate on a specific piece of real estate. The codes were input and the data flowed up or down, depending on the government's requirements.

Five days after Yasi had been kidnapped, a high ranking White House official sent a request to have a U.S. spy satellite, already orbiting other areas in the Middle East, to shift its focus to central and southwestern Saudi Arabia. The request was endorsed by both Secretaries of State and Defense. The message was sent "Flash" with the highest Agency priority code. Agency in-house analysts organized a "Red" team to quickly interpret any data that would be received. Intelligence assets from other agencies were assigned to assist with the task. Yasmina al Amar, code name "Abacus," was being searched for by the most efficient information gathering system in the world.

Almost four weeks after her abduction, a distress signal appeared on a covert agent designated line with the appropriate doomsday code. It was weak, and had faded in and out a half dozen times before its digital fingerprint could be locked onto. The analysts were surprised to see their computer highlight the signal's location as the northwest corner of Yemen, on the southern Saudi Arabian border. The geographic region was a desolate and unpopulated area just short of the main Yemeni mountain range. How Abacus had gotten there was a mystery, but the Agency's job was to get her out. It took only a few minutes to put local assets on full alert and brief them on their mission. A Blackhawk helicopter with a combat team aboard lifted off from inside Yemen and a Predator drone was launched in tandem with the "Go" order.

The satellite whirred overhead on its silent and dedicated orbit, signaling its handlers that it had new intelligence to transmit. During the last terrain scan, it had detected an unidentified moving object on the desert floor, only a few miles away from the designated extraction zone. Orbiting in the lower reaches of outer space, the satellite zoomed in with its multi-lens cameras and sensors and transmitted a high definition image of a HMMWV M998 (Humvee) speeding across the flat terrain at sixty miles per hour. The ground temperature recorded by the satellite was 110 degrees Fahrenheit. The GPS indicated the vehicle's location was within five miles of Abacus's last known location and closing rapidly. Within seconds, it sent this and millions of other bits of new data to its home computers at Ft. Meade, MD.

At the Red Team Ops center, a senior analyst scanned the latest data from the orbiter, looked at the new digital images and quickly picked up the Director of Operations, or DO's, direct line. He spoke carefully and with emphasized diction.

"Sir, we have a serious problem with Abacus. Condition Red. Condition is fluid and hot. An unidentified vehicle is closing on the extraction site at top speed. Not identified as a friendly asset. Repeat. No known Saudi or Yemeni military involvement. UAV on site. Advise."

The response was immediate. Earlier, a UAV (Unmanned Aerial Vehicle) Predator Drone had been dispatched from the USS Nimitz as the ship cruised a few miles off the Yemeni coastline. The Predator had been kept in a holding pattern behind the foothills of Yasi's position, hovering low along the forward ridge line as it sent back live video feed and updated GPS positions of the approaching vehicle to its control pilots still onboard the ship. The pilots watched the latest video display. It showed two men in military uniforms driving a Humvee toward Abacus's position. Live feed now showed the vehicle begin to slow its speed and confirmed the driver was scanning the foothills with digital binoculars, trying to acquire a target along the ridgeline. A second man on the passenger side of the Humvee was waiting to fire an RPG, or rocket propelled grenade launcher, on his commander's order.

One hundred fifty yards from the cave, the GPS guided Hellfire Missile hit the Humvee with the explosive force equivalent to one quarter ton of TNT. The explosion's concussion and intensive heat rolled upward into the narrow opening of the cave, throwing Yasi back against the rear wall. She howled, rolling her body from side to side on the cave's floor covering her ears and head. When the explosion ended, her ears filled with a dull clanging and her mouth had a gritty metallic taste. Instinctively, she had gotten onto her hands and knees and tried to crawl into a corner to get away.

The Blackhawk was two minutes from their target when they saw the explosion.

"What the hell was that?" growled the Spec Ops Captain into his radio.

"Predator Sir, three o'clock. Looks like it just made a kill," the Blackhawk pilot answered.

"Get me there, pronto!" he barked.

He turned to his team. "We go in on repel. Get hooked up. Once we set down on the ridge, I go first, then Achmed and then Abdullah." The men hurriedly checked their gear.

Thick, black smoke spiraled upward from the spot where the Humvee had stopped. At first, nothing could be seen until the desert wind began to blow, clearing the air and spinning the explosion's dense smoke westward. Yasi crawled over to the cave's opening and looked down. At first, she could not see anything, but slowly her eyes focused. Looking down at the area below her, she wasn't quite sure of what she was seeing. Debris had been cast for dozens of yards into the surrounding desert and what had been the Humvee was unrecognizable, with only twisted pieces of blackened metal remaining. The ground around it was scorched and blackened and, although the blast was over, small fires burned everywhere. Yasi was stunned at the total destruction. Her stomach heaved and she retched when she realized that one of the fires still burning was a human body part. As she turned her head to vomit, she saw blood dripping down onto her shirt sleeve. Her face had been cut by shrapnel. Dozens of small pieces of metal and rock had been blasted into the air during impact of the missile and had left wounds covering her face and neck. The cave's small opening kept her from receiving more serious injuries, but it was the shock of the blast itself that had affected her most. She could not hear. Her ears were clanging loudly and ached. She rewrapped the filthy gutra tightly around her head, trying to stem the flow of blood from her face.

Her mind was on the verge of exploding with the knowledge of how deadly a predicament she was in. Sitting down on the floor of the cave, she began to shake uncontrollably and rocked back and forth trying to comprehend what had just happened. Mohammed's men had just killed the soldiers who had been sent to rescue her. The bastards were out there and would come for her, next. She took deep breaths, purposely slowing down her breathing, calming her thinking.

She remembered during the explosion she had dropped her pistol by the back wall of the cave. Turning around, she saw the gun lying on the rock floor, a few feet behind her. Moving away from the mouth of the cave, she dropped down to her hands and knees to pick it up. If they were coming to kill her she would, at least, take a couple of them along with her.

She never saw the black faced soldier repel his body through the cave's opening. He slammed into Yasi, knocking her onto the floor of the cave, immediately grabbing her hands tightly in his gloved fists, forcing his body on top of hers, pinning her down. She struggled but he was more powerful. The weight of his body suffocated her, his torso ground her into the cave floor. Her screams sounded like grunts from the back of her throat. She tried to break free, but the soldier sat astride her body and held her down. She kicked her legs in the air and tried to bite him but he stayed far enough away so that she could not. She tried to lift her torso, but he kept her pressed to the stone floor. Her head flailed from side to side as she swore and tried to bite his face. She became a wild thing, grunting and snarling, twisting and arching her body. It didn't make any difference. She was trapped. She knew he could kill her at any moment.

Yasi stared at the blackened mouth poised above her head. She could see the cords in the soldier's neck tighten as he moved his mouth, but all she could hear was clanging in her ears. He seemed to be yelling something at her, but it was in pantomime. He mouthed an identical pattern, over and over. Sounds began to fade in and out of her hearing, but they were only bits of words and she couldn't recognize what they meant. It didn't matter anymore. She couldn't breathe. It was over. She fell into blackness.

She dreamed she was drowning, while she was sitting in a living room chair. Jolting back to consciousness, she found herself sitting on the floor of the cave while someone poured water over her face. She tried to drink the wetness away, but gagged. She struggled to open her eyes, forcing herself to breathe in both water and air but threw the fluid up. Hands rubbed her wrists. She could hear bits and pieces of far away sounding voices. When she opened her eyes, she saw two Middle Eastern men standing in front of her, one holding a military water bladder. She glared at them and struggled to get to her feet, but was forcibly held down. Another soldier was seated behind her, his arms around her, her back pressed hard into his chest. He held each one of her balled fists in his. She couldn't see his face but heard him, crooning softly. "Yasi, it's okay. Yasi. Yasi, it's okay."

Yasi? She recognized her name, but she did not recognize the other words. The man repeated the words over and over in singsong fashion. Her ears were now only buzzing, the clanging fading away.

"It's okay, Yasi. It's okay."

English. He was speaking English. The man was crooning to her in English. She hadn't recognized the language. What was English doing being spoken in the cave?

"Yasi, it's Mark. Yasi, it's Mark. Yasi, it's okay."

She twisted her battered body around and stared into the blue eyes of Mark Harrison.

Mark had never revealed to Yasi what his real orders were. He felt guilty leaving her in D.C. thinking he was on his way to Afghanistan as a military liaison officer, but his orders were clear. His mission was classified and he could not tell anyone where he was going.

Although technically still a Captain in the United States Army, he'd been temporarily assigned to the Agency. Al Qaeda had gotten a powerful start in Yemen and had an army of operatives already in place. It was his mission to find them, hunt them down, and kill them. He was also tasked with the training and consolidation of local Yemeni tribesmen. They would remain in place as military assets and fight against the terrorists. It was the job of his dreams.

After arriving in Yemen, he called Yasi every week, pretending that he was in Afghanistan. They conversed about her finishing her thesis and his new job. The lies he told her bothered him and he found himself both concerned and relieved when a couple of months later, she told him that she had decided to take a low level State Department job in Riyadh, Saudi Arabia.

When he asked how her family felt about her moving to Saudi Arabia at such a dangerous time, she quipped that she was sure that her father's newspaper would wait a year for her to get her valuable first person experience in international relations. She offered she had never ruled out the Foreign Service as a possible career and, ever since 9/11, she always felt she should be doing more to help. Certainly by filling a junior consular position in the American Embassy in Riyadh, she would free up an Arab speaking career employee for the more critical job of translating top secret terrorist communications.

Her answer seemed somewhat flip, but Mark was so excited about being able to see her again that he put away any doubts he had. Yasi did not know that while she lived in Riyadh, they would only be a short military flight away from each other. If things worked out, Mark could probably fly to Riyadh every month. Of course, Yasi would think he would be flying in from Kabul, but that was not a problem. She would be in Saudi Arabia soon and, if everything went as he hoped, he would fly over in the next month or so and surprise her with a visit. He ached for her and the thought of her naked body sent his mind reeling.

He had been on the ground in Yemen for six months, working with both his US and Yemeni teams, hunting al Qaeda. The Yemenis expertly ferreted out dozens of al Qaeda subversives during that time, most of who were turned over to be interrogated. Occasionally, a tribal blood feud would interfere with an arrest and Mark would arrive at a village only to find a dead body proudly presented to him instead of a prisoner. Other successes had been tempered by a few key enemy subversives fleeing over the border to Saudi Arabia before they were caught.

Mark felt his Yemeni tribesmen were more than a match for whatever al Qaeda had. Local people were slowly making the country of Yemen unpleasant for al Qaeda operatives. Yemenis would no longer accept the slaughter of innocent women and children for a false holy war they did not believe in, by men who cared nothing for their people or their country.

The month before, at an intelligence briefing, he was told that Saudi Arabia based HUMINT operatives were being systematically hunted down and eliminated by al Qaeda. The senior Agency operative in Riyadh was reported killed by a hit and run driver, but it was known by the intelligence community that al Qaeda had executed him. Mark knew Yasi had arrived in Riyadh during the same time but convinced himself that as a glorified embassy clerk, she would be safe in the Diplomatic Quarter.

Three months after the Sanaa briefing, an emergency extraction order had been received "Flash: Top Secret" at the American Embassy in Sanaa. Mark was out on patrol and was contacted by secure phone with orders to take all necessary steps for an immediate emergency extraction of a covert agent exiting Saudi Arabia. Terrorist forces were known to be operating in the region and closing in on the agent's position. Time was critical. The only additional information he had been given was the extraction had the highest priority.

Mark and his team departed within the hour. He knew the agent would be well armed and edgy. While waiting for his extraction, he might mistake the good guys for the bad guys. Mark did not want anyone on his team injured so he planned to use shock and awe during initial contact. Once in position, he would rush the agent's location, physically immobilize the man and then identify himself. His team would provide cover from the enemy.

The Blackhawk set down on the top of the ridge and the three men repelled down a rocky slope toward the agent's last location. Mark sighted the cave's entrance. He crashed through on repel and grabbed at what looked like a young Bedouin fighter kneeling on the cave's floor, reaching for a revolver. The boy jumped at the sight of him and lunged for the weapon. Mark flung the agent down, pinning him with his body as he held his hands in his fists. He yelled out his name and rank as loudly as he could. The boy fought him like an animal, cursing at him in Arabic, trying to bite his hands and face. As Mark held him away from his body, he was surprised at how strong he was for his small size. He was

emaciated and obviously suffering from dehydration, but continued to
fight ferociously. Immobilizing the agent, he sat astride the slim body
and yelled directly at the boy's face that he was an American soldier
here to rescue him. His captive acted as if he did not hear and only
redoubled his efforts to throw Mark off, continuing to struggle. Mark
forcibly held him down until he felt the body underneath him shudder
and go limp. As Mark moved to give the boy room to breathe, the gutra
fell off the young Arab's head, and Mark saw short matted hair framing
a bloody face.

Yasmina? Was it Yasmina? My God. Yasi. It was Yasi! What was she
doing here? Why was she fighting him? Was she the agent? What was
going on? He sat up against the cave's wall, and pulled her small limp
body up into a sitting position, his arms cradling her. As he gently
pressed her against his chest, he felt how thin her body was, and
grimaced when he saw her wounds. Her face was cut in a dozen places
and her breathing was labored. My God, he thought. She's half dead.

He motioned to Achmed for the water bladder and started to wash
her face, hoping she would wake up and drink. The Arab held the
bladder spout and squeezed a small amount of water into her mouth.
She started to come to, shook her head violently, and threw up.

"Yasi, it's okay. It's me Mark." He crooned softly, repeating the
phrase. "Yasi, it's me, Mark," he nuzzled into her ear. "Yasi, it's okay.
It's Mark."

She started to struggle again and then suddenly stopped, her body
becoming stiff and motionless. He kept whispering to her. He was
holding her firmly, chanting her name into her ear. He realized that
she finally heard him when she twisted abruptly in his arms, and staring
wildly into his eyes, breathed his name.

CHAPTER 14

Yasi awoke in the pristine whiteness of the American Embassy's infirmary, her eyes immediately irritated by the bright overhead lights. Turning her head to one side, she noticed an IV in her arm. There was a doctor standing by her bed. He smiled and offered her a cup of water. She drank deeply.

"Hello," he said. "Welcome back."

"Where am I?" She tried to lift her head, but the room spun.

"Stay down. You're in the American Embassy in Yemen. You've had a rough time. There's nothing for you to do right now, but to sleep and get your strength back." He smiled down at her and patted her shoulder.

"How did I get here?" her lips had a salve on them.

"Captain Harrison and his team brought you in last night. You were really out of it."

"Mark?" She remembered his voice chanting to her, his arms around her. *Oh Mark, how did you find me?*

"I want to see him." It was a direct order to the doctor.

"Not now. He'll be here later. You need to sleep." He adjusted the

IV drip and she tumbled backward into blackness.

She awoke to the smell of food. There was a tray by her bedside and a nurse smiled broadly while she adjusted her bed.

"It's only a soft food diet." The young woman smiled apologetically. "The doctor wants to see how you handle digesting it. If all goes well, dinner will be a lot more fun. I'll be back later." The nurse smiled again and bustled off. Yasi ate everything on the tray and asked for more.

"Hello Yasi." The voice took her away from her dark sleep. She turned her head and looked up into Mark's blue eyes. His handsome face was tanned and more angular than she remembered, as if he had gotten older. He smelled of soap and aftershave.

"Hi!" She smiled at him warmly and reached out her hand. She wanted to climb into his lap and sleep forever. He kissed her forehead, looking down at her with a concerned expression. "You're looking a lot better. You've got some color back in your face. I would have bet it would have been a week or so before you even woke up. You were pretty strung out." His voice was unemotional, flat.

"Thanks for rescuing me," she squeezed his hand and smiled. "I guess I'm not going to win any beauty contests for awhile. They gave me a mirror earlier. I think I look like Frankenstein's girlfriend with all my stitches." She watched his face. There was no reaction.

"What's wrong?" She sat up, adjusting her body as she raised the back of the hospital bed. "Am I that bad?"

"No, no. Not at all." He looked at the floor. "I'm just glad my team and I could be of service. You were close to being done in." Lifting his head he stared at her face with narrowed eyes. "Why didn't you tell me you were working for the Agency?"

"Why didn't you tell me you were assigned to the Agency yourself, and oh, by the way, stationed in Yemen and not Afghanistan?" She answered hotly.

His face colored beneath the tan.

"You knew I was in the military and subject to changes in orders. I still am. I'm just temporarily assigned here." His eyes flashed. "You, on the other hand, never told me you had joined up. Even before I left you were immersed in training with the Agency. My God, we were still together in Washington when you signed up. You lied to me Yasi." There was pain in his voice.

"Oh well, you lied. I lied. We both lied." She sing-songed her answer.

"You know the rules for operatives, since you're one yourself." She was surprised how hard and sarcastic her voice sounded. She wanted him to hold her, to tell her he loved her. She wanted to disappear into his arms and never come out. She sat upright in the bed and exhaled in frustration.

"I loved you," he said quietly.

"And I loved you. We just had lousy timing." She looked at him with soft eyes. "Things changed Mark. September 11th changed them forever. We shouldn't have gotten involved with each other when we did. It wasn't in the cards. You already had your orders and I was given the opportunity to serve. I know we couldn't tell each other the truth, we both understand that. Lying was obviously the most convenient choice we had." Her voice quavered. "What we are doing now is much more important than who we were then. Maybe if we give ourselves another chance in the future, take some time off to be together again. Would that work?" She watched him, waiting.

He thought for a moment, shifting his weight from one foot to another. She could see him struggling with his emotions. The mood passed. His voice was at once professional. "I've been told to update you. We've had a breakthrough. The Saudis have found out where the al Qaeda chieftain who kidnapped you is hiding, and they are willing to cooperate with us so that we can snag him. He's in Syria. We should have a team together in a couple of days to go after him."

The effect on Yasi was electric. She swung her feet down and jumped out of bed before Mark could react. He put his hand on her arm to steady her, thinking how small and malnourished she looked. "Whoa, where do you think you're going? Hold onto me, you're a little shaky."

She steadied herself. "I'm getting out of this bed so that I can get dressed and get moving. I want to be ready to move with the team." Her voice was filled with anticipation.

"No way, Yasi!" It was a command. "I'm the designated mission commander for this operation and I'm pulling rank on you. You are not only not coming with me, but I am going to suggest to the Ambassador that you be MEDEVAC'd stateside immediately. Look at yourself. You're in no condition to participate in anything. I will not risk my men's lives by having you with us."

She reached out touching his arm. "Mark you don't understand." She pleaded. "There are too many things to tell you now, but I have an obligation to be there when Mohammed is captured. Things happened to me during my kidnapping and escape that make me understand who I really am, and what I must do. Mohammed must be held accountable not just to me, but to everyone he has tortured and murdered." She stopped. Her breathing was measured, the emotion of her statement washing over her. Mark looked at her, questioningly.

She continued. "Mark, it's my right. I know you can't understand all of what I'm saying, but capturing him is something I have to do. Every person he's tortured or murdered has the right to know that reprisals are in store for him. They are dead. They can't be here, but I can carry their message of vengeance." She wanted to shake him, to make him understand what she was telling him. Her eyes were bright and watery.

He looked back at her. "I don't know about your rights, or the needs of dead people, but this raid is a military action and I'm in command of it. I will take only men who have the combat skills I need for the mission. As far as I'm concerned, you're not a military asset and you don't have the necessary physical conditioning or training for combat. You'd be a detriment to the team's success." He had spoken in a flat emotionless voice, but then softened slightly. "I hope you continue to feel better and get well quickly. I'll get back here and touch base with you when it's all over." He leaned down to kiss her cheek but she turned away. He left quickly, his boot steps echoing down the hallway.

If the American Ambassador in Sanaa had been astonished that the Senior National Security Advisor to the President of the United States, Mr. Hunter Farrington had personally called to inquire about the condition of agent Abacus, he was flabbergasted when Yasi demanded and got access to the N.S.A.'s secure line in Washington, D.C.

She did not wait on protocol. "Mr. Farrington. I'm asking you to intercede with the military plan to capture Mohammed bin Fasheed. You must allow me to be included in his capture."

A cultured voice purred over the secure line. "Yasmina, first of all congratulations on your successful escape and the exposure of Mohammed bin Fasheed as an al Qaeda chief. We are all proud of your incredible success, but I am especially proud. You have dealt the terrorists a huge blow." He paused. "Given that, I fully understand your motives to finish what you have started, but I do not think it would be conducive to have you on the military mission. You are in a weakened physical condition. The men would be distracted by worrying about your safety and your presence could inadvertently cause casualties. I do think however...."

She interrupted him sharply. "Mr. Farrington may I remind you of your own personal history. My father worked closely with you to accomplish the unification of Yemen. After he was marked for assassination, you helped him and my mother escape from Yemen to the United States so that they could live their lives in safety and freedom.

Because of your actions, my brothers and I were born Americans. My father, Adel al Amar, a direct descendant of one of the most honored and respected tribal dynasties in Yemen came to love his adopted country of America enough that he gave you permission to recruit me for the Agency. My mother, Suhair bint Faisal al Jouf could trace her blood line directly back to the Queen of Sheba, and yet the one thing she was most proud of was the naturalization papers that made her an American citizen. My father and mother were murdered on Mohammed's direct orders. They were killed in retaliation for me being uncovered as a covert agent and threatening to close down his network within the Kingdom of Saudi Arabia.

I was kidnapped and brutalized, not only because I jeopardized his terrorist actions within Saudi Arabia, but because he wanted revenge. Mohammed ordered my death to be slow and painful in order to show the world that no American, especially a woman, could successfully challenge him, and the power of al Qaeda. I was to be tortured, mutilated, and executed. Held up as an example of the weakness of the decadent West, my execution would be an icon for the absurdity of an American woman trying to combat al Qaeda!

Mr. Farrington I will tell you this. Even though they will continue to wage jihad against us, and have successes from time to time, al Qaeda must now be forced to begin to feel pain from our reprisals. They have indiscriminately murdered our families and citizens around the world. Until now, we have only fought back within the rules of civilized nations. We have to make the price they pay for their unholy acts of terrorism more devastating to them than their attacks upon us. We must begin to make them fear our reprisals. To fear us.

As a student of Arab culture, you understand the reasons for the ancient tradition of tribal retribution. It was to deter your enemies from making war upon you in the future. The tribes knew that if the acts of blood vengeance and reprisal were more terrible than acts of war, men would think twice before declaring war.

You asked me to volunteer as a covert agent because you knew that within me lay a combination of the old and new Middle East, intermingled with powerful American strength. You were hoping that my talents would prove fruitful for gathering information but your people miscalculated where I should serve. You never counted on the warrior skills and blood lust of my ancestors to be as deeply ingrained within me as they are. I am not just Yasi al Amar, an American. I am also Yasmina al Amar, proud daughter of the Maerb and al Jouf tribes of Yemen. You must allow me to bring the retribution of both my cultures to this murderer of American and Arab peoples. Under ancient tribal law I claim it as my right. Under American law, I need your permission."

Hunter spoke in a patient tone. "Yasmina, you never gave me a chance to finish the sentence I started, in what now, seems like ages ago. Your eloquent argument is not only a testament to your fine education, but emotional and heartfelt dedication to your country and family. Yes, I have studied the traditions of Middle East, and I do understand the cultural forces that flow through you from your ancestors. I also understand that some of what you have said is true about America.

We have not made our enemies pay enough of a price for their slaughter of innocents, but make no mistake, they are afraid of us. It is because of people like you. I cannot overrule what the military has planned for the capture of Mr. Fasheed, but I have a proposition for you."

Later that afternoon she was summoned to meet with the Embassy's chief anti-terrorist officer. He gave her an operations briefing in preparation for a sanctioned flight to Syria, and introduced her to the soldier who would accompany her. The Yemeni warrior was Ali bin Salman, a lean, swarthy man who proudly led a local group of Yemeni fighters against al Qaeda. That night, the two of them would fly to Damascus on an Agency jet and meet with Syrian agents. The Syrians would take them to where Mohammed was being held. The anti-terrorist chief also told them Mark and his combat team would not depart for Syria until the next afternoon at 1500 hours. She would have her time with Mohammed first.

In order to obtain the Saudi's cooperation in Mohammed's capture, the Agency ensured the royal family had been properly briefed about his plot to assassinate the Crown Prince and take over their country. Mohammed was identified as the chief architect, as well as prime beneficiary of the proposed coup. A deal was struck between the two allies and it was decided that the Americans would capture and retain custody of Mohammed first. After debriefing him, they would deliver what was left of him to the Saudis for final dispensation.

Mohammed bin Fasheed had wired millions of American dollars into the personal Singapore bank account of Achmed al Assad, the Syrian Minister of the Interior, in exchange for a secure villa in an upper class Damascus neighborhood. He knew the Americans were hunting for him, but would not be able to coerce the Syrians into cooperating. The Syrian government had no appetite for dealing with the United States, and had already provided many other terrorists a safe haven. His plan was to stay in Damascus temporarily, until he made other permanent arrangements. What Mohammed did not know was, one day after he had made his payment to the Syrian minister, a representative from the Saudi royal family paid the same minister ten million American dollars more to turn his back on Mohammed and assist the Americans in his capture.

Yasi approached the Gulfstream V dressed as a Bedouin fighter. She had a new M9 Beretta tucked into her belt next to the old man's dagger, and carried a small leather bag. After she and Ali climbed into the jet and settled in, she undid the gutra that had been wrapped around her head and face. Ali grunted mumbling to himself in his local dialect that she was a "pretty looking boy." He sat bolt upright as she spoke back to him in the same dialect.

"I ask that you do not make light of me, son of Yemen. I am proud that I'm an American by birth, but my ancestors came from Yemen. My father, a sheik's son, was Adel bin Jamal al Amar of the Maerb. My mother, also the daughter of a sheik, was Suhair bint Faisal of the al Jouf. The son of a jackel Mohammed bin Fasheed and the butchers of al Qaeda murdered them as well as hundreds of other innocent people under the guise of jihad. Mohammed's real motives however, are his own greed and obsession for power. He tortured and attempted to kill me. I claim the ancient right to avenge my parents' deaths and to deliver the retribution he is owed in the name of all the innocents he has harmed."

Ali's face looked stricken, his eyes wide with shocked surprise. Offering his hands palm upward as if to pray, he intoned, "May god be praised! I am Ali bin Salman of the Maerb. My father was murdered over twenty-five years ago when our village was attacked by hired

Communist assassins. His name was Salman bin Faisal al Amar. His cousin was named Adel. You are of the Maerb tribe. You are of my family." He bowed his head and gestured in reverence to her. "I embrace you my cousin, Yasmina al Amar. I am your servant unto death."

Yasi was speechless. The world was indeed, a small place. She had the old man's dagger tucked in her belt, a 9mm strapped to her hip, and Ali as her new protector. If the ops plan worked as it was supposed to, Mohammed would be waiting for her. The only thing that could have been better would be to have Mark by her side.

Syrian agents met the jet at touchdown and escorted Yasi and Ali to an SUV. As they drove off, they were each handed a cell phone.

"When you are finished just push 000 and we will return for you. We will come back for three of you or whoever is left alive." They smirked.

"Where is Fasheed now?" Yasi asked.

"The illustrious Mohammed bin Fasheed dined with our Minister of the Interior earlier this evening," they chuckled. "He is still sleeping off his dessert."

On the drive to the villa the Syrians explained how they had laced Mohammed's food with a powerful drug. The Syrian security service quickly and efficiently killed his body guards and he was carried unconscious to his bedroom. The villa had been cordoned off from the main road by soldiers. The guards left inside the villa were mercenaries being paid by the Saudis and had been told to follow Yasi's orders.

Mohammed's suite was luxuriously decorated and furnished. A gas log fireplace blazed in the air conditioned room. He was lying akimbo atop a king sized bed, out cold and snoring loudly. Yasi checked the time. It was okay. Mark could not get here before the next day. She ordered the Saudi guards to stand outside the suite and allow no one past the doors. When they left, she instructed Ali to find something to tie Mohammed up in a sitting position. Returning with a heavy rope and rawhide Ali wrapped the rope around Mohammed's chest and waist hoisting him up against the heavy wooden headboard. His arms and legs were then separately tied to opposite bedposts with the heavy rawhide thongs. When he was finished, Ali checked the tensions and nodded his approval to Yasi.

Yasi went to Mohammed's desktop computer and started to download files, putting each flash drive into her bag after it was filled. When she was finished, she took all the cell phones and pagers she found in his center desk drawer and then began to rummage through others looking for his laptop.

The photograph had been hidden beneath some paper files in the top left desk drawer, and finding it took Yasi's breath away. She tried to pick it up, but could not seem to make her fingers work. It was if it had a strange power over her, and her hand shook as she brought it closer to her face. When she finally saw the picture she felt herself go very still.

It was a photo of her, naked and unconscious, taken the night Mohammed kidnapped her in Riyadh. It had been taken in the suite at the Hyatt where she was tortured. Mohammed's face was twisted by hatred as he leered at her, his left fist gripping her long hair, pushing her bruised and badly beaten face toward the camera. Her face was grotesquely swollen; her eyes black and badly cut; her mouth lacerated and bloody. In his right hand he held a pair of scissors. She could see the gruesome wounds on the side of her head where he had gouged off her hair, leaving her scalp bloody and torn. She remembered how viciously he had raped and sodomized her. She remembered the unending pain. His cruelty and the cruelty of the desert camp would stay in her memory forever. The camp was the place she was supposed to be killed and dismembered but became the place where she killed her captors and escaped.

Holding her breath, she took the photograph and put it carefully in her pocket, her hand grazing the single gold coin she had taken from the old Bedouin's chest the day she escaped. It was part of the blood money Mohammed paid him to maim and kill her. She purposely kept it with her every day as a reminder her torture and death were paid for with Saudi Sovereigns. God, it all seemed like a lifetime ago. She walked over to the roaring fire and placed the photograph and the coin on top of one of the asbestos logs. She watched as the horrible picture burned and curled itself into a black ash, the coin glowing warmly in the midst of the black waste and lapping flames.

Ali broke her reverie when he sharply asked what she wanted to do next, jerking his head in Mohammed's direction. The antidote to the drug had been left in a syringe on the bedside table. Yasi picked it up and jabbed it hard into Mohammed's neck.

He began to come to. Moaning, he tried to move his arms and legs, struggling weakly against the rawhide. Yasi stood to one side, next to his head. She took the gutra off, her short brown hair framing her bruised and sutured face. She slid the ancient dagger out of its scabbard and put the point of it on Mohammed's jugular, pricking the skin. Ali watched with slitted eyes.

"Mohammed bin Fasheed," she whispered hoarsely in English. "Open your eyes."

He blinked his eyes open as if on her order and then stared at Ali standing at the foot of his bed. He could not quite see who held the dagger to his throat without turning his head into the blade.

"The voice I heard was a woman's, and she spoke to me in English." He seemed amused. "It must be you who holds a sharp dagger to my throat, my beautiful Yasmina."

She moved the dagger back a little, allowing him to move his head. He turned toward her and smiled.

"Ah, yes, it is you. What a surprise that you survived all that I have put in your way. You're not as beautiful as I remember, but considering what you've been through.....ow!" She jammed the point of the dagger forward making his neck bleed. She wanted to kill him. He turned his head away, blood falling from his neck onto his shirt.

"Yasmina, no, no. You can't kill me. I know it's not that you don't want to, but you Americans have so much to gain from keeping me alive." He was almost laughing at her. Her hand shook with the effort to keep from driving the dagger home.

"I'm too valuable a prisoner for you. After all, how many high ranking al Qaeda commanders have your people captured up to this point? I'm a prize!

I know much that will help your government defeat my brothers in terror and I'll be happy to negotiate with them and offer new and important information. I have great confidence that they will want to hear all that I am willing to tell them. After all, governments are whores for power at heart. They'll do anything to make themselves stronger. Eh? Here, let me give you an example of the depth of my knowledge. I'll volunteer information about...." He started rattling off names and places of al Qaeda contacts in Saudi Arabia. Yasi moved to the foot of his bed and locked her eyes on his face. Interrupting his soliloquy, she spoke in a deep and deadly voice.

"Be quiet. It is time for me to give you information. Your plan to assassinate the Saudi Crown Prince and depose the royal family has been uncovered and the Saudis now know of your intent. Your carefully constructed al Qaeda network has been destroyed; your agents are being hunted down and killed as we speak. Every aspect of your international business cartel has been uncovered, your businesses and personal accounts confiscated. All of your money is now in the hands of the United States and its allies."

Mohammed's face paled. He yanked at the thongs that held him in place. Ali jabbed him hard in the gut with his rifle and Mohammed stopped moving.

"It was your plan to take over the Kingdom and replace the royal family with you and your heirs. You never had any interest in jihad or in al Qaeda. You don't care about any religion. Your goal has always been to amass billions and to control the oil of Saudi Arabia as the leader of a brand new dynasty. You wanted to hold the world hostage to your will.

You had your infant sons taken to Switzerland to be raised by your brothers and ordered their mothers murdered as a precaution against any interference. But, your brothers are now dead, a courtesy of your Saudi countrymen. We have found your sons and they have been taken away. They will be adopted separately by families who will be given information that they are orphans of a North African businessman and his wife who were killed in an automobile accident. Your sons will never know who you were, or that they were your sons. As we speak the Saudi royal family is erasing your ancestors names and any mention of your family from their written history. When they are finished the name Fasheed will no longer exist.

You will be taken from here and debriefed. When your brain no longer holds any information that is of use to us or to our allies, you will be turned over to your own countrymen for final disposition. You will be held accountable for all the suffering and deaths that you have caused and final retribution will be doled out at the appropriate time.

As of this moment you are a dead man. It is only a matter of timing as to when the sentence is carried out to its conclusion."

"You whore of a pig mother!" Mohammed screamed. Ali pointed his rifle at Mohammed and cocked it, but Yasi nodded no.

She crossed the room and using the fireplace tongs took the now white hot coin from the fire. Signaling Ali, she started to speak as she approached the bed holding the tongs in front of her.

"You once said to a Bedouin that killing me was worth 150 Saudi gold Sovereigns, but only if he beat and tortured me, cut off my fingers one at a time, and sent them to you as proof that I was still alive and suffering. You ordered my innocent parents to be killed by being beaten to death, and then taunted me with their murders. When you found out I was an Agency asset and close to uncovering your position with al Qaeda you raped and brutalized me for your own sadistic revenge. You were one of the architects of September 11th and responsible for killing thousands of innocent people to further your own despicable plans for wealth and power." She paused. "There is not enough evil to repay you for your actions, but I claim the right of retribution for myself, my family and all the nameless innocents who were your victims.

Mohammed strained with all his strength against the ropes. "Yasmina, you stupid bitch! I've raped you more than once! That first time in Georgetown, when I took your virginity. You didn't give it to me, you stupid woman, I took it. I gave you GHB, I .... "

She drew the Beretta and quickly walked to the head of the bed slamming the butt of it into Mohammed's head. He went limp. She ordered Ali to cut off his trousers.

She took the tongs that held the red hot glowing gold Sovereign and placed the coin on Mohammed's penis holding it in place. Ali grunted as the coin burned its way through Mohammed's flesh and imbedded itself in his organ. Mohammed thrashed in agony spewing filth and hatred, howling for mercy.

Yasmina switched to Arabic, the local Yemeni dialect her father had taught her, the language of Ali's tribe. "You told me that I could not kill you. You were right, I can not. As an agent of my government, I am forbidden to take your life without permission. It is true you have information you will be able to give to us that we desperately need in the war against terror. It is my duty to make sure you stay alive, and make it available." She paused, staring at the sobbing, tortured man in the bed. Her voice seemed to come from somewhere deep inside of her body and resonated throughout the room.

"Hear me Mohammed bin Fasheed, coward of a man and son of the most despicable of living things. Your blood line has been erased. Because of what I have done to you today, you will no longer be able to spread your seed. The coin I leave embedded in your body is only partial payment for the pain you caused my country, my family and innocent people of the world. I am Yasmina al Amar of the Maerb, daughter of Adel bin Jamal of the Maerb, and Suhair bint Faisal of the al Jouf. I have now exacted part of the blood debt owed to my murdered family and the unnamed innocent victims of your evil acts. All men will be told of your evil and of your punishment." She turned, and motioning for Ali to follow, left the room.

Six hours later, Mark and his team found the badly injured Mohammed still tied to his bed, bleeding and groaning in pain. When they saw his wound, the hardened soldiers on the team wondered who could have tortured him so savagely. Although it was not a killing wound, the damage would obviously require surgery to extract the coin. The possibility of a penile amputation along with an agonizing recovery period had every man on the team shuddering as they peered sheepishly at Mohammed's butchered manhood. The Americans were positive it was Saudi retribution but they were told not to mention it in their after action report, in case of political reprisals.

The Saudi intelligence colonel stationed in Riyadh read his soldiers' Syrian after action report for the second time. He shook his head in puzzled amusement. He had never heard of such outrageous behavior from a trained Western agent. An untried Western woman, a young agent of the Americans had mutilated Mohammed bin Fasheed and rendered him almost a eunuch. The report stated his guards overheard an American doctor saying it would take multiple operations to correct the damage. It was fortunate for Mohammed that the Americans' medical team had the expertise to save him from hemorrhaging while he was being transported.

The officer smiled in admiration. He did not know what the royal family had in store for Mohammed's final dispensation, but he knew they would have a grudging respect for the unique damage this young woman had inflicted upon their family's sworn enemy.

Six months later, American interrogators notified their Saudi counterparts they finished questioning the prisoner, Mohammed bin Fasheed # 911234. His mental examinations and debriefings had been successful and included notes on both his physical and mental condition. Pertinent classified information had already been sent to appropriate American and Saudi government agencies.

His medical report noted that he had completely recovered from his penile wounds. Although operations to repair his urethra had been successful, he had been left with an erectile dysfunction disorder. Otherwise, he was pronounced in good health and physically capable of traveling.

A particularly cooperative subject, he had attempted to establish friendships with his interrogators. To maintain their objectivity, American personnel had been rotated on a weekly basis to deny the prisoner any sympathetic response. The latest psychiatric evaluation noted that although his mental state was stable at the moment, he was prone to fits of depression and anger.

When the Saudi Secret Police detail arrived to take him into custody Mohammed appeared well fed and was dressed casually in clean clothes. Recognizing who they were, he immediately ordered them to notify the royal family that he wished to speak to the Crown Prince. The soldiers did not reply, but expertly handcuffed and shackled him. His mouth was then taped shut and he was pushed outside toward a waiting helicopter.

After he was lifted up into the rear seat of the custom designed Sikorsky S76C, the policemen seated themselves on either side of him. His eyes adjusted to the darkness of the cabin and widened in surprise as he saw one of the more important royal princes sitting across from him. He was a man that had been one of his boyhood friends, Prince Khalid. Their fathers had been as close as two brothers.

As the helicopter's rotor began to turn, a set of headphones were placed on his head. The copter lifted up, began to hover and then moved off toward the southeast. He heard his childhood friend's voice in his ears.

"The Americans have taken good care of you Mohammed. I am satisfied that they have farmed your brain successfully for any information about our enemies and yet left enough of you for us to dispose of."

Mohammed began to make grunting sounds and pleaded at his old friend with his eyes. The Saudi held up his palm in front of Mohammed's face.

"Stop, or I will have you beaten unconscious! You are only to listen, dog. I refuse to hear your sniveling, lying voice, and would cut out your tongue, if I could." Mohammed stared at his friend's face with questioning eyes.

"You are a traitorous pig. May you be damned for all eternity for the part you played in the slaughter of the American innocents on 9/11 and in the murder of our people as well as other Muslims around the world! You have practiced treason against my family and our nation. You have plotted with our enemies to murder us and usurp our throne. You would rule in our stead. You have disgraced your family's name and now it is forever obliterated from our history. With your greed, need for power, and thirst for blood you have dishonored our country and placed it in terrible jeopardy from the evil forces of terrorism. In punishment for your traitorous actions, the rest of your family has been killed or exiled with all their estates and properties forfeited. Your ancestors' names no longer exist in any record of our history. You are the consummate traitor and will suffer a traitor's death.

I have been sent here to inform you that you will not have the easy death of a beheading. You will be dropped into the middle of the Empty Quarter of our country with one small water bottle. The water will help to slow your death from exposure. With no shade available for protection from the desert sun and no hope of escape, it is our fervent wish that you suffer before you die. When you are lifeless and carrion have begun to feast on what is left of your rotting flesh, the sands will blow over your bones and mankind will finally be rid of the filth of you. I spit upon you, and wish you a long, suffering death." As the prince's spittle landed on his face, Mohammed never saw the weapon that crashed into the back of his skull.

When Khalid told him that he would be thrown into the desert of the Empty Quarter to die Mohammed had felt a surge of hope for the first time since his capture in Syria by the Americans. Now, as he walked through the deep sand he thought how stupid the man was, but Khalid had never been very bright, even as a boy. It was asinine to think that they could kill him by letting him loose in the desert. He was amused at their clumsy attempt. He would survive and strike back, killing all of them.

As far as he could tell, he had walked about twenty miles east the previous four days. The last seventy-two hours had been more difficult, the blazing sun beginning to take its toll, blistering his face and hands and causing his tongue to swell. It was now late morning on his fifth day and he found himself once again digging a hole in the sand with his bare hands in order to bury himself until the sun began to go down. The liter water bottle he had been given was almost empty and there still was no sign of life anywhere in the desert. He had vainly watched for birds or a sign of antelope, knowing that if they were around there would be water nearby.

As he lay in the newly dug sandy grave shading his face with his hand, he smugly remembered he had money hidden in places that no one could have found. All he had to do was get to it. He also found hope in the fact that smugglers often crossed the Empty Quarter because it was not patrolled by any nation's soldiers. If he could keep himself headed east toward the border of Oman there was a good possibility he might run across a band of them and barter for his escape. They would know his name, and in knowing that, they would realize he could pay them for their trouble. All he had to do was make the water last and keep moving toward the east.

The next day saw him make a small amount of headway but on the seventh day, the sun renewed its attacks with fiery heat, the wind shredding his skin with sand blasting gusts. He drank the last few drops of his water, but when he tried to dig a sand cave to escape the worst of the day's afternoon sun and wind, he was too weak and lay down on top of the burning sand with his head in his arms. The blast furnace heat of the afternoon baked his brain and he faded in and out of consciousness.

The Blackhawk circled for a few minutes, the pilot deciding exactly where he wanted to land. After he touched down, Yasi was out the door, her Glock 31 pistol in one hand, and a rubber water bladder in the other. She walked briskly to the unconscious body lying on the sand and gave it a hard shove with her boot. Purposely shading Mohammed's face with her shadow, she called his name and prodded him until he came to. He looked up, but could only see the silhouette of the figure in front of him. Rubbing his sand sealed eyelids open, he spoke through cracked and bleeding lips, barely able to speak. "Who is it? What's happening?"

"Yasmina al Amar," a woman's strong voice answered.

"You! What do you want?" his voice cracked.

"Your death. Since you have been put out here we've kept track of your progress with a transponder implant. It was put in place before we released you to the Saudis. As it stands, your progress has not been very impressive but, if it had appeared that you were going to get lucky and meet smugglers, we would have intervened to prevent it. This is your executioners' ground. I have come to finish what I began with you in Syria, what I owe to the memory of my family and all the victims that you and all terrorists have murdered. I now leave you at the end of your evil life. You are a dead man. Your sons have been given away to others. You and your name have been scoured from your country's history. Your family and possessions are forfeit, and the earth shall be salted so that nothing of you can survive. Enshallah." She threw the water bladder down in the sand next to him and strode off back to the waiting helicopter.

He heard the whirring sound of the helicopter's rotor fading away and felt on the ground next to him for the water bag. Why would she leave him more water? Did she think having water to drink would make him suffer more? She was an idiotic bitch. He would use what she'd left to get to the border. Screw the implant. He would escape.

Mohammed picked up the bladder, flipped off the covering cap and pointed the spout to his mouth. Nothing happened. He hefted it and tried again. Nothing. With great annoyance he unscrewed the entire spout, turned the bladder upside down in his mouth and shook it hard. Salt gushed forward, each grain adding its tiny bulk to the one next to it, instantly filling his mouth with white crystals, spilling out onto the brown sand, salting the earth.

His piercing scream skimmed over the desert sand and disappeared into the oncoming wind. "Yaaaasmina!"

EPILOGUE

Far above, the Blackhawk helicopter's infrared sensors showed no life signs emanating from the prostrate body lying on the desert floor. It was over. Mohammed was dead. Yasmina put the Steiner 8x30 binoculars down and ordered the pilot to head back to base. They would be back in Qatar in less than an hour, and she would be on the next Agency jet to the United States within forty-eight hours.

Bone weary but satisfied with the final success of her mission, she'd had her vengeance by not only killing Mohammed but also by dealing al Qaeda a crippling blow within Saudi Arabia. She'd survived the torture and death sentence inflicted upon her and retaliated by taking Mohammed's operatives into custody as she helped dismantle his carefully built terrorist organization. Al Qaeda had fled the country. The American HUMINT network in Riyadh was back up and gathering information once again.

None of this gave her as much pleasure as knowing Mohammed died realizing it was her, Yasmina al Amar who arranged his death. It was as it should be. She had kept the promise she made when she found out he ordered her parents tortured and murdered. She fulfilled the brutal prophesy of the tribes with sheer force of will sustained by genetic strength from her ancestors. The blood of the ancient tribes of Yemen warmed in thoughtful reflection on the revenge she exacted upon him. She felt their approval wash over her from beyond the edge of time. She had fulfilled her obligation to them by the ferocity and finality of her actions. She had also helped to protect her country. She knew the West would be grateful for her help in bringing about the defeat of one of the most powerful and dangerous terrorist networks in the world.

The ordeal of her imprisonment and torture had changed her. She was a woman who now knew pure good and pure evil, having experienced both. Her thoughts drifted to the love she felt for Mark. She wondered if he was safe. Was he still in Yemen? Was he still her Mark? She didn't know. Since departing from Yemen, she had not heard from him. She prayed for his safety every day. She would try to contact him again after returning home.

Home. Like the character Dorothy in The Wizard of Oz, home was where she wanted to be more than any place in the world. When she got back to Michigan, she would do what her parents would want her to do. She would be an anchor of strength for her family and take control of the future. She would pull what was left of the al Amars together and make a home for all of them. She wouldn't let them down. Enshallah.

The End